Nothing Compares to the Duke

"I'm not the girl I used to be," she said on a breathy whisper.

Yet she still didn't move. She remained astride him, one hand fisted in the fabric of his shirt, the other pressed to his chest. The weight and heat of her felt delicious. So good he had the wayward notion of bucking up to get her closer.

"What is it?" If she remained on top of him, she'd soon know exactly the direction of his thoughts. Was he misreading the look in her eyes for desire? He was more than prepared to remain pressed against her all day, but he knew the crinkle in her brow meant there was something she wished to say. "Tell me, Bella. What's wrong?"

Rather than speak, she acted. Her finger came down on his lower lip and that single touch sent a shiver of pleasure down his spine.

She was so soft, so warm. And she wanted him. There was nothing hidden in those expressive eyes of hers now. He'd promised himself he wouldn't do this with her. But he did want her, and he'd wished for her to look at him just like this for longer than he'd ever let himself admit.

By Christy Carlyle

The Duke's Den Series
A DUKE CHANGES EVERYTHING
ANYTHING BUT A DUKE
NOTHING COMPARES TO THE DUKE

Romancing the Rules Series
RULES FOR A ROGUE
A STUDY IN SCOUNDRELS
HOW TO WOO A WALLFLOWER

The Accidental Heirs Series
ONE SCANDALOUS KISS
ONE TEMPTING PROPOSAL
ONE DANGEROUS DESIRE

NOTHING COMPARES TO THE DUKE

A Duke's Den Novel

CHRISTY CARLYLE

AVONBOOKS

An Imprint of HarperCollinsPublishers

NOTHING COMPARES TO THE DUKE. Copyright © 2020 by Christy Carlyle. All rights reserved. Printed in the United States of America. No part of this book may be used or reproduced in any manner whatsoever without written permission except in the case of brief quotations embodied in critical articles and reviews. For information, address HarperCollins Publishers, 195 Broadway, New York, NY 10007.

First Avon Books mass market printing: June 2020

Print Edition ISBN: 978-0-06-285401-8
Digital Edition ISBN: 978-0-06-285398-1

Cover design by Patricia Barrow
Cover illustration by John Paul Ferrara
Author photograph © 2001 Paul F. Blouin

Avon, Avon & logo, and Avon Books & logo are registered trademarks of HarperCollins Publishers in the United States of America and other countries.

HarperCollins is a registered trademark of HarperCollins Publishers in the United States of America and other countries.

FIRST EDITION

20 21 22 23 24   CWM   10 9 8 7 6 5 4 3 2 1

To my mom. Thank you for always believing in me. Your love and encouragement mean so much.

Acknowledgments

From the bottom of my heart, thanks to my editor, Elle Keck, for your wisdom, insight, and patience. You always help me make a book better.

NOTHING COMPARES TO THE DUKE

Prologue

August 1843
Hillcrest, country house of Viscount Yardley and his family, Essex

𝒜rabella Prescott flattened herself against the drawing room wall and held her breath until the footman passed by. Her heart beat so fiercely inside her chest, she was certain every servant in the house could hear. She'd run all the way from the garden. That was possibly the worst of her sins so far today.

Her mother didn't mind if she wasn't good at dance lessons or spent too much time with her nose in a book. Mama loved books too, after all. But running was a grave misdeed, particularly in a pink beaded taffeta gown specially commissioned from a famous London modiste.

Today, of all days, she'd be expected to display the

ladylike refinements learned through all the years of tutors and governesses. Bella knew the rules and she was good at keeping them. She liked pleasing her parents. As an only child, there was no one else to make them proud. But she didn't need lessons to know it wasn't proper to skulk through drawing rooms when she was supposed to be attending to guests at her eighteenth birthday party.

The problem was one guest had gone missing and he was the only one who mattered to Bella.

After peeking around the threshold to make sure no one was about, she lifted the long skirt of her gown and dashed down the hall to the library.

Rhys Forester didn't love reading as she did, but they'd made a kind of haven out of the library together. It was where they'd go when she helped him decipher words in books which had challenged him since he was a boy, and it was where he'd listen patiently while she talked through a new idea for one of her riddles.

The room was large enough to find a private corner where they could talk for hours and Bella searched all those nooks now, only to find them empty. Stopping at one of the long windows, she pulled the drape back and looked down at the guests milling around the garden. From this high above, the party looked elegant. Tables laden with food and enormous punch bowls were arranged around a central area that servants had cordoned off for dancing. Another square of lawn had been pressed and trimmed for lawn tennis.

Down there, amid the flurry of guests and servants,

it felt far different. Less elegant and more panic inducing. She could only focus on the dais that had been assembled for her to stand on and give a little speech of thanks to everyone for attending. The thought of it made her stomach tumble.

Speaking in front of others was not her skill, but she knew someone who did it naturally. Effortlessly. He'd even helped her craft what she would say. In the farthest nook of the library, the one with the cushioned window seats, they'd worked together just two days prior on the speech her mother expected her to give today.

And now he'd gone missing.

She'd searched every drawing room, the conservatory, the morning room where they sometimes used her mother's desk when Bella helped him with writing. He wouldn't be upstairs, and he was nowhere to be found in the gardens.

"Looking for me?" Rhys's deep voice sent a shiver down her spine.

She turned so quickly her skirt tangled around her ankles. "I thought you'd gotten bored and gone home."

"Miss Prescott." He pressed a hand to his chest and winced dramatically. "Your lack of faith wounds me. I would never abandon a friend and I'm determined to celebrate your day along with everyone else."

"Where were you?" Bella untangled her skirts by shaking out the fabric and moved closer.

"Looking for you, of course. You're the lady of the hour. The girl of the day." He pulled something from his waistcoat pocket, cupped it in his hands so she couldn't see, and hid it by sliding both hands behind his back.

"If that's a gift for my birthday, you're meant to wrap it and present it to me properly, not hide it away."

Her pulse quickened as she thought of what he might give her. Then she looked down and the way his shirt buttons strained across his chest made her breath speed too. Lately she was aware of everything about him in ways she'd never been before. More specifically, she'd become intensely aware of his body.

Like now, when she noticed that the stubble on his chin glittered gold in the sunlight. How he smelled of fresh air and the cinnamon biscuits Cook had made for the party and that unique deeper scent that was all Rhys.

"I'm not sure you'll like it, Arry. You are known to be rather picky."

Arry was a nickname only Rhys used. He wasn't satisfied with Bella, as everyone else called her. He insisted on something unique.

"How dare you? Everyone knows you're the pickiest man in the village." Bella pushed playfully at his chest as she'd done dozens of times over the course of their friendship.

This time was different.

He wasn't a little boy anymore and she was no longer a little girl. That he was four years older had never mattered much when they were children, but over the course of the previous summer, she'd begun to think of him as a man. The inescapable fact was that he'd grown very appealing. And very handsome. Her feelings for him had grown too, into something she was afraid to voice.

But now, standing inches from him, she found she didn't want to pull away. Under her palm, he radiated heat and it was as much of an enticement as discovering whatever gift he concealed behind his back.

"You're so picky, none of the girls in the village can catch your eye." Her heart leaped in her chest as she waited for his reply. A part of her dared to hope *she* was the reason no other girl could tempt him.

"It took you a month to decide which color of dress to wear today," he teased.

"Mama said it was the most important dress I'd ever wear, at least until the start of the Season. But she is dramatic when it comes to fashion."

He laughed and the sound was infectious. She always laughed when he did. But the sound was richer now that she could feel the reverberation against her palm.

"Show me what it is," she insisted with a gentle push.

Rhys tipped his head and looked down at where she touched him. She felt his response. His heartbeat raced faster. When his eyes met hers again, their cool blue shade seemed darker.

"Turn around, Arabella," he said on a husky whisper.

Bella did as he requested without protest or hesitation. That was new too. Usually they debated everything.

Her breath snagged in her throat as she waited, listening to the rustle of fabric as he brought his arms forward. A little squeak sounded in the high-ceilinged library, like the metal-on-metal rub of a hinge giving way.

A hinged box? Bella's mind went to jewelry and then to the image of a ring and her deepest most secret wish that she was almost afraid to admit to herself. She was expected to have a wildly successful coming-out Season. Her mother had been planning for months. Years. But since her change of heart toward her best friend, Bella's dream was an uncharacteristically rebellious one.

Deep down, she hoped her Season might be unnecessary because Rhys would ask her to be his.

Her parents couldn't disapprove. They'd known Rhys as long as she had and loved him as a son, not to mention that he was heir to a dukedom. As her mother had told her a hundred times while they discussed eligible noblemen who might be promising prospects for the coming Season, "nothing compares to a duke."

It would come as a shock to no one to discover that he'd had her heart for years. Even Rhys couldn't doubt that. But it had always been a friendship kind of love.

Now it was so much more.

He swept his fingers across the back of her neck and Bella gasped.

"Are my hands cold?"

"N-no" was all she could manage. Her skin tingled where he'd touched her and a ribbon of warmth spread out from that spot and slid all the way down her back.

She felt his other hand come up and he stretched one arm over her shoulder, then the other. Cool metal landed gently against her neck and then his fingers were fumbling at her nape again, brushing against the wisps of hair that had escaped her coiffure.

He'd hooked a necklace and the thin chain tickled against her skin.

"There," he said softly, pressing the flat of his hand to the curve between her neck and shoulder. When he let go, the chain slid down, almost to her cleavage.

Bella lifted the pendant and tilted it up. A daisy flower, its petals made of opal and its center a round of etched gold.

"Will it suit you? Daisies are your favorite flower, aren't they?"

"I love daisies." But they weren't her favorite flower. Lily of the valley was her favorite and always had been, but she couldn't bring herself to tell him.

He came around to stand in front of her and took her hands in his. "They're as sweet and lovely as you are."

"Thank you." For a long awkward moment, she couldn't get any more words out. She struggled so long that his encouraging smile faltered. "Rhys—"

"Arry, I know you're nervous about the speech. But don't be. We practiced and you'll pull it off beautifully." He glanced behind her at the clock on the wall. "You should head down. It's almost time."

"*We* should head down." She'd come looking for him because she could not imagine speaking to all the guests from that dais without being able to look out and focus on his face.

He reached up and cupped her chin, tilted her head gently, and stared down at her as tenderly as he'd ever looked at her in the decade they'd known each other.

Bella held her breath. Her gaze flitted down to his lips. This was it. This was the moment of her very first kiss. There would never ever be another and there was no man she would ever want to kiss more than Rhys Forester.

"You," he said emphatically, "are so much more than you know. More clever, more talented, more beautiful than you even yet realize. I hope when the Season comes a dozen men tell you so. There will be many vying for your heart and your hand."

No! Everything in her shouted the word. A dozen men didn't interest her in the least.

Only one. This one.

"Don't break too many hearts, my sweet lovely friend." He smiled again and bent forward.

Bella leaned toward him too, stood a little straighter, and stretched up to meet his kiss.

But rather than touch his mouth to hers, he pressed his lips to her forehead, lingered a moment, and then pulled back.

"Return to the party." He spoke gently, less of a

command than an encouragement to do something he knew she dreaded. He dropped his hand from her chin and took a step back and to the side, clearing a path for her to the library door.

"Are you not escorting me down?" The words came out far sharper than she wished, but her heart ached. There was so much she wished to say, so many feelings burning inside her, but now she feared there would never be an opportunity to confess any of them.

"There's someone I must speak to and then I'll join the celebration. I promise."

Bella had no notion who he planned to speak to, but there were half a dozen guests that Rhys knew as well as she did. A cousin of Bella's had been one of his university classmates and the Debley twins, who'd idolized him when they were girls, seemed just as smitten now.

Reluctantly, Bella nodded and started toward the library threshold. "If you're not about when Mama calls me to the dais, I'm coming to find you."

He laughed, a shallower sound than his usual chuckle. "I have no doubt."

"COME, BELLA. WE can't dally any longer," her mother said as she waved Bella's father away from the punch bowl. He loved the lemony concoction, but sweets never agreed with him. "We told guests the party would break up at three and you'd say a few words before we sent everyone on their way."

"Soon, Mama." Bella twisted the daisy pendant between her fingers and stood on her tiptoes to look out past a cluster of guests onto Hillcrest's garden paths that were lined with tall box hedges. It wasn't quite a maze, but there were places to sit and a few guests had wandered off to rest on shady benches or converse privately among the flowers.

She'd seen Rhys come out of the house nearly half an hour ago, but Vicar Eames had engaged her in conversation and she'd been unable to get away.

"My girl," her mother said with barely restrained irritation, "it's rude to make everyone wait."

"I must find Rhys."

"Arabella." Her mother let out a long-suffering sigh and closed her eyes. "When the Season begins you won't be able to spend so much time with Lord Huntley."

"Precisely, Mama, which is why I intend to do so now." Bella didn't wait for a reply before moving past her mother and heading for the tall hedges. She had a hunch she'd find him there.

The Debley twins were sitting on one of the stone benches, and looked up at her guiltily as she approached. "We were just planning to return to the party, Miss Prescott. Daisy felt a bit fatigued," one of the twins said while gesturing to the other.

"I'm much better now," Daisy insisted.

"Good." Bella managed a smile while glancing each way down the hedge rows. "Have you seen Lord Huntley, by any chance?"

The dark-haired twins exchanged a glance before

Dorothy said, "We did a while back. He went that way."

Bella didn't have to go far before she heard voices. A woman and then a gentleman's raspy reply. Laughter filtered through the leafy wall of the tall hedges, a low and resonant rumble so infectious it tickled in her own belly.

Rhys's laugh.

She picked up her pace, lifting the skirt of her gown to keep from tripping. The daisy pendant bounced at the base of her throat. As she drew closer, she heard a feminine moan. She rounded the corner and bile rose in the back of her throat. Blood rushed so fiercely in her ears it blocked out every other sound.

Rhys shot up from the bench where he'd been reclining, nearly on top of the redheaded widow next to him. Lady Nelson pushed her skirts down and began fussing with her hair. She kept her eyes focused on Rhys and couldn't manage a single glance Bella's way.

Stumbling back, Bella clutched at her throat. She couldn't breathe.

"Arry—"

"No. Don't call me that." It was a silly nickname. "What a childish fool I must seem to you."

He lifted a hand toward her. "Never a fool."

"A child, then?" Bella glared at Lady Nelson, who'd stood and composed herself.

"No."

The moment Rhys stepped toward her, Bella had to escape. She couldn't bear to look at him, to hear his voice. She didn't want explanations or apology. Getting away and trying to forget what she'd seen was all she needed.

She stumbled along the stone path. Tears came so hot and quick her vision blurred, but she could see clearly enough to note that the Debley sisters were no longer on their bench. Bella swiped at her cheeks and nose and noticed someone waving in the distance. Her mother stood at the edge of the garden paths, gesturing her forward.

A little keening sound bubbled up and her throat burned. She couldn't give her speech. She couldn't pretend as if her heart wasn't shattered.

Rather than head toward her mother, Bella veered left toward the house. Before she could get halfway there, footsteps rushed toward her from behind and Rhys gripped her arm.

"Arabella, please. Listen to me."

Even turning to face him took effort. She feared if she looked at him, she wouldn't be able to walk away.

"I know what you must think of me." He let go of her and ran a hand through his hair. "And of Lady Nelson."

"I don't give a damn about Lady Nelson."

"No, of course not, but—"

"Leave." Saying the single syllable brought a pain in the center of her chest so sharp, it felt as if getting the word out had cut her from the inside.

"Arry—"

"Just go. Go!" She didn't even realize she was shouting until he jolted back and began glancing around, as if worried she'd attract notice their way.

Looking at him was too hard. Standing this close, all she ached to do was reach for him. Even now, after the unequivocal proof that he did not care for her. That he didn't care for his own reputation. That he wasn't a proper honorable sort of gentleman at all.

And despite everything, she still wanted him. She still wished he wanted her.

He bowed his head and nodded once, then walked away.

Bella wrapped her arms around her chest and bit down to stop a wave of shivers. The afternoon had turned warm after a day of unclouded sun, but inside she felt chilled. Empty.

She looked up when she realized his footsteps had slowed. He'd stopped and stood looking back at her.

"Good-bye, Bella."

She said nothing. There wasn't anything left to say.

Bella willed herself to stand still when he walked away, not to call out or run after him as her heart insisted. She couldn't find her usual rational self. This wasn't a riddle she could unravel. Pain and confusion clouded everything, but intuition told her he wasn't just walking out of her party.

Rhys Forester had just walked out of her life.

Forever.

Chapter One

July 1848
London, Lyon's Gentlemen's Club

Rhys Forester, Duke of Claremont, was a lucky man.

He told himself as much as a blade cut the air a hairs-breadth from his cheek, its glinting silver flashing in his periphery. A streak of heat whispered against his skin and his heartbeat spiked before the knife lodged in the wooden board at his back.

Partygoers crowding the opulent private room in Lyon's Gentlemen's Club let out a murmur of relief. Rhys swept his gaze across the assembly of noblemen and their paramours, forcing a rakish smile. One of the young lords he'd invited tightened an arm around his lady companion's shoulders when she let out a flirtatious giggle.

He understood the man's worry.

Rhys had spent years earning his scandalous reputation, and he'd had a hell of an example to follow.
The late Duke of Claremont had been known for his
decadent tastes and very few morals. Rhys had never
been close to his father, but now he'd grown used to
the same whispers about his own behavior.

Reckless affairs earned him constant mention in
scandal rags and at least two breach of promise suits.
Ridiculous luck at the gaming tables caused some to
claim he cheated at play. But most of all he was known
for the nightly revels he hosted. Parties so wild there
had been injuries, infamies, and drunken brawls leading to fisticuffs and more than a few illegal duels.

For years, infamy had sustained him. He'd loved
the endless parties. The attention of beautiful women.
The envy of other men. Laughter filling his ears because he'd put on the best celebration his guests ever
attended. He excelled at very little, but amusement he
did well. That and giving pleasure. Giving people an
excuse to have fun. Filling his nights with so much frivolity that he could push away thoughts of the duties
he'd have to face when daylight came.

Of late those responsibilities were piling so high no
amount of revelry could keep them at bay, but he was
damned well determined to try. Now that he'd inherited a dukedom, he was compelled to make each party
grander than the last.

He'd always been as willful as he was wayward,
but what he could no longer deny was how tired it all
made him.

This was the fourth party in as many nights with very little sleep in between. His eyes were dry as dust, his throat burned, and there were far too many hours left to go until this soiree died down. The circus theme had been a grand success, but now guests were inebriated and eager for more daring feats from the performers he'd hired.

"Throw another!" a drunk lordling shouted for the second time from the back of the room.

The muscles of Rhys's arms and neck were stiff, tautened by tension, but when he shifted, the lady flipping a knife in front of him shook her head.

"Stay still, darling." Jess, one of the music hall performers he'd hired as entertainment, winked at him. "Wouldn't want to mar that pretty face of yours."

"You wouldn't dare. You're too fond of my face just as it is."

"Handsome man, you are. Can't deny it." She returned a knowing smile, one full of promises he considered holding her to later in the evening.

Party guests laughed at their repartee and gathered close to watch her toss another blade. Hosting a party in a private room at Lyon's Gentlemen's Club had *seemed* a good way to celebrate his latest investment triumph. The Duke's Den had given him an opportunity to expand the wealth he inherited from his father even further via investments in England's brightest entrepreneurs. But now that he was bleary-eyed, his patience for standing against an unforgiving wooden board and hoping Jess's aim was as good as she claimed was waning.

"Above his head!" a gentleman called out.

"Between his legs," his pretty redheaded companion said with a mischievous grin.

"I shall land this blade near the opposite ear." Jess narrowed her eyes and drew back her arm to throw the next knife.

A nobleman's buxom paramour gasped.

Rhys held very still and reminded himself once more that fortune was ever on his side.

Jess loosed the knife and it came at him so fast, he only heard the thwack as it struck the board. Then a pinpoint of pain bloomed at the side of his head. Rhys winced. Jess covered her mouth with her hands, eyes widening.

Reaching up, he swiped at a trickle of blood at the edge of his ear.

"Just a scratch," he told her, and then louder for the guests leaning close, whispering worriedly. "A tiny knick. No harm done."

"Lucky that," one man shouted.

"No man is as charmed as the Duke of Claremont," a brunette said, her eyes wide.

"Another!" Lord Southwell called out. "Let's see if his luck can hold."

Jess looked unsteady as she drew the final knife from the belt she wore. Her hand shook when she lifted the implement. Rather than aim and toss the blade, she held his gaze and offered the tiniest shake of her head.

"Go on," another man urged.

Rhys was on the cusp of calling it off. Jess's mouth quivered, her facade of confidence faltering.

"Claremont, may we have a word before this young woman impales you?"

Rhys recognized the voice. Aidan Iverson had been invited to the party, but Rhys had given up on him attending. He was happy to see his friend, if only because it meant freeing himself from further target practice.

Though now that Iverson was here, he didn't look at all festive. And he wasn't alone. Nick, Duke of Tremayne, stood beside him. Both of Rhys's partners in co-ownership of Lyon's lingered on the threshold of the crowded room, their faces a grim contrast to the evening's gaiety.

"Please, everyone, carry on." Rhys gestured toward the quartet of violinists in the corner of the room and stepped down from the platform. "Time for music and dancing."

He cast a look at Tremayne and Iverson. They definitely wouldn't be dancing. Their gazes were so serious that he dreaded whatever news they'd come to deliver.

"Quite an impressive performance, Your Grace."

Rhys looked over his shoulder and found the brunette who'd called out to him earlier watching with an assessing gaze. She'd come with a friend, a viscount who had been a member of Lyon's for years. He couldn't bed her, but she possessed a porcelain beauty that was hard to ignore.

"Everyone says so."

One gossip rag claimed he possessed all the qualities a bon vivant nobleman could ever require: charm, wealth, an insatiable appetite for pleasure. He was renowned throughout London as the blazing spark of any party. A man whose smile could charm a lady from across a crowded ballroom. The most daring investor of the Duke's Den.

Rhys almost believed the stories others told about him. Almost.

A good tailor helped with the appealing facade he presented to the world. An adept valet was a godsend. Being a lucky man, he possessed both.

Wealth had come easily. As the firstborn son of the Duke of Claremont, he'd been afforded the best education. Excellent tutors. Long-suffering types who remained in their post no matter how difficult it was to teach a duke's son who couldn't read or memorize his numbers like other children. University had been a bit of a nightmare, but the allowance from his father had started then. With those funds he'd been lucky enough at gambling to grow a sizable wealth of his own.

And now, atop all of his other blessings, he'd added his father's title. A dukedom could only enhance a man's merits.

He was the most favored of men.

Which was why he'd confided to no one that the weight of the responsibilities that had been heaped on his shoulders in the past weeks were crushing him like a millstone.

He glanced back at the brunette, her long shiny ringlets swaying in a sinuous fall above a petite waist and shapely hips. She turned as if she sensed his notice and a wicked smile curved her lush lips. When he winked in reply, he fought a wave of fatigue that made him want to close both of his eyes and lean heavily against the nearest wall for a short nap. How long had it been since he'd tasted a bit of the pleasure he was renowned for seeking?

No. He could do this. He'd hear whatever news his partners had for him and then return to his guests.

Revelry was his talent. Revelry and the instinct to know when an investment might go well and turn a profit. Unlike Iverson and Tremayne, he didn't rely on facts and reports or carefully calculating the return on his investment. He simply felt his way through decisions. And he applied the same principle at gaming tables and to every amusement life had to offer.

And he excelled at all of it when he wasn't so bloody exhausted. The fatigue that weighed on him like ballast had begun a month past on the evening he'd received news of his father's death. An estate, tenants, a seat in Parliament, a coterie of servants—all of it had passed to him overnight, along with a pile of unexpected debt.

He admitted to no one that his nerves jangled like the traces on a runaway carriage.

"What is it?" he said as he approached his friends, trying to temper the panic welling up in his chest.

"We need to talk." Tremayne glanced around the room. "Not here. The balcony."

Rhys followed the men, each step building a wave of unease. Upon reaching the private space high above the gaming tables of Lyon's, Iverson gestured toward a cluster of upholstered chairs. "Shall we sit?"

Rhys ignored him and headed for the drinks cart. "Don't coddle me. Let me get a swig of whiskey down and say whatever you must as quickly as you can. The long looks on your faces don't give me much hope for pleasant news."

Iverson took up a position near the cart, boots firmly planted and arms crossed.

The same nervousness making Rhys's hand shake as he lifted a glass to his lips was also radiating off of Tremayne, but Iverson simply stood, still and calm. He'd always been the steadiest of the three of them.

"When was the last time you were in touch with your sister?"

Rhys cocked his head and locked eyes with Iverson. "Is she unwell?"

"No." Iverson lifted his hand in a calming gesture. "Nothing like that." He gazed over his shoulder at Tremayne. "But you haven't brought her to London or taken her back to the estate in Essex?"

Two drums began a fearsome tattoo in Rhys's head, one behind each temple. "My sister is at finishing school in Hampshire."

"She's finished," Tremayne said drily. "Lady Margaret sent me a letter because she hasn't heard from you. She graduated nearly a fortnight ago and was expecting a carriage to escort her home."

"Christ." Rhys scraped a hand through his hair. He'd been living so hard of late the days had merged together. So much so that he'd bloody forgotten the date and his only sister. "I'll send for her immediately."

"Already done," Nick told him in the voice he usually reserved for frustrated noblemen who came to complain that they'd lost too much at the club's gaming tables. "She should arrive at Edgecombe tomorrow."

"Thank you." Rhys let out a sigh of relief but none of the tension in his body loosened.

Meg had inherited their mother's kindness along with a full measure of their father's impatience. He could well imagine the words she'd have for him when she returned home. He deserved them all.

"She's concerned about you," Nick added in a gentler tone. "We all are."

Rhys looked up. He deserved whatever disappointment his longtime friend felt for his irresponsibility. But Tremayne lowered his head and stared at the carpet. He couldn't look Rhys in the eyes.

"There's more. Don't spare me. Just say it."

Iverson crossed his arms and rocked back on his heels. "You recall Mr. Carthorpe?"

"Yes, of course." Rhys didn't have Tremayne's aptitude for numbers or Iverson's shrewd head for business matters, but his memory rarely failed him. "The horseless carriage chap."

Rhys recalled him as young and fidgety, but the man's invention was an exciting prospect and every member of the Duke's Den had been eager to invest.

"Don't tell me he's run off with our money."

Nick cleared his throat and then rubbed a hand along the edge of his jaw. It was a tic Rhys had observed many times in the Den. The gesture was the same he used when he was loath to tell an inventor that none of them wished to invest in his or her device.

"Out with it," Rhys barked, too exhausted for delicacy.

"Carthorpe did not receive our full investment," Iverson told him in a firm voice. Then he paused and cleared his throat. Rhys could virtually see whatever else he wished to say lodged in the man's throat.

Iverson dipped his head and flicked back his suit coat to place a hand on each hip. When he finally looked up, his eyes were filled with what Rhys thought looked a great deal like regret.

"Your bank reported that the amount you promised could not be fulfilled."

"That's not possible," Rhys scoffed. The air rushed out of him in another bluster of denial.

The claim was absurd.

He wasn't in daily contact with his banker and had no real notion of the balance in each of his accounts, but that was precisely the point. His funds on hand had always been so healthy that he'd never worried about paying an invoice or offering his money to an inventor in the hopes of getting a generous return.

"Your bank hasn't contacted you about this matter?" Tremayne asked.

"Not that I'm aware of." Rhys stared at Nick but in his mind's eye he saw the stack of unopened letters he nudged aside every time he sat at the desk in his study. "The post *has* piled up in the last few weeks." Letters, invitations, and notes of condolences had arrived in a flurry after his father's death. He'd struggled through reading a couple before allowing them to accumulate.

"Avoiding your post? Forgetting the commencement of your sister's studies. Unaware of your finances." Iverson's usually calm voice ebbed toward concern. "Is something amiss, Claremont?"

Every damned thing, apparently.

"How could it be?" Rhys forced a rusty chuckle and shrugged his shoulders, wishing he could dislodge the tightness that had taken root there. "I've inherited a dukedom."

"And yet you remain here in London," Iverson pointed out unhelpfully. "Have you returned to Essex at all since your father's funeral?"

Mention of the funeral made Rhys long for another finger of whiskey, but Iverson stood like an enormous red-haired oak tree blocking his path to the cart.

The funeral had been as bleak as any event Rhys had ever attended. The duke had isolated himself in his later years and those who'd come to see him laid to rest had done so out of duty rather than affection. Guilt weighed heavy on Rhys. He too had been among the dutiful, rather than those who'd felt any warmth toward the old man. Only Meg had cried genuine tears for their father.

It hadn't always been that way. Once upon a time, Rhys had looked up to Tarquin, Duke of Claremont. Idolized him. He recalled the duke's visits to the nursery, the occasional encouraging pat on the head, and how his father often gifted books for Rhys to read.

That was where it had all gone wrong. As soon as his struggles with learning became evident, his father lost interest. A duke's son who couldn't read properly? Unthinkable.

"Enderley was a shambles when I inherited," Nick admitted in a tone that was far more sympathetic than pitying. "What is the state of Edgecombe?"

Rhys hated admitting that he hardly knew. Without his mother and sister to brighten its halls, the old estate had all the charm of a mausoleum. He'd stayed in a guest room the single time he'd visited and departed as soon as he was able.

But thinking back to his conversation with the estate's staff, Rhys was beginning to form a theory. "There were debts attached to the estate." He scrubbed a hand through his hair before looking at each of his friends in turn. Fortunate, he may be, but he knew his faults. Even admitted them once in a while. To himself, if no one else. He had a tendency toward irresponsibility and a refusal to be anything but the feckless nobleman others expected him to be, which left very little room for anything he truly wished to be.

Disappointing the friends who'd stood by him when

others in polite society called him a ne'er-do-well and a cad? That was a fresh low.

"I directed the steward to contact my bank and see to any financial obligations my father had yet to meet."

Nick's dark brows arced up. "How steep were the debts?"

Rhys turned to Nick, intending to offer one of his charming smiles. His typical devil-may-care reassurance that all was well in hand. But the muscles of his face rebelled.

Weariness washed over him and honesty was the only thing that took no effort. "Apparently mountainous."

Nick let out a heavy sigh.

"Is there more?" Rhys had known the two men long enough to sense there was a great deal Tremayne and Iverson were leaving unspoken.

"You agreed to fund two other inventors after Carthorpe," Nick said. "They've received nothing yet, but Iverson and I can see to your share between us."

Rhys tried to concoct reasonable excuses, rationales for why his accounts had been drained and he'd somehow been too busy to notice. But they knew his reputation. His ducal town house was such a mess from the last party, he'd been forced to host this one at Lyon's.

They deserved more than justifications.

"I'm sorry," he heard himself say. The words were unfamiliar and felt misshapen on his tongue.

He lifted his head. Both men deserved more than a simple apology. All of society knew he was a man who sought recreation rather than rectitude every day of his life, but perhaps it was time to stop playing a role and assume the responsibilities he'd become so good at outrunning.

Casting a glance at Tremayne, he caught his own reflection in the gilded mirror on the wall. Dark circles smudged the skin under his eyes. His hair wasn't its usual artful tumble. It was downright disheveled. And the snow-white collar of his shirt was dotted with blood.

Iverson took two steps closer and surprised Rhys by placing a hand on his shoulder. "Whatever's troubling you, we wish to help."

It was tempting to confess the truth to both of them. But if his father had taught him anything, it was to never admit weakness.

Sensing his friends' stares, Rhys wielded the familiar skill of scoffing at whatever challenge came his way.

"If you're any example," he told Tremayne, "a man can become a decent duke in a matter of weeks."

The smile came slowly, inch by inch, but eventually softened Tremayne's grim expression. "I became a duke as you did. Unexpectedly and long before I was prepared to assume any such responsibility. Embracing duty didn't come easily. I credit my wife with whatever decency I've managed."

"Having known you for years before you met her," Iverson quipped, "I agree she deserves a great deal of credit." He turned a sardonic look Rhys's way. "I suppose you'll be needing a wife soon yourself. Any likely prospects in the countryside?"

An image filled Rhys's mind, a memory so sharp, he felt a stab of pain under his ribs.

Auburn curls, green-gold eyes, a contagious laugh, and a smile that came rarely with others but easily with him. She would be there when he returned to Essex, but Miss Arabella Prescott would have no smiles for him anymore.

He pushed the thought of her away. As he had for five years.

"Let me find my feet before I get myself leg shackled." He gestured vaguely and drew in a deep breath. "I must go to Edgecombe. Whatever I find at the estate is mine to sort out." He pointed at Iverson and then Tremayne. "I will repay you both. The dukedom's debts could not have drained my accounts entirely. I maintain others. I may be a reckless pleasure-seeking fool, but I know a man shouldn't put all his coin in one purse."

Iverson stared at him for a long silent moment, assessing him, then turned his back on Rhys and filled a glass from the drinks cart. Several glasses. One for each of them.

"Safe travels, Claremont," Iverson said as he handed Rhys a half-filled tumbler.

"I have some notion of what awaits you." Nick stepped forward to take his glass and lifted it in a toast. "Good luck, my friend."

Rhys swigged back his finger of whiskey and savored the trail of heat racing from his throat to his middle. He needed a bit of fire in his belly. Nothing but his own selfish indulgence had motivated him for years. Exhaustion still nipped at him, worry still rode his shoulders, but he managed a grin.

"They do say I'm a very lucky man."

Chapter Two

August 1848
Hillcrest estate, Essex

With a satisfying swipe of her pencil, Arabella Prescott struck another task off her list as she strode toward the dining room. Her family's long-planned house party was imminent, and Bella's list had been a long one. She loved helping her mother with party preparations, or any project that involved order and structure.

She should have set herself to conquering her list earlier, but she was so close to finishing the first draft of her book. She'd barely left her room in days. Just a few more details and she would be ready to consider submission to Mr. Peabody, the London publisher her mother had introduced her to the previous summer.

The past months had brought a reviving change.

After a series of failed Seasons, she no longer had to worry about social rounds or spending months in London while her parents put her in the way of every eligible nobleman on the marriage mart.

There'd been no talk of matchmaking all summer, and she could finally focus on her dream of publishing the conundrum book she'd been adding to off and on for years. The project had nothing to do with duty or her parents' expectations. Some in society would no doubt frown upon her harboring ambition for anything other than marrying well, but the book mattered to Bella. She needed to prove to herself that she could be something more than the doted upon daughter of Lord and Lady Yardley. A book of cerebral puzzles and logic problems written by a nobleman's daughter might be difficult to sell, but she was determined to try.

Now that her parents accepted her status as a spinster, her choices were her own. She only needed to get through a fortnight of being sociable to family friends and then her time would be her own too.

In the dining room, Bella discovered the staff had outdone themselves. Porcelain and silverware glinted in the late afternoon light and a centerpiece of flowers scented the air. Peonies, lilacs, and freesia blooms overflowed the edges of etched silver bowls.

She circled the table, moving from chair to chair to admire the perfectly arranged place settings. She loved symmetry, evenness, order. Every plate and glass and implement were in their right place. She let out an appreciative sigh, but then the name cards caught her interest. Stark white rectangles with gilded edges and names written in a bold hand. She examined the next and the next. The more she looked, the further her heart dropped.

Gripping the back of one polished wooden chair, she scanned the table again, her mind whirring.

Bella had always been good at solving puzzles. From childhood she'd excelled at mathematics and all the logic problems her governess devised to test her. She'd become so adept at unwinding riddles, she'd even published a few of her own in ladies' magazines.

The Puzzling Miss Prescott, one newspaper called her during her third Season. Of course, the society columnist had been referring to the mystery of why she'd refused five offers of marriage rather than her analytical mind.

Studying the cards the servants had carefully arranged in front of gleaming plates, she could see the trap she'd stumbled into, as unsuspecting as a rabbit rushing headlong into a blackberry bramble.

"Too many men," Bella whispered to the empty room.

Her heart lodged itself in the back of her throat. Her parents were still scheming to marry her off.

After four failed Seasons, she thought it was over, that they understood. But it seemed their patience had worn thin. She knew they were frustrated every time she refused a suitor or an invitation to London. But she couldn't regret her decisions. The five men who'd offered for her would have made dreadful husbands, and she would have made them a miserable wife. Her parents could have insisted, but they never had. They'd married for love and wished for her to do so too.

She'd accepted that she wouldn't, but clearly they hadn't given up hope.

When her parents suggested a house party to celebrate her twenty-third birthday, she'd been pleased. Not that she wished to make a fuss about her birthday. Since the debacle of a garden party five years past, she'd wanted the date to pass with little fanfare.

But *this*—plot—had never crossed her mind.

Gentlemen. A bevy of them. Four prospective suitors. They had to be. The only ladies who'd be in attendance were Bella, her mother, and her cousin Louisa. Since Louisa wasn't yet out, she couldn't be the object of this munificence of men.

At the sound of someone clearing their voice, Bella spun to find her cousin hovering at the dining room threshold.

"How angry are you?" Louisa stepped inside the room and slid the pocket doors closed behind her.

Bella pressed two fingers to her temple. "You knew about this and said nothing?"

Louisa blinked and her blue eyes widened. Rather than answer, she plucked nervously at a satin ribbon on the front of her gown.

Four years younger and far more eager for romance than Bella had ever been, Lou was sweet natured and rarely prone to duplicity. They were as close as sisters, and Bella understood why she'd gone along with the plan. Bella even sympathized with her parents' desperation, but she had to make them understand.

"Where are they?"

"I saw your mother in her sitting room a quarter of an hour ago. I suspect they'll be in the drawing room greeting guests soon, but I've just come from there and no sign of them yet."

"I need to speak to them before this all starts." Bella hugged her notebook to her chest, pushed her pencil into the crook above her ear, and swept past her cousin.

Louisa called out a soft hesitant "Good luck."

Marching toward her mother's sitting room, Bella rallied logical arguments in her mind. Explanations. Rationales that would help her parents accept that she was not meant to marry. Some girls, like Louisa, stacked all their hopes on matrimony, but Bella didn't entertain those dreams anymore.

By the time she stood outside her mother's door, she knew exactly what to say, but she hesitated with her fingers on the handle. Voices came from her father's study across the hall.

Good. Both of her parents in one place was exactly what she needed.

She approached the study but stopped short when her mother began shouting. Bella pressed her ear to the wood.

"You must speak to her, Edmund. Tell her the truth."

"Bah," her father grumbled. "Perhaps she'll take a

fancy to one of the gentlemen you've invited for the fortnight. Then everything will fall into place, just as we hope."

"My dear." Her mother used the long-suffering tone Bella had become very used to. "Our daughter has stubbornly refused every offer put to her. Shouldn't we tell her what you must give up if she continues to do so?"

"She might opt to accompany us," her father said, his voice pitched high and hopeful.

"Bella wishes to publish her book. She won't want to be away from England so long and I won't leave her unchaperoned. Unmarried."

"My sister Iona—"

"Is ailing in Scotland and must look after her health rather than our daughter."

Bella couldn't stand it anymore. She turned the latch, pushed inside the room, and faced her startled parents. "What aren't you telling me?"

Her father heaved a long sigh and settled into his desk chair, then popped up again and removed two books he'd apparently deposited there and forgotten about. For a moment, he struggled to find an empty space where he could rest the two volumes. As usual, his desk was covered with maps and sketches of ancient Greece. He'd tutored others in the language for years, but his true passion was Hellenistic art and architecture.

"Mama?" Bella turned to her mother. Of the two of them, she was the most effusive. As a poet, she understood the value of words more than most. But today she was uncharacteristically quiet. Pressing her lips together as if forcing herself not to speak, she turned her gaze toward Bella's father. Whatever they were hiding, it seemed he would have to be the one to tell it.

"I didn't wish it to come out in this manner, my girl." He flattened the edge of a sketch and placed the books on top before sinking into his chair. "I've been offered an opportunity," he said softly.

"In Athens," her mother blurted.

"That's . . ." *So far away* was Bella's first thought, but it was a selfish one. Her father longed to visit the lands he'd been studying for decades. "Wonderful news."

"It's a teaching role." He gave her that searching gaze of his with jade green eyes the same shade as her own. "The offer is for three years."

Years? Bella had never been parted from her family for more than a few months when she'd gone away to a finishing school in the north, loathed it, and returned home early. And they'd never traveled farther than London or the seaside at Brighton. Travel had never been her passion, but she had no wish to keep her father from his. Her mother, she suspected, would find much inspiration for her writing among ancient ruins too.

"I wish you to go, Papa. Both of you. But I can't accompany you, and I don't think the marriage plot house party will work."

"Hardly a plot, Arabella." Using her given name

meant her mother's patience was wearing thin. "We invited a few gentlemen to round out the numbers."

"Far more gentlemen than ladies."

Her mother sighed and rubbed her fingers against the fob watch on a chain around her neck. "They're decent gentlemen," she said with a hopeful lilt. "Well-bred. Well educated. We thought in lieu of another Season—"

"I never want another Season, Mama." The words were out too quickly and too loudly. "You know my plans. My hopes. I've done my round of Seasons." Bella let out a sigh that was more sadness than frustration. "Do you truly expect me to do it all again?"

"My girl," her father spoke up, his voice soft, almost pleading. "We wish to see you settled before we would ever consider leaving England. Neither of us can bear to think of you here alone." He glanced across the room, his eyes meeting her mother's. "I assure you marriage is not a terrible fate."

"Not for some, but I've accepted that it won't be my fate." Once she'd longed for marriage as much as any debutante, but she'd discovered a flaw in the whole nonsense of Seasons and balls and matchmaking. Her heart was stubborn and she'd pinned her hopes on the one man who would never fulfill them.

"It still could be." Her father gripped the edge of one of his books so tight his knuckles whitened.

Bella moved close and laid her hand on his. "Are you all right, Papa?"

"I'm well." He nodded once, but Bella didn't like how pale he looked. He'd taken ill the previous year and had not yet recovered his usual vigor for study and teaching.

Bella looked toward her mother. "Is there more you're not telling me?"

"Dr. Bell did comment that a bit of Greece's sun may do your father well."

Every emotion Bella had entered the room with— guilt, frustration, determination—turned to fear. She didn't want her family to go, and yet she wanted her father to be well. She couldn't lose him.

"The house party is a hope that you might finally find the happiness we wish for you. And you must forgive us for not telling you of your father's news. We wanted to find the right moment."

"You know I do." Bella had learned the danger of holding on to hurt.

"If I'd said anything you would have commandeered a pony cart and ridden off to some distant village where no one knew your name."

"I still might." Bella quite liked that idea.

"Bella, please."

"We must give her at least one good reason not to," her father said playfully.

Hearing lightness in his tone eased the worry weighing on her heart.

Her mother let out a half-hearted chuckle. "Because we have house guests arriving who expect to be entertained for a fortnight?"

And just when I have a book to finish. Dozens of slips of paper decorated the wall in her sitting room.

Some were riddles, others contained word problems or logic conundrums. Every time she thought of a new one, she added it to the collection and then to the pages of her manuscript. She was so close to adding finishing touches.

"You needn't choose any of them," her father told her in his rumbling baritone.

"Edmund, we've discussed this." Mama's quelling glance would have given other men pause, but her parents had been married for two decades and her father wasn't a man to be put off easily.

"They're all fine young men, of course," he conceded. "Your mother chose with care."

"But without consulting me," Bella couldn't stop from blurting.

Her mother strode forward. "What would you have said, dear girl? Would you have agreed to meet them? We do not wish to force your hand."

"And yet four men are descending on Hillcrest and I had no choice at all." Her voice had taken on a reedy quality she hated. Petulance didn't suit her.

"The choice shall always be yours to make." Her father's firm unwavering manner always made her believe him. "We only long to see you happy."

"I'm happy as I am." Bella felt the hollowness of the claim even as she spoke it. Loneliness weighed on her more often than she liked to admit. She kept busy and there were always things to do. But at moments, just every once in a while, it felt as if something was missing.

"Marriage does have its merits." It was rare that her father fell into the softer tone he'd used when she was a child, but he wielded it now as he approached to stand next to her mother. His gaze turned soft, filled with warmth. "You are our only child. We wish to see your future secured, with a home and a man who is worthy of you."

Bella swallowed the protest that welled up.

"Who are they?" Bella had learned long ago that one couldn't form a strategy without information.

"You will meet them soon enough. Guests have been arriving for the last hour. By six they will all be gathered in the drawing room, my dear." The smile her mother offered was encouraging, but her eyes gleamed in that way they did when one of her plans had turned to triumph.

Bella's father stepped forward and offered his arm as if he meant to escort her to the drawing room immediately.

"I will greet them, of course, as visitors to our home. But I make no promises," Bella told them with the same vein of stubbornness that made her want to bolt from the room. "I saw no names I recognize at those place settings. These men are strangers to me."

"Arabella, don't be churlish—"

The moment her mother's voice began to rise, her father spoke up. "We ask only that you meet them, my girl. Speak to them. Consider that they came here because they wished to make your acquaintance. No different from the young bucks you encountered at all those silly balls during your Seasons."

"Better not to mention those gentlemen," her mother added.

With a little grumbling sound, her father came forward and took her hands in his. "You deserve the finest of suitors, my girl. And I've yet to convince myself any of them deserve you. But do consider whether any of the lads downstairs might suit you."

Bella clasped her father's hands.

They'd been endlessly patient. She knew of parents who arranged marriages with more concern for titles and bloodlines than their daughters' happiness.

She longed to tell them the truth, but it was one she could barely admit herself.

Clever young women who hoped to publish their own book one day did not allow their heart to be smashed by a man who hadn't even bothered to send a letter in five years. A man who'd become a duke and probably didn't even remember her anymore.

"I should prepare to greet our visitors," she told her parents. Then more softly to her father, "I'll do my best."

Perhaps it was time to let go of Past Bella, that silly girl so infatuated with her childhood friend that she'd convinced herself he returned her affection when all he truly wished was to bed as many women as it took to prove his prowess.

New Bella knew better than to trust such a man ever again.

She let out a long breath, trying to release all the tension knotting her muscles. But some deep vein of unease remained and Bella could only think of how appealing it would be to go back to her room and work on her book.

She sensed her parents anxiously watching her and pushed the errant thought of escape away.

There would soon be four gentlemen awaiting her presence in the drawing room, and all of them possessed at least one important quality in their favor.

None of them were Rhys Forester.

Chapter Three

Rhys gave one shove with his bootheel and four heavy volumes crashed to the tiles in a terribly pleasing pile of bent spines and crumpled pages. This corner of the conservatory was blasted cold so late at night, but his mother's desk and chair in the airy open space were far preferable to the cramped stuffy confines of his father's study.

His eyes ached, his head throbbed, and he couldn't make heads or tails of the numbers and notations in the estate's ledgers. The books were as much use to him on the floor as they'd been after hours of perusing their pages.

He was glad to be rid of them and sank with a sigh into the creaking leather of his chair. Folding his hands behind his head, he stretched his legs out atop his mother's ormolu desk. He closed his eyes and tried to appreciate the silence, both the stillness of the space and the quieting of his mind.

It lasted approximately fourteen seconds before a frustrated groan rose in his throat.

Who was he trying to fool?

He loathed silence, and he hated being alone. Since coming to Edgecombe he'd encountered a nearly endless supply of both. His sister still hadn't quite forgiven him and spent most of her time visiting friends in the village or holed up in her chamber.

The single attempt he'd made at a sincere apology had caused her to cry and rush off to the library, her haven as a child and now too apparently.

As if his thoughts had summoned her, Rhys heard her approach.

"When I was little, I used to love lying on the cool tiles to read." Margaret's slippered steps sounded behind him. "Though now I don't think I'd enjoy getting down on my elbows to read."

"Sounds uncomfortable to me."

"Not as uncomfortable as those ledgers look. You've bent the pages."

"Serves them right."

"And why are we angry at the ledgers?" Meg came to stand beside his chair, arms crossed as she stared down at him.

"I'm outnumbered by them."

"Might I help?" She asked the question softly. Tentatively.

"The responsibility is mine. You have a Season to plan."

He couldn't tell her. Rhys had no doubt the answers

to every question regarding their father's indebtedness were between the ledgers' pages, but it was not a trouble he planned to visit on his sister. She was too prone to worry as it was.

"Speaking of which"—she clasped her hands together and her voice pitched with excitement—"my friend recommended a clever modiste who's made gowns for several prominent debutantes. She's in London, so we must make a trip there soon. I will need to order dresses, shoes, hats—"

"I know." The sigh he let out was tinged with regret. "Why not start in a week?"

She unfolded her arms and began plucking at a ribbon at the wrist of her wrap. "If something's amiss, you should tell me. Papa never told me anything and I loathed it."

Rhys looked up at her and noted the lines of worry creasing her forehead. How miserable it must have been for her here alone with their father in a rambling lonely estate. The thought came that he should have visited more often or brought her to London once in a while. But that was foolishness. His reputation would have ruined hers.

"Please don't worry. I'll ensure that your first Season is a grand success." He had no idea *how* he'd achieve that claim, but he would.

"There were debts, weren't there?"

When he didn't reply, she took a step toward the ledgers.

"Leave them, Meg. Trust me. All will be well." He

managed a smile and she gave a little nod of silent agreement that she would press no more. At least for tonight.

The topic would come up again. He had no doubt. His sister was tenacious, if nothing else.

"Then if you promise not to throw anything else this evening, I shall return to bed."

"Sleep well."

After she'd gone, all he could think about were the damned ledgers. Kick them to the floor, throw them out a bloody window, and the facts would remain the same. There were irregularities. Even with his ineptitude in mathematics, it was clear the columns didn't add up. But the numerical notations were hell to decipher. Not only were they scribbled in a messy hand, some had been scratched out. Even the bits that were legible challenged him. Over the years, he'd gotten better at deciphering words on a page. He'd improved at jotting down his own thoughts too, but when he was exhausted, when problems stacked themselves up over his head, everything was a damnable pain in the arse.

What he needed was someone with a mind for numbers and fine details. He didn't trust Edgecombe's steward. Not only had the man hied off on a holiday prior to Rhys's arrival, but he was either oblivious to the errors in the estate's ledgers or he'd been swindling the Claremont dukedom for years. He'd met him once years earlier, and despite impeccable manners, the man hadn't impressed.

Now the only question was whether Mr. Radley

would return to his post or disappear with Claremont money, if he was indeed the one diverting funds from the accounts.

"Bloody blighted hell."

Rhys lowered his boots to the tiles and stood, eyeing the bottle of bourbon he'd emptied earlier. He considered calling a maid to fetch another, but a fuzzy mind wouldn't help him unravel the mystery before him.

He'd always been damned awful at puzzles, unlike the girl who'd brightened every day of his childhood. Instinctively, he turned his head left, staring at the glass and metal walls of the conservatory but seeing much farther in his mind's eye. He looked past Edgecombe's brick facade toward Hillcrest, the neighboring estate.

What might she be doing this evening?

The last day he'd seen her, she'd been happy, celebrating. Her parents had spared no expense for the elaborate garden party and, for once, Arry had allowed herself to relish the kind of attention she normally shied from.

He clenched his hands into fists when the memory sharpened. The disappointment in her eyes. The tears she swiped away with the back of her hand.

God, what a wretch he'd been. And he'd never even apologized.

On instinct, he reached for his suit coat and didn't bother with finding his discarded neck cloth. He exited the conservatory and kept striding, the click of his bootheels echoing through Edgecombe's empty marble-lined halls, until he reached the front door.

Hillcrest was too far off for him to see the estate, even on a clear moonlit night, but he knew the route by heart. His pulse thudded faster, anticipation nudging him out the door and down the steps. Deep inside, a guilty voice of warning whispered to turn back, but Rhys dipped his head and started off against the cold breeze.

If he was going to remain at Edgecombe for any amount of time, if he intended to be any kind of duke at all, making amends with the most prosperous and well-loved family in the village made sense.

Not that he was sensible. Taking a carriage and not showing up on their doorstep disheveled and unshaven would have been sensible.

But he followed his instincts and his gut told him not to stop.

He kept on, striding through the fields west of Edgecombe. He could see lights now, the long windows of Hillcrest's facade illuminated with a warm glow. He stumbled over uneven ground and realized he'd walked so far that these were no longer the neatly pressed lawns Edgecombe's gardener took pride in under his feet. He'd reached the stony fields, an unforgiving patch of earth that forever provided a plentitude of rocks for the mile-long fence dividing the ducal acreage from its neighbor.

The bulky outline of the wall stood out in the moonlight. So much smaller than it loomed in his memory. How many times had he scaled the jagged structure to reach the Prescott estate? How many times had he helped a girl with copper-colored curls scramble over to his side?

Before Meg came along, his childhood had been a lonely round of nannies and tutors. It was natural that Arabella had become his playmate, his closest companion. She'd merrily joined Rhys's childhood antics, a partner to romp with across the countryside. Four years his junior and she'd still been able to best him at everything. Fearless and too clever for her own good, she'd been adventurous and the most loyal of friends.

She'd been the only one he'd confided in about his struggle with reading and how desperately he wished to please his father. Only Bella had been allowed to read the scraps of poetry and unfinished stories he'd felt compelled to write in his youth. She'd never laughed at him or lost patience. Indeed, she'd encouraged him in every endeavor.

Rhys could feign blind confidence well enough, but Bella Prescott was a woman who truly could accomplish anything she set her mind to.

Unfortunately, she'd put her mind toward avoiding him. And he'd just as determinedly tried to ignore her. She'd once attended a ball he'd been a guest at too. At one point he'd been certain she noticed him, but then she'd turned away. They'd never acknowledged or spoken a word to one another.

He understood. The memory of what he'd done filled him with disgust and he was loath to revisit it.

Bella had idolized him, looked up to him, and as he had a tendency to do with all those he cared for, he'd disappointed her. So severely he'd broken all the trust and camaraderie they'd built over years of friendship.

He'd been so young and brash, he hadn't even expressed real regret. She'd been too angry to let him.

Five years seemed long enough to leave that task undone.

"YOUR MOTHER HAS truly outdone herself," Louisa whispered as she leaned closer to Bella on the settee they shared. She was a frenetic young woman, always on the move, and tonight she was virtually vibrating on the cushion next to Bella's.

"She certainly outwitted me." Bella smiled. Or rather she continued smiling. The truth was she'd been smiling so long, she feared her face would soon freeze in an expression of unconvincing mirth.

"Lady Yardley isn't usually the scheming sort. You've made her desperate, Bell. She's organized the next fortnight like a military maneuver."

"Oh, I'm well aware." She was also aware that she should be working on her book and drafting letters to publishers, but instead she found herself seated in her family's best drawing room with several pairs of masculine eyes turned her way.

She had agreed to try, but three days into the house party and she knew nothing for certain except that none of the men her mother had invited made her want to change her mind about matrimony.

"Two are missing," Louisa noted.

"Perhaps they don't care for musical evenings." Her mother had provided for entertainment on each night of the house party. Tonight, one of the gentlemen visitors was doing an admirable job performing Schumann on the room's grand piano. "They departed as soon as the music started. They'll be back."

Bella suspected her mother had informed each suitor bluntly that their only purpose during the fortnight was to vie for her affection. Some had already begun the onslaught. Lord Wentworth had the temerity to burst into song when he'd come across her in the hall, apparently trying to win her heart with an exceedingly long aria. Another had presented her with flowers this morning. Roses that she'd planted and preferred on the stem where she could look at them during her walks rather than watching them wilt in a vase.

Over the sounds of the piano, Bella could almost hear the gears in the gentlemen's minds spinning, trying to find the chink in her armor. The way into her heart, as her mother would put it. Lady Yardley was nothing if not a hopeless romantic.

When her mother approached, Louisa stood. "I'll go and see what the missing bachelors are up to."

"Mr. Nix isn't titled, but he may be the handsomest of them all," Bella's mother whispered as she settled next to her on the settee.

"Handsome men have proposed marriage to me before, Mama."

"I know." Her mother patted her arm. "And I under-

stand you prefer a man of wit and intelligence. So do
I. Why do you think I married your father?"

"Papa *is* handsome."

Her mother's mouth curved into a mischievous smile.
"Indeed, he is. But he isn't perfect. No man is."

"I don't seek perfection." What she desperately wanted
to add is that she wasn't seeking a husband at all. But
they'd had the conversation so many times her mother
could probably recite the arguments from memory.

As if she could sense the turn of Bella's thoughts,
her mother changed tack. "Seek kindness, my dear. A
kind man will bring you contentment and a home and
family of your own."

The old Bella had been just the sort to build those
dreams up in her mind. She'd even sketched pictures
of the home she wished to have, the children. One
boy and two girls. Of course all of them would have
Rhys's blond locks. Recalling how naive she'd been,
how thoroughly she'd let her fancies run away with
her, all of it stung.

New Bella would never give in to such romantic
nonsense again.

"Lord Hammersley is a viscount, of course. I did
try for a duke." Bella's mother had been speaking,
reviewing the merits of the various gentlemen she'd
wrangled into spending two weeks in Essex. "But I
thought it best not to invite the Duke of Claremont."

"No," Bella said sharply. She needed to get used to
hearing the title and realizing it was Rhys's now. But
she wasn't there yet. "We shouldn't invite him."

"You were such close friends once." Her mother's gaze was steady, too inquisitive.

Bella had never divulged the details of that day to anyone, but it wasn't difficult for her perceptive mama to note her tears and Rhys's hasty departure. But to Bella's relief, she'd never pressed for more. She'd made overtures about inviting the duke or Rhys to a dinner event now and then, but those stopped too when word of Rhys's reputation got back to Essex and spread through the families in the village.

"We *were* friends. Once. Not anymore."

Louisa slid to a stop at the edge of the settee, her cheeks flushed, as if she'd dashed the whole way back from wherever she'd gone. "Forgive me, Aunt Gwendoline. I must speak to Bella."

Her mother narrowed her eyes but offered them both a tiny nod of approval. Bella stood and followed Louisa to the edge of the drawing room.

"I found them," she said in an agitated whisper.

"I had no doubt you would. In the billiard room? I hope they aren't in their cups this early in the evening. And if they're smoking in that room, Mama will have—"

"No, none of that. Well, they may be drinking, but what's important is what they said. You need to know what I overheard."

Bella arched a brow when Louisa said no more.

"Tell me, Lou." Her cousin did have a flair for the dramatic but Bella was too out of sorts to have the patience for it tonight.

Louisa leaned in. Bella took a step closer. But rather than telling her what she'd discovered, her cousin looked around the drawing room, reached for Bella's hand, and pulled her into the hallway.

"Loui—"

"You need to hear for yourself. If we're quick, they'll still be at it."

"At what?"

Rather than answer, Louisa broke into a dash and pulled Bella along with her. At the billiard room threshold, she stooped and turned back to Bella, a finger pressed to her lips.

The men weren't difficult to hear. Their booming laughter echoed into the hallway. Mr. Edgar Nix, the wealthy mill owner her mother claimed was the most handsome of all the gentlemen guests, and Lord Teasdale, a widowed viscount with eight thousand a year and a crumbling castle in the north of England.

"One poor fellow claimed she wouldn't even shake his hand after she refused him. The lady is a cold one."

"It's true," Nix agreed. "Gent I know still tells the tale of the time he tried to kiss her. She didn't flinch. Didn't push him away. Just turned to offer him her cheek. He said her skin was cold as winter."

A scream welled up and Bella felt anything but cold. The words stoked a familiar anger inside her to white-hot fury.

Both men chuckled, echoing each other.

"Perhaps we should increase the bet. Two hundred pounds? We must have some reward. After all, we'll have our work cut out for us and a rather chilly prize if we win."

"Two hundred pounds it is." Glasses clinked. More belly-low chortles followed. "Hardly worthwhile for a lady to be such a beauty if she hasn't an ounce of passion in her."

Bella's whole body vibrated. Heat rushed across her cheeks and her heart beat in her ears loud enough to drown out the men's chuckles.

She moved past Louisa, pushed the billiard room door open, and marched toward the two men.

They turned as one, eyes wide, backs stiffened in what she hoped was shame. Maybe they weren't so craven that they were capable of embarrassment.

"Lord Teasdale." He was the one who'd called her passionless. She was proud of herself for getting his name out in something less than a shout.

Bella strode toward him. He couldn't look her in the eyes, but he was mumbling. She didn't stop. Anger drove her, a vibrating outrage that was more instinct than thought.

"Miss Prescott, I don't know what you heard—"

Bella lifted her arm to strike. Teasdale reeled back.

"Arry, don't do it." The voice came from behind her. Deep and warm and achingly familiar.

Bella froze. Her arm still raised. Goose bumps spread across her skin.

It wasn't possible.

Teasdale lifted his gaze to the man who'd entered the room. The look in his eyes, a mix of consternation and begrudging deference, told her that the voice she'd heard wasn't some conjuring of her mind.

Bella lowered her arm, breathed deeply, and glanced over her shoulder at the man she should have slapped five years ago.

Chapter Four

$\mathscr{A}$rabella Prescott was not at all as he remembered.

The girl he'd disappointed at that long-ago garden party had been all softness and sweet innocence. Her hair had hung down in loose ringlets, arranged over the shoulder of a frilly candy-sweet pink gown. The same rosy shade had colored her cheeks and tinted her full lips.

The woman who stood before him now was all bold colors. She wore a rich blue velvet gown buttoned to her chin, revealing nothing of her freckled skin. A wash of crimson colored her cheeks and her wavy auburn hair was trapped under pins, though a few strands gave off a fiery glint in the candlelight.

Rhys swallowed hard. Until this moment, he'd had no notion of how much he'd missed the sight of her.

When she turned to face him, the green-gold gaze that speared him held none of the warmth he'd once found in her eyes.

"Didn't know you were invited, Claremont." Lord Teasdale's nasal voice was high, defensive.

Rhys had beaten him at cards often enough for the man to loathe him for that alone, but since inheriting his father's title, he'd found that men's loathing now came with a tinge of jealousy.

"He wasn't."

"I wasn't." He and Bella spoke nearly in unison, their gazes never wavering from each other's. Emotion flickered behind the fierceness in her eyes, but he couldn't tell whether it was surprise or something else.

"Miss Prescott," he asked, "may I speak to you? Alone."

She gave no reply, but her shoulders tightened. The soft curve of her jaw drew taut.

When neither of the gentlemen made any move to depart, Bella's cousin, Louisa, spoke up from where she stood next to Rhys on the threshold.

"Gentlemen," she began in a commanding tone, "my aunt will consider you long absent from the drawing room. I'm returning there now. I suggest you follow." She cast Bella a look, eyebrows raised in curiosity.

"Won't that leave Miss Prescott unchaperoned?" Mr. Nix asked.

Rhys sensed Louisa watching him and turned to find her giving him a scrutinizing perusal.

"The Duke of Claremont and my cousin were childhood friends and haven't seen each other for many years." She waved the two gentlemen from the room, and they shuffled out with their chins up, chests puffed as if they hadn't almost been slapped by the angry daughter of their host.

Rhys was tempted to close the door behind them, but he knew it wasn't proper. God help him, he thought of those things now.

He waited, expecting her anger. There was a great deal they'd left unsaid.

After staring at him a moment, she turned and strode toward the back of the room. He expected her to approach the window, so that she could look out onto anything rather than face him. But instead she went to a case that held billiard cues and took one down. After a long still pause, she turned toward the billiard table and began arranging the balls, as if she'd just come into the room for a game and he was merely an incidental distraction.

Rhys tapped his boot against the carpet. Tapped his fingers against his thigh. Reading was his bane but he usually knew the right words to say. "Silver-tongued," one lady he'd wooed had called him. Now the words wouldn't come. The feelings were all there, heavy on his chest, but they wouldn't arrange themselves into polished sentences.

"Arry—"

"Don't call me that." She turned to face him. "No one calls me that." She tipped her head down, stared at the carpet, and then at him again.

"Bella—"

"Do you remember how to play?"

Images filled his mind instantly. Memories teeming with laughter and wagers that were for stakes no higher than lemon scones and based mostly on childhood bluster.

"I remember that you always won," he admitted.

Her mouth twitched, and Rhys hoped it meant she was tempted to smile.

"Shall we see if you've improved at all?" She gestured to the cue rack and tipped her head in a way he'd seen her do a hundred times. Her voice was cool, emotionless, but her nod was a gesture of challenge. And if she knew him at all, she knew he could never say no to a challenge.

Rather than answer, he shrugged out of his coat and tossed the garment onto the back of a chair. Then he began rolling up his sleeves as he approached the cues. She watched him steadily but without giving anything away. Then she went back to arranging the balls on the green felt billiard tabletop.

"What are we playing for?" he asked, approaching the opposite side of the table.

Her high-necked gown hid much but he noted that she swallowed hard and squared her shoulders before answering.

"A favor."

Rhys wondered for a moment if he'd heard her correctly. A favor was precisely what he needed from her.

"I'll agree to that."

"Without knowing what I intend to ask?"

"I have one of my own but I'll tell you after I win."

"*If* you win." She frowned at him. "Why are you here?"

It was a simple question, arguably the first she should have asked but it left his mouth dry. "I . . . wished to see you, Bella. It's long overdue that I say—"

"No, why are you in Essex?"

He didn't want to talk about the estate. Not yet. He moved to the end of the table, risked a step closer, and was relieved when she didn't retreat. The candlelight caught the gold in her eyes and they sparkled, less fierce than when he'd entered the room but still not warm. Still not welcoming.

"Right now, I'm only here to do what I should have done years ago."

She inhaled sharply as if she dreaded what he'd say next and then gestured at the table. "Shall we begin?"

Rhys didn't expect her to be so unwilling to hear his apology, but to say the words would be tugging at old wounds. If she preferred a game of billiards, it was the least he could do. Having any excuse to remain in her company suited him.

"Ladies first."

"That didn't used to be your policy."

"Perhaps I've become more civilized." Now, that was the farthest thing from the truth he'd said in years. She seemed to know it too. One auburn brow winged high.

"Not according to London gossip."

Rhys chuckled at that. "Have you begun reading tattle rags?"

"Of course not," she snapped. "But people talk."

Ah yes. There'd been a time when he'd liked being the name on everyone's tongue. Infamy was far better than others laughing at your foibles. But he'd never thought any of it would find its way back to Bella. She hated gossip.

"And when the talk was about me you listened?" he asked her softly, a little too hopefully.

She smirked. "The Debley twins visit and they've always enjoyed their London tattle rags. I listen to be polite."

Without waiting for his response, she bent, positioned her cue against her white ball, and took her shot. Her ball bounced against his.

"First point. Your turn, Your Grace."

Your Grace? Good God, were they as chilly as titles now?

He angled his arm, imagined where a strike would land her ball, and sent his spinning toward hers. The ivory spheres clicked when they collided but he barely dislodged hers an inch.

"One point each," she said.

She moved closer to take her next shot, and Rhys's pulse built a faster tattoo as she did. He watched her as she calculated. When Bella was thinking, it was almost as if one could see all the brilliant thoughts organizing themselves in her head. She pursed her lips, two little divots formed between her brows, and the notch in her chin became more pronounced.

She was concentrating so determinedly that she moved close enough for her arm to brush his.

He could have stepped aside. He should have, but he craved the contact.

Bella didn't seem to agree. "Pardon," she said softly. "I need to stand where you are."

He wasn't a proper gentleman. He'd rarely even tried to be, but he knew that if anyone deserved an attempt, she did.

Stepping back, he gestured for her to take his place near the edge of the table.

A little nod was all he got in the way of gratitude before she bent over her cue, took her shot, and sent his ball spinning to the opposite end of the table. The grin she gave him over her shoulder made him want to let her take the next turn too.

Rhys positioned his cue stick but he couldn't focus worth a damn. She was a terribly appealing distraction. Not only for all that was unsaid between them, but because the attraction that had sparked the moment he saw her again only built the longer he was close to her.

Rather than take his shot, he straightened and held her gaze. "Bella, I'm sorry for how I conducted myself that day years ago. I'm sorry I ruined your party." He was on the cusp of saying more when she began to move.

To his shock, she made her way around the table

and approached him. There was such intensity in her gaze, he readied himself for the slap she'd intended for Teasdale. If she chose to strike, he deserved it but he couldn't help but notice she was carrying her cue.

"You're not planning on using that on me, are you?"

Her lips trembled and her eyes glittered in the candlelight. Rhys steeled himself for tears.

But no sobs came. She wasn't on the cusp of crying. She was bristling with frustration.

"Do you truly think I cared about my party?" She took one step closer. "I never wanted a grand event in the first place. I've never cared about parties the way you did." She took another step, close enough for him to see the lovely pinpoint spray of color along the cut of her cheeks and the bridge of her nose. He'd always adored her freckles despite how much she loathed them.

Gorgeous. The thought came, unbidden and unexpected, and it surprised him.

Bella had always been pretty, but now she was something more. She exuded confidence in the way she carried herself, a poise that made the beauty she'd always possessed more pronounced. She'd become a formidable woman and the realization unsettled him. It was a bloody inconvenient time to realize his childhood friend had become a stunning beauty.

Rhys was used to women looking at him with heat in their gaze, but the sparks in Bella's eyes weren't appreciation.

"Do you know what I cared about?" she asked him. "Why I was so upset?"

He did know. He'd sensed in the months before her birthday that she'd begun to notice him in a different way. She'd always thought far too highly of him. But by that day on her birthday, he'd already begun earning a reputation among the ladies in the village. It was a side of himself she couldn't know, and he'd been determined to protect her.

So he'd ignored her youthful crush, and that day she'd discovered who he really was.

She lifted her brows, impatient for his answer. Rhys sensed that what he said next could change everything between them. He knew now that she didn't want his apology so much as for him to understand her feelings.

"You still don't know." There was real wonder in her voice and for a moment she sounded like the curious girl he'd once known.

But she looked like a fearless woman. Her gaze still fixed on his, she took a final step that brought them toe to toe.

Rhys licked his lips. Tried and failed not to glance at her mouth. She smelled like cinnamon and the autumn air, and he felt something he'd never felt for her before. Desire. The rush of it was so intense it left him breathless. Aching.

"You're a fool, Rhys Forester."

Yes, that sounded right. His name on her lips. He'd

missed her calling his name and hadn't realized how much until this moment.

"I am inarguably a fool." He sometimes thought of himself as high society's jester, but *fool* worked too. "I was thoughtless and I'm asking you to forgive me."

In the beats of silence that followed his request, his breath caught in his throat. He watched her eyes, willing the steel he saw there to soften. She didn't blink. He couldn't look away. Nothing had mattered to him in a long while the way Bella's response did.

He needed to know she didn't hate him. He needed her forgiveness.

She blinked. One quick fan of her thick dark lashes. But she still said nothing as she watched him. Then, finally, she parted her lips and drew in a sharp breath.

"I can't." She spoke on a shaky whisper and even in those two quick syllables he heard emotion. Pain that he had caused.

"Please, Bella." God, how he wanted to reach for her. She was close enough and he'd once touched her without so much as a thought. But as near as she stood, so close he could feel warmth radiating off her body, he sensed the chasm between them. "I'm not much good at groveling, but I'm willing to try."

He'd never gotten on his knees with a woman for any purpose that didn't include pleasure. But he'd accept a dose of humility for Bella's sake.

Bending his knee, he began to lower himself in front of her.

"Don't do that." She slapped him on the shoulder,

gripped his lapel, and pulled him back up. "I'm not saying I'll never forgive you."

Once he was on his feet again, she didn't let go of his lapel. He leaned closer and color bloomed in her cheeks, but still she held him. Breath quickening, he told himself not to give in to the urge to reach for her or the more inappropriate urge.

He wanted to kiss her.

Too soon, the spell broke and she released him, taking one step back in retreat.

"I don't need you to beg, only to understand. Back then, I'd become convinced that—" She caught herself and pressed her lips together.

He willed her to go on, even shifted his gaze from hers to let her know he'd simply listen. It was better if she said it than he.

But silence fell between them. Silence and a tension that made him yearn for the right words to make things better.

BELLA BIT DOWN until her jaw ached. She'd come so close, but she couldn't bring herself to admit how silly she'd been.

For years she'd imagined this moment.

His apology had come as easily as she expected. Deep down, she knew he'd never wished to hurt her. They'd always protected each other, defended each other, kept each other's secrets.

But when she imagined this moment, she'd seen herself aloof. An impenetrable wall of calm and poise.

But now he was here. So close she could touch him. So near she could smell his familiar scent. And she wasn't doing anything she'd vowed she would do. Her heart was betraying her, aching in that old familiar way. Not as sharp as it had once. A duller pain. But enough to make her realize this could never work.

Playing nice, resuming their friendship, pretending as if all the rest hadn't passed between them—it was as impossible as walking downstairs and agreeing to marry a stranger.

His gaze was full of tenderness, yearning. "I was wrong, Bella."

"I was foolish too."

"You?" His mouth curved. "Even at eighteen, you were the least foolish young woman I'd ever known. I can't imagine how clever you must be now." He swallowed hard. "It's bloody terrifying."

"I *am* cleverer." Bella straightened her back. "And more clearheaded than the girl you used to know."

For a long silent moment neither of them spoke, giving her another opportunity to study him. He was still the most handsome man she'd ever seen. There were lines at the corner of his eyes, a few curving at the edges of his mouth, but they only made him look more dashing. Laugh lines, of course. No one enjoyed frivolity more than Rhys Forester.

No, he was Claremont now. Perhaps it was time to let the past go. Time to let go of the anger and hurt she'd held on to for so long.

They could never be friends again. She would always remember how much she wanted more. He still affected her too much. But it felt right to make peace.

"I forgive you." Once they were out, the words loosened something in her. As if they weren't simply words but a key that dissolved the pain and uncertainty she'd harbored.

They seemed to free him too. He let out a relieved breath and smiled. Not one of his dashing meant-to-charm smiles, but the genuine one. A bit crooked and imperfect, with no pretense.

He was far too appealing. He always had been.

Best she ended this unexpected visit and put the Duke of Claremont out of her mind.

"I fear we must stop our game. We have guests, but I appreciate your visit." Returning to the drawing room and attempting charm among strangers was not what she wanted, but it was what she'd promised to do.

They had nothing left to offer each other. The favor she'd thought of asking him was silly, and would only prolong a connection it was wiser to sever.

All the warmth drained from Rhys's expression. "This wasn't merely a social call, Bella. It's ten in the evening and I wasn't invited to your party."

She'd been so overwhelmed by the sight of him that the oddness of him bursting into a house party unannounced hadn't yet crossed her mind. Earlier she'd asked him why he'd returned to Essex, and he hadn't even answered that question directly.

"I need your help."

Her heartbeat had steadied the moment she'd forgiven him, but it thudded faster now.

Her silence prompted him to step closer. "Is it selfish of me to come after all this time and ask that of you?"

When she took a breath to answer emphatically yes, he lifted a finger and held it hovering over her lips.

"Don't answer that. I know it is, but there's no one else I trust."

Every word he said was true. Bella could see it in his furrowed-brow expression, hear the earnestness in his voice. He wasn't employing any of his usual charm. She sensed there wouldn't be any jokes or clever quips to undercut his statement.

"Surely there is someone else," she said, and couldn't help glancing down at where he still held his finger dangerously close to her lips, "for whatever reason you require assistance."

The man was a duke with servants at his beck and call, ladies prepared to swoon at his feet, and gentlemen eager to curry favor.

"No one like you." His voice had gone low, not much above a whisper. "You know who I am. My failings and flaws. Many of which are your strengths. Mathematics, for instance."

Bella frowned.

"And London Seasons," he added, then finally moved his hand away to begin ticking off items. "Ordering gowns, negotiating with haberdashers, hats, shoes, who knows what else. That is precisely the point. I have no notion of what Meg needs. You do."

Mention of his sister made Bella smile. In cutting off her friendship with Rhys, she'd missed any connection to his sister too.

"I would be happy to meet with Lady Margaret. She could visit me at Hillcrest if she's in residence at Edgecombe."

Now it was Rhys's turn to frown. "But it's more than Meg." He pressed a hand to his chest. "*I* need you. You know I can't read or juggle numbers worth a damn and—"

"That's not true. You're better than you think you are." The instinct to reassure him came without thought or intention. An old habit, yet she still found the words to be utterly sincere. He'd never seen himself as she saw him, never understood the man he could be.

"You still believe that after all this time?"

"Unless you've changed significantly in the last five years, I probably do."

"I appreciate the sentiment, but I still need your aid. The ledgers at Edgecombe, Bella. They're a nightmare. I can't make heads or tails of them and I must. There's been theft or perhaps simple mismanagement. I'm not certain. Nothing is certain." After his rushed ramble, he shoved a hand through his golden waves. He looked as exhausted as she'd ever seen him. "If you'd just examine them and speak to Meg. I've nothing to offer in return. You'd have my gratitude, but you've had that since the day we met."

The desire to help him was almost as compelling as a need. But that was exactly why she couldn't. A few minutes in his presence and tender, foolish feelings were already there, waiting to resurface and shatter all her resolve.

Perhaps they would always be there.

"What was it you wished to ask of me?" he said softly. "Name it, and I'll agree."

No, she couldn't continue this. It was too much like picking at a wound that had finally healed over.

"Please tell Meg to call. Despite the house party, I would welcome her any day." She took a deep breath before saying the rest. "Beyond advising her, I cannot help you."

He closed his eyes a moment, pursed his lips, and then began to nod. "I understand. You owe me nothing, but I've always been a selfish man, haven't I?"

"I never thought so."

That little smile came again, tip-tilted and charming. "You thought too highly of me."

"Yes."

"But not anymore?"

"It's not that." What was the point of explaining feelings that no longer mattered? "I'm sorry, but I must return to our guests."

He nodded and worked his jaw, then it was as if a breeze swept the clouds aside on a sunny day. He smiled, but it was the false one. The beautiful beaming facade. "I'm a selfish bastard, and I've kept you too long." He reached for her hand.

Bella bit back a gasp at the contact. His hands were bare. Hers too. And his skin was warm.

"I bid you good evening, Miss Prescott."

"Good-bye, Your Grace."

He let her go and moved past her toward the door. Bella didn't turn, didn't breathe, as she waited for him to depart. Then his footsteps stopped.

"What was the favor?" he called from behind her.

Bella turned to face him. "It was nothing. Nonsense."

In a flash of rebelliousness, she'd thought to invite him to the dance and dinner her parents had planned for tomorrow night. Her birthday fete. But the impulse had been pure mischief. For a moment, she'd wondered if a single waltz with the infamous Duke of Claremont might convince the men her mother had invited to abandon their pursuit.

"I'd be more than happy to exchange favors, Bella." His smile was wicked, unlike any he'd ever offered her before. "If you change your mind, you know where to find me."

Chapter Five

Rhys stifled a yawn, planted his boot a step higher on the rolling ladder, and stretched to tug at the books on the top bookcase shelf. Every muscle ached and he deserved it for getting the only hours of sleep he'd achieved while draped across an overstuffed settee in the corner of his father's study.

After meeting with Bella, there'd been no possibility of returning to his chamber and falling into anything like restful slumber. Guilt and regret still chased him, hours after their encounter.

He could no longer pinpoint what had possessed him to go to Hillcrest and ask for her help.

What didn't surprise him at all was her refusal. Of course she'd refused. Bella owed him nothing and he had nothing to give her in return even if she'd agreed to assist him. It wasn't hard to see the irony. He'd gone seeking to make his responsibilities feel like less of a burden and yet facing Bella made him more determined than ever to embrace duty and be a better duke.

He'd decided to search his father's study for any clue to why the Claremont finances had taken such a downturn in the previous year. He dreamed of finding a journal the old man left behind, preferably one explaining that the steward was a thief or that he'd been cheated in some investment by a scoundrel.

But instead of answers, he'd only discovered that his father liked subterfuge. He'd squirreled away documents in the oddest of places. Random drawers, hidden compartments in his desk, and tucked behind the rows of books on the tall shelves that lined one wall of the study.

Rhys gripped the edge of one finely tooled leather-bound copy of Herodotus with his fingertips and pulled. The volume came easily but he nearly dropped it when a feminine voice called up from below.

"Shall I bring your morning repast here, Your Grace?" Edgecombe's ruthlessly efficient housekeeper, Mrs. Chalmers, had taken to delivering his breakfast personally each morning. He suspected it had something to do with how foul tempered he'd been since arriving in Essex and her desire to spare the younger staff from his churlishness.

She also had a unique talent for overruling his directives. Though she showed him all the necessary deference when other staff were about, she fussed over him like he was still the boy she'd once known when no one was about as a witness.

"Strong coffee is all I require, Chalmers."

"Excellent. We've just pulled out fresh crumpets and there's a bit of ham from last evening's meal."

Rhys shot her a raised-brow look which didn't seem to intimidate her in the least.

"Will you be working from the study now, Your Grace? Shall we move all of your writing implements from the conservatory?" Chalmers had always had a way of phrasing her suggestions as questions. She was grayer now and the sharp angles of her face had softened with age, but she still knew how to spark his guilty conscience just as she had when he was a child.

"I already have." Rhys descended two steps on the rolling ladder attached to the wall of bookcases and was rather proud to point to the ink pot, pen, and various crumpled pages littering his father's desk. He'd managed a short note to his bank directing the transfer of additional funds and inquiring about a clerk to be sent out to Edgecombe to review the estate's accounts. "I still need to retrieve the ledgers."

"I'll have one of the footmen see to it. Have you been able to review the invoices, Your Grace?" She gestured to the corner of the desk.

Rhys hadn't even noticed the neat little pile of documents there.

"They've been waiting for some time." He understood the older woman's impatience. She'd probably accomplished more in the few hours since daylight than he would all day. Though he'd been up early, the search of his father's study had proven futile.

After replacing Herodotus, he descended the ladder attached to the bookcase, jumped off the last step, and reached his hands over his head to stretch the muscles of his back. Aside from his hours in the Duke's Den, he hadn't spent so much time sitting on his arse in years. He longed for movement. Activity. Anything that didn't involve perusing documents and deciphering tightly scribbled handwriting.

Rhys stared down at the mess of a letter he'd been working on for the better part of an hour. A few words to his banker had been easy enough, but the note he'd begun to the Duchess of Tremayne had proved a challenge. He planned to ask her to shepherd Meg through her first Season, but he'd crossed out and rewritten so many lines the letter was no longer worthy of anything but the rubbish pile.

Reaching out to crumple the latest attempt, his hand stilled as he looked at the doodle he'd sketched at the edge. Bella's profile. Her round chin, elegant nose, and waves of auburn hair. He hadn't sketched her in color, but he would always see her that way.

He balled up the unfinished letter, aimed for the bin near the door behind Chalmers, and tossed the crumpled paper in a perfect arc that landed with a soft thud on top of the others he'd already tossed there.

She made a little harrumphing sound of chastisement but said nothing.

"Tell me about the invoices."

"They are nothing more than routine monthly expenses, Your Grace, but Lady Margaret has asked the staff to prepare a special luncheon for three of her lady friends next week, and we should see to the deliveries soon." Rather than wait for him to retrieve the documents, she lifted the pile and held them out.

He couldn't take the time to decipher every word, but he skimmed a few and decided they all related to food or supplies for the ducal larder.

"You see to some of the estate's invoices, and I take it Mr. Brooks sees to the others?" Between Chalmers and Edgecombe's long-serving butler, Rhys couldn't imagine that any of the estate's financial woes could be ascribed to their mismanagement. But if co-ownership of Lyon's had taught him one thing, it was that people will always surprise you.

"Quite so." Mrs. Chalmers's face puckered in a frown. She was a clever woman. Rhys suspected she could see through his ham-fisted interrogation and sensed there was something more afoot. "Mr. Brooks and I were allowed to purchase as we saw fit."

"What was left to Radley?" Rhys was due to meet with the estate's steward in the afternoon and longed to know if his previous impressions of the man were shared by others.

"Only when an expense was out of the ordinary would we consult Mr. Radley, and he spoke to His Grace on our behalf when necessary." Her dark eyes narrowed behind her spectacles. "Is anything amiss?"

Rhys liked her suspicious mind. It made him certain the staff were not aware of whatever shenanigans had gone on with the dukedom's finances.

"Mr. Radley is relatively new to the role of steward, is he not?"

"Your father hired him nearly two years ago."

Two years during which Rhys hadn't spoken to his father and exchanged only a handful of letters with his sister. If the dukedom was struggling, he'd never been informed.

He scooped up the paperweights off the edge of his father's desk. Polished rounds of jade he suspected his father liked more for their beauty than their usefulness. He began juggling the three disks. Concentrating on the task allowed him to focus his thoughts.

"Do you like him, Chalmers?"

"Not for me to say, Your Grace."

"I command you to say."

Her graying brows winged up high and she pressed her lips together.

More gently, he tried, "You're a discerning woman." She was so clever, he had half a mind to ask her to have a look at the estate ledgers herself. But he didn't want the staff alarmed if it was something as simple as an accounting error. "I trust your judgment, so may I have it?"

"He's a bit odd. Went away rather a lot. Disappeared for weeks at a time."

"Why?"

She shrugged. "Can't rightly say. We all wondered why he was allotted so many holidays or whether he was off on business for your father. I do recall mention of property the duke thought to purchase. There was talk of who among the staff might go to the new house."

"New house?" Rhys gestured around the spacious study. "Edgecombe has twenty-three bedrooms, three drawing rooms, and the largest ballroom in the county. Why would my father need another house?"

"The seaside. There were whispers that he wished to buy a house for holidays. Mr. Radley did make several trips to the seaside and spoke of the temperate weather."

"Do you trust him?" He expected her to hedge about answering again, to demure and say it wasn't her place to cast such a judgment. Instead, she held his gaze a long silent moment.

"Now that you ask, Your Grace, I do have my suspicions about the steward."

Rhys fumbled a stone but caught it before it fell. Leaning toward his housekeeper, he whispered eagerly, "Tell me more."

NOTHING MADE SENSE.

The previous day, Bella had organized her book into three distinct parts and today the words seemed to run together on the page. Sorting and arranging, which usually gave her such pleasure, only stoked the irritation that had been stewing since opening her eyes.

She could blame fatigue or the distraction of having strangers in her home, but mostly she blamed Rhys for bursting back into her life uninvited.

How dare he disturb all the poise and contentment she'd been working toward for years? And without even a bit of warning. Even now, hours after they'd parted, she felt like a kaleidoscope being twisted, its pieces tumbling one over the other.

Five years should have been sufficient. More than long enough to put her foolishness aside. Seeing him again shouldn't have disturbed her peace of mind one iota. She'd fought for that peace, practiced it day after day until it was a habit every bit as firmly ingrained as her desire to speak to him every day had once been.

She'd pushed thoughts of him aside so often that she told herself she'd forgotten how he looked and sounded and smelled, his unique spice and leather scent.

But it wasn't true.

She remembered him completely, but memory was nothing to seeing the man in flesh and blood. Rhys had always exuded a vibrant energy she could feel from across a crowded room, but last night the billiard room had been empty. His nearness had surrounded her like a soothing warmth she hadn't known she needed. Somehow, unfairly, time had lent him more appeal. Even as disheveled and exhausted as he'd looked, he was handsome. Devastatingly so. Especially when he smiled. That lip-tilted smirk of his was perhaps what she'd missed most of all.

For so long she'd told herself what she felt for him was childish nonsense. The infatuation of a girl with no real sense of what love or romance meant. She'd vowed to be unfeeling if they ever crossed paths again.

Forgiveness, yes. She could offer him that, but nothing more.

Last night, he'd expressed regret and she'd accepted his apology. That should have ended all that remained unresolved between them.

So why did nothing feel resolved?

One thing she knew with unwavering certainty: she couldn't help him, despite how much the impulse gnawed at her. The girl who gave in to every whim and fancy was gone. New Bella had plans and they were set as firmly as the stones in the rough-hewn wall separating Yardley land from the Claremont acreage.

Setting her manuscript aside, she stood and put on her jacket then glanced at the mirror and decided the simple knot she'd pulled her hair into would have to do. Breakfast was long over and at this hour guests would be assembled outdoors for croquet.

Outside, Bella found the late summer sun shining on a freshly manicured lawn of vibrant green. Her mother and Louisa were consulting with servants about tables that had been moved out onto the veranda. The gentlemen seemed engrossed in the middle of a game.

Bella was pleased to note that Teasdale was not among their number. She'd hoped embarrassment and shame at their behavior would drive him *and* Mr. Nix to depart early.

Unfortunately, the wealthy mill owner remained and, as usual, he was talking. He and the other gentlemen stood with their backs to her, unaware of her approach.

"Some would call a woman ruined for Miss Prescott's behavior last evening." Nix's voice had a whiny pitch to it, and Bella bit her tongue to stop from revealing *his* behavior the previous evening. What would the others think of him for plotting to wager for her like a filly at Tattersall's?

In truth, Bella was thrilled by his disdain. Let him judge her a hoyden for speaking to an old friend. She looked at the situation strategically. With Nix and Teasdale out of consideration, she only had to contend with playing polite debutante to two gentlemen. Hammersley, who was far too old, and Lord Wentworth, who was far too quiet.

"I must agree," Hammersley said as he rolled up his shirtsleeves. "Claremont is hardly proper company for Miss Prescott. Or any decent young woman. Alone in a room together for God knows how long. The man's the worst sort of scoundrel."

"She's clever," Wentworth added quietly. "Miss Prescott cannot be unaware of his reputation."

"I begin to doubt her sense of propriety." Hammersley positioned his mallet near the blue-ringed croquet ball and lined up his aim. "No man wants a wife without a whit of good sense. Never mind how pretty she may be."

Bella went to the rack and selected the yellow-ringed mallet.

The taciturn Lord Wentworth spoke while Hammersley took his shot. "The lady is known for her cold demeanor. I don't imagine Claremont got very far."

"He didn't," Bella said brightly, and watched each man jolt in shock and consternation. "Good morning, gentlemen."

"Miss Prescott." Wentworth nodded solemnly. He did seem to have the least to be embarrassed about.

"I understand there is some concern about the Duke of Claremont." Bella waited a moment to ensure she had every man's attention. "He was not invited but his presence in our home is nothing out of the ordinary. As a child, he spent many days at Hillcrest."

"He's hardly a child anymore," Nix put in unhelpfully.

No, he most definitely was not. Bella got lost for a moment thinking of all the ways the man she'd faced in the billiard room last night was different from the boy she'd once known. The bravado was much the same, but something was missing. He wasn't as quick to smile or tease. One could almost see the dukedom weighing on his broad shoulders.

"We must start a new game, gentlemen, so that Miss Prescott and I can join," Louisa announced as she approached with the green mallet that perfectly matched the ribbon on her dress.

Wentworth acknowledged her arrival with a nod but the other men ignored her.

A thwack sounded behind Bella and Hammersley

let out a low belt of laughter. "I shall win our wager yet, Mr. Nix."

"Another wager," Bella mumbled under her breath.

"Men do enjoy winning," Louisa said as she came to stand close enough for them to whisper.

"Teasdale is gone. I wonder why Nix chose to remain after last evening."

Louisa moved an inch closer. "I believe he wishes to make an arrangement with Hammersley to fund a new mill in the north near the viscount's estate."

"Do men do nothing but make deals?" Bella bit her lip as soon as the words were out.

Rhys's visit had left her so out of sorts that the entire house party felt like a farce. She wanted it to end so she could get back to her puzzles and conundrums. Solving riddles made far more sense than navigating gentlemen suitors.

She also had to find a way to convince her parents to set off for a warmer climate.

The truth was that she wanted an arrangement too, preferably with a reputable publisher who believed in her work.

"Ladies, we're starting a new match if you wish to join," the usually quiet Lord Wentworth called from the edge of the first wicket. He watched both of them cross the grass, but Bella noticed that his gaze fixed on Louisa.

"I suppose we all make bargains, don't we?" Louisa mused as she walked beside Bella. "Is marriage itself not a deal of sorts?"

Bella narrowed an eye at her cousin. "You make me nervous when you become philosophical."

Louisa laughed. "I promise I'm not playing matchmaker. To be honest, I'm dubious any of these gentlemen will suit you. Your mother meant well but she couldn't choose as you would."

"On that, we're agreed. At least the field has narrowed to Hammersley and Wentworth."

"And what is your strategy?" She grinned the way she did when Bella was on the verge of explaining a new conundrum.

"Do I need one?"

Louisa stopped, pulled Bella to a standstill and shot her a dumbfounded look. "You're a puzzle maker, Bell. You always have a strategy. And you're practically an expert at turning down offers of marriage."

"Thank you." Bella frowned. "If that was praise."

"Oh it was." Louisa smiled mischievously. "You must teach me that skill in case I need it during my first Season."

"You won't need it." Bella knew her cousin's first Season would be a grand success.

Louisa was lovely, clever, and eager to fall in love. No past hurt held her heart hostage.

"If I do, I'm coming straight to you for aid." She glanced toward the men assembled near the first wicket waiting for them to start a new match. "Now, how may I help you with these three?"

Bella assessed the men too. "My only goal is to

end all of this as soon as possible and get back to my work."

"Do you not fear your parents will arrange for another Season?"

"Yes, but shall I marry Hammersley instead?" The fear of another Season chased at her mind relentlessly. But the fear of a life with any of the men standing on her lawn was far greater.

"So you must dissuade Nix, Wentworth, and Hammersley from any further pursuit." Louisa pursed her mouth thoughtfully and tapped a finger against her cheek.

Bella knew the answer. She'd considered it last night, and the gentlemen's earlier conversation made it clear how well it would work. They'd been appalled by Rhys's unexpected visit, and it had apparently unsettled Hammersley almost as deeply as it had shaken Bella.

What would they say if Rhys joined them for dinner as an invited guest and danced with her at the musical evening her mother had planned?

"There it is," Louisa said excitedly. "The gears are working. What have you come up with?"

"A bargain."

Louisa tilted her head. "With one of these gentlemen?"

"No." Bella drew in a deep breath and placed a hand over her middle. "He'd insist he's not a gentleman at all. A scoundrel, some would say."

"Claremont." There wasn't even a hint of surprise in Louisa's voice. "But you sent him away last night, didn't you? Why would he return?"

"He asked me for something."

"So you'll make a deal."

Bella smiled and the fluttering in her belly eased. This wasn't even a terribly difficult problem to solve. He needed her help and now she needed his. Rhys was reckless and completely impulsive, but he could be practical too.

"Are you joining us, ladies?" Nix's impatient whine grated on Bella's nerves.

Wentworth stepped in front of him and gestured Louisa and Bella toward the first wicket. "As it is your birthday, Miss Prescott, you must take the first turn."

Louisa began to step toward the men, but Bella stayed her with a hand on her arm. "I'm going to make an excuse to step away. I need to compose a note to the duke and have a servant deliver it before it gets too late in the day."

"Let me do it," Louisa whispered. "These gentlemen have come to spend time with you. Just tell me what to say."

"No, I must do this myself." Bella wondered if he'd remember the date, the anniversary of the last moment they'd spoken in five years. Until last night.

In that moment, she decided a note wouldn't do. He'd come to her, so she'd go to him.

Now that the shock of their first encounter had worn off, seeing him again wouldn't disturb her at all.

"Forgive me, gentlemen, but I must attend to an errand this morning."

Rhys would welcome her visit. And maybe if he did this one thing and freed her from the pressure to marry a man who didn't suit her, it would truly make up for that day.

Chapter Six

The man was late.

Rhys paced the length of his father's study but it did nothing to burn away the frustration that had been building since his return to Edgecombe.

Glancing out the garden-facing window, he spotted Meg, who'd set up an easel to paint flowers in the sunshine. Getting out of doors might do him good too. Maybe a gallop across the fields on one of his father's stallions. The stables were apparently full of fine horses and there was a man-made lake on the property his father had commissioned but Rhys had never seen.

In many ways, Edgecombe was a mystery. He'd avoided the place for years, and during that time his father had made expensive changes. Discovering why and solving the problem of its finances was proving an even greater quandary than he'd expected. Unlike his clever neighbor, Rhys had never been good at unraveling riddles.

He glanced at the clock again. "Where the hell are you, Radley?"

He refused to be confined inside on a fine day because his suspicious steward declined to show his face. The man's reticence made it more and more likely that he was the culprit in siphoning the estate's funds. Ah, how bloody grand it would be to wrap up the whole matter quickly.

Then he could focus on Meg and her Season, speaking to tenants, making repairs to the estate, a visit to the House of Lords when it was in session. Good God, how had the list of duties grown since he'd arrived?

Making amends with Bella Prescott ran through his mind unbidden.

She was there at the top of his thoughts. To think of anything else, he'd ruthlessly pushed her aside all morning. Had she always smelled like violets? Had she always had such fire in her gaze?

He shrugged out of his jacket, laid it across a chair, and began rolling up his shirtsleeves. He needed air. To move and put distance between him and Edgecombe's thick stone walls. A walk would put some heat into his bones and give him an opportunity to examine the outbuildings and elaborate gardens his father had put in the place in the past few years.

Good God, when had he started thinking practically?

He unwound his cravat and began pulling it from his neck but stilled when he heard footsteps in the hallway.

The steward. Finally.

His steps were firm, a loud clatter on the polished hallway floors. Rhys considered going out to greet the man, but he decided it was far better to remain and exude the kind of authority his father would have. The objective was to put the man on edge and get him to confess his misdeeds.

He strode to his father's desk, settled his backside against the edge, and crossed his arms over his chest. If his father was any example, Claremont ducal arrogance involved pretending you knew everything, puffing your chest out as if you were the burliest man in the room, and laughing at insults as if they mattered not a whit. Rhys could do all of that. He'd always been good at pretending.

As soon as the door latch twisted, he boomed out the man's name.

"Mr. Radl—" Rhys's voice faltered and his mouth went dry.

It wasn't Mr. Radley who stormed into the room.

Bella stepped inside and closed the door behind her. She vibrated with energy, and smelled of lemons and fresh air.

"You walked all the way from Hillcrest." Rhys was no detective, but her cheeks were flushed a delicious pink.

"Of course." She caught at a few loose strands of hair and tucked them into pins. "One of us used to walk back and forth every day. Sometimes we even raced each other. Have you forgotten?"

"I haven't forgotten." Just like back then, her boots

were dirty and the hem of her skirt was dotted with mud. Neither of them had ever minded about such matters. It made him ridiculously pleased to find that she still didn't.

As he studied her, the blush in her cheeks deepened. Mercy, how he'd missed that.

If she'd blushed last night, he couldn't tell in the low light of the billiard room. But he found he liked both Bellas. The fierce, sharp woman of last evening, and this one, beautifully disheveled and still breathing hard from her trek across the fields.

"I'm glad you've come." The gladness poured through him like fine whiskey, warming his insides.

She didn't seem to share his feelings. The determined set to her jaw told him she'd come with a plan. He didn't know what part he was to play in her schemes, but he suspected he'd agree. He needed her help and after the previous evening's encounter he feared they'd go back to avoiding each other. After parting from her, he'd felt like a fool who'd mucked up a chance to make amends with the girl who'd once been the most important person in his life.

"I've changed my mind." She lifted her chin a notch after making the declaration as if the words were some sort of challenge.

Rhys waited. There had to be more.

Her confidence gave way to a frown. "You said you'd be willing to exchange favors."

"I did." He swallowed hard recalling how he'd given himself away in that moment. Never in his life had he imagined his apology would turn to flirtation. "I am still willing."

"Excellent." She rubbed her hands together, and Rhys had his first moment of pause.

"Wait. Tell me what I'm agreeing to first."

"A visit to Hillcrest."

Rhys stepped forward, arms still crossed, and gazed down at her flushed face, savoring the excitement in her green-gold eyes. Only he got to see her like this. With others she was always careful. Proper. But when they were alone, he saw this side of her. Reckless, eager, full of ideas. "Tell me the rest."

She stared at him, assessing. "I'm hoping your presence this evening will dissuade the rest of the suitors Mama invited to the house party."

"Suitors?" Plural. "How many do you have?"

The notion of her having any made a muscle jump at the edge of his jaw and he wasn't entirely sure why. Protectiveness, perhaps. He'd failed at it woefully with her but the impulse remained.

"My mother invited four men. Two of whom you saw in the billiard room last evening. Lord Teasdale departed this morning, and I'm hoping Mr. Nix will decamp soon too." She drew in a sharp breath. "But that leaves two others."

"And my presence will do what?" Possibilities whirled in his mind. "What is it you wish of me?"

Bella shrugged. "Be yourself. Converse. Tell amusing stories. Dine with us." She gnawed her lower lip a moment and added, "Perhaps dance with me."

They'd never danced in all the years they'd known each other. There had been endless days spent together rambling the countryside, confessions of hopes and fears as they explored all the nooks and crannies of Edgecombe, and yet in all those years they'd never stood in each other's arms and danced.

His pulse quickened, and he wasn't certain whether it was nervousness or anticipation. Dancing was one of his few talents, and one that he enjoyed. He wasn't sure of Bella's opinion though.

"Do you like to dance?" Suddenly he was desperate to know.

She blinked and her eyes widened as if the question surprised her. "Not particularly but it's expected."

"Enduring the company of suitors your mother has chosen for you is expected too, and yet . . ."

He'd heard of Bella's reputation for rejecting suitors. She may deny caring about news of him, but he'd determinedly sought news of her through mutual acquaintances during the Season. A lingering sense of guilt and unease had made him determined to confirm that she was well. The first time he overheard a man at a soiree recount a proposal to her and the cold manner of her rejection, Rhys struggled to reconcile the description with the woman he knew.

"Yet?"

"You've rejected a few."

She tipped her head down and he wanted to take the words back. He'd always appreciated that she knew her own mind and it didn't surprise him that she'd reject any man who didn't suit her. But as the only daughter of a viscount, he understood that her parents would not stop until they saw her well matched and happily settled.

"This time, I promised my parents I would try."

That he understood too. Her parents doted on her and she'd been dutiful despite her independent nature. Which made her request all the more confusing.

"Yet you're hoping my presence tonight will thwart their plans on purpose."

He could almost see the conflict inside her, the struggle between acceding to her parents' wishes and pursuing her own happiness.

"I *will* need to marry," she admitted in a begrudging tone. "But not any of these men. Hammersley is too old and stuck in his ways. Lord Wentworth is too taciturn."

Rhys stifled the impulse to ask what he was. But he already knew. Too reckless. Too debauched. And, of course, too muddle-minded to decipher a few estate ledgers, though he knew she'd never let him speak of himself that way to her aloud. She'd always been his staunchest defender and she'd never minded when he needed her help.

As if she sensed the turn of his thoughts, Bella said, "I'll assist you in return, of course. With Meg and the ledgers." She turned to glance at the messy pile of scribbled notes and open books on his desk. "We could begin tomorrow."

"Tomorrow, it is. And tonight we will celebrate your birthday and I will play the role of suitor." He winked at her, as he'd done a thousand times before. In the past, it had drawn a giggle, a punch on the arm, or a wink in return.

Today she looked horrified.

"YOU'RE NOT A suitor." Bella hated the way her cheeks caught fire and her voice went raspy.

She wasn't inviting him to Hillcrest to woo her. Not in any true way. She wasn't even asking him to cause a scandal. Hopefully his mere presence would disturb Hammersley and Wentworth enough for them to give up any thought of pursuit.

The Claremonts had always been a family that trampled the bounds of propriety. The ducal title had simply allowed Rhys's father to do as he pleased with more impunity. From all that she'd heard of his London shenanigans, Rhys had spent the last few years trying to outdo his father's infamy.

Men like Hammersley and Wentworth wouldn't wish to associate with him privately, or marry a young woman who counted him a friend.

"Bella?"

Her mind had wandered while she'd stared at him, and he'd stepped closer without her noticing.

"I'm banking on your reputation. Being pursued by you never crossed my mind."

"I see." He wore an irritatingly amused expression,

as if he knew some great secret she did not. "But you are *aware* of my reputation."

"Of course. You throw a lot of parties and drink to excess and there are a great many women."

He tipped his head and glanced up at the ceiling thoughtfully. "Accurate enough that I won't quibble." When he looked back at her, his gaze had changed. No more amusement, just seriousness. "My concern is for *your* reputation." He paused, pursed his lips, and then continued. "If I dance with you, they will think we're enamored."

"That's ridiculous." The entire notion made her pulse jump at the base of her throat. A single dance meant nothing. "People dance at balls who don't even like each other. I assure you, I've partnered with many men I've never spoken to again."

Rhys dragged a hand across his jaw and stared at her dubiously.

"Fine," she told him a little too loudly. "We needn't dance."

The more she thought about it, the more the prospect seemed a step too far. Face-to-face, body to body, hands clasped and his palm against her waist. That much nearness was entirely unnecessary.

"I'm not saying I don't wish to, but rumors will start soon after."

Bella laughed. "You're very sure of yourself."

"I am." He spoke the two syllables without a hint of bravado.

For a man who'd once doubted his intelligence and let his father's disdain weigh on him, she was pleased to hear the confidence in his tone.

But he was wrong if he thought they'd start a scandal.

"Louisa knows why I'm inviting you, and my parents still think of you as the boy who spent his days at Hillcrest. No one will think we're paramours. I promise."

"If you say so." His smile was too knowing, but then he turned away from her and lifted his cravat from the back of a chair. "The steward was due today, but I don't think he'll appear. I'd be pleased to join you for dinner."

She desperately wanted to inquire why he was in such a state of undress, but held her tongue. He slid the fabric around his neck and then focused on the task of rolling down his sleeves.

The motion drew her attention to his bare forearms. To the muscles flexing as he moved and the dusting of blond hair against sun-kissed skin.

For a man she'd once known well, she found herself intensely curious about him. In the years since they'd last spoken, he'd lived much more than she had.

How many raucous parties had there been? How many ladies?

Good grief, she'd never even been kissed.

Lifting a hand to her mouth, she willed the thought away. Then she found herself staring at his lips. His was a generous mouth, always twitching into a smile or bravado-filled smirk and rarely turning down in a frown.

But what would it be like to kiss those lips?

He let out a little chuckle, and she realized he'd caught her watching him.

Bella moved toward the messy desk in the center of the room.

Ledgers. Numbers. Those were things she understood.

She opened one of the large leather-bound books to a page that had been crumpled and torn at the edge. A tally of expenditures from four months past. Some lines had been struck through, some amounts crossed out and then rewritten. Always in a lesser amount. Either the account keeper was error prone or the cost of goods had changed drastically.

Bella lifted the book into her arms to examine some smaller notations and turned the page.

"You needn't look at those now." Rhys approached from behind.

Bella jumped at the sound of his voice and lost her grip on the heavy ledger. One side flipped open and bumped the others stacked precariously at the desk's edge. As the thickest on top slid off, Rhys reached around her and caught it, his body pressed to hers.

He was all heat and firm muscle and it frightened her how much she wanted to lean into his warmth.

"I've got it," Bella told him as she clasped the volume's front cover. She pushed back against him and he retreated instantly.

It took her a moment to catch her breath.

"We can have a look at those," he said quietly, "another time."

"I know."

After taking one deep breath and vowing not to let her gaze snag on his bare neck or full lips, Bella turned to face him, bumped another of the ledgers and sent the whole pile tumbling onto the carpet.

She knelt down to collect them. Rhys knelt beside her.

When she grabbed for a spine of a ledger, he reached out too and his hand brushed hers. Rather than pull back, he wrapped his fingers around hers.

"You're trembling." He swept his thumb over the back of her hand. "Don't worry, Arry. I'm sure you're right. My attendance at the party will disturb Hammersley and the others so thoroughly, they'll scurry back to London at first morning light."

Bella slid her fingers free of his and the friction sent a jolt of warmth along her arm. "We will see."

She did her best to ignore him and continued gathering the ledgers. He wouldn't let her do the task alone and moved in front of her to retrieve one that had fallen farthest.

"You don't trust me anymore," he said quietly.

Bella snapped her gaze to his and the pain there struck her like a blow.

"I'd like to earn that back."

"Rhys—"

"I understand," he said before she could finish. "You've put me out of your mind for years."

Bella collected several of the ledgers and pivoted to face him.

"Here." She held out the volumes and he took them, then she reached for the last. As she leaned forward, she felt something catch at her neck and raised a hand.

The daisy pendant was cool against her fingers. She closed her fist around it quickly, but she was too slow.

Rhys fixed his gaze on her neck a moment before he reached for her.

Bella opened her hand and let the pendant drop. He caught it between his fingers and stroked the opal petals with his thumb, almost as tenderly as he'd stroked her hand.

"So you didn't hate me," he said on a husky whisper.

Bella's heart pounded so hard it hurt. She tugged on the chain of her necklace and the flower pendant slipped from his fingers. She got to her feet, ignoring his offered hand to help her up.

When Bella stood before him, Rhys remained kneeling, as he'd attempted to do the night before. His full, far too appealing mouth flickered into a hesitant smile that faded almost as soon as it appeared.

"We were friends for so many years, but I'm not certain you ever knew me at all." She should call the whole thing off. The invitation she'd come to extend would just lead to more of this. Her heart in her throat, all the old feelings that she should have banished years before welling up as if they'd never left at all.

Turning on her heel, she started toward the study

door. The most logical solution was to walk away and move forward rather than looking back. But on the threshold, she looked at him over her shoulder.

"We'll gather in the drawing room at six. Dinner starts at seven."

Chapter Seven

*R*hys had never hesitated to walk through Hill-crest's thick carved maple door in his life.

Lord and Lady Yardley's country house had often felt more like a home than his own. They'd welcomed him, not as the neighboring dukedom's heir but as a young man who'd befriended their daughter. And they'd encouraged him to visit nearly as often as Bella had.

If not for the Yardleys, he would have had no real notion of family after the loss of his mother when he was a boy. No notion of a loving family anyway. They'd striven to make him feel a part of theirs, and as a child he'd wanted nothing more than to be included in their conversation-filled dinners and silly parlor games.

He loved Hillcrest and everyone who inhabited the manor house.

Yet tonight he paused on the steps, pointlessly adjusting his cravat, which his valet had already arranged impeccably, and scraped a hand through his hair as he'd done half a dozen times on his carriage ride over.

He'd thought about Bella all day. The way she'd shuttered herself earlier haunted him. The stony set of her jaw and the way her shoulders trembled, betraying whatever emotion she wouldn't let him see.

She'd always been that way. Where he'd been brash and let every emotion slip out, she'd been quiet. Observant. Calm when he wasn't. But he knew her well enough to know she wasn't placid or emotionless. Bella was every bit as passionate as he was, or at least she had been once.

He wasn't sure at all who she'd become in the years they'd been apart but he very much wanted the opportunity to find out.

Through a half-open window, he could hear conversation in the front drawing room. Her cousin Louisa's lively laughter and the voices of several men. Those bloody suitors Lady Yardley had selected in the hopes they might woo Bella.

Why did that fact irk him?

Stepping toward the door, he knocked twice. A moment later the doors creaked open and Mr. Lewes stood on the threshold. The Yardleys' longtime butler had always been kind, and Rhys was ridiculously pleased to see recognition in the old man's eyes.

"Your Grace, it has been a very long while." He offered a little half bow and gestured for Rhys to enter.

"I trust you've been well." The man looked far more hail and hardy than Rhys did after a week of London soirees.

"I've no complaints, Your Grace."

The honorific still made Rhys want to glance over his shoulder to see if his father was there, but it sounded more right on Lewes's tongue than it had on anyone else's.

"Where is she, Lewes?" His question should have been familiar. It was the one Rhys had asked whenever he came to visit Bella.

"Miss Prescott has not yet come down, Your Grace." Lewes stared at him and then glanced at the long stairwell that wound up to the family's private rooms.

Rhys couldn't count how many times he'd bound up those stairs to find Bella in the nursery or her sitting room.

"Guests are gathering in the drawing room," Lewes told him quietly. "May I announce you?"

Propriety dictated he join the other guests. Dashing up to the family's private quarters might have been forgivable when he was twelve and Bella was eight, but they weren't children anymore. She was a proper young lady.

Unfortunately, he'd never been a proper gentleman for a single day of his life.

"Not quite yet. Good to see you, Lewes."

The old man gave one curt nod, and Rhys stepped past him and headed for the stairs. The path to her chamber felt as familiar as if he'd tread the path yesterday, yet when he reached her door, he didn't knock.

What the hell was happening to him? He wasn't a man who ever hesitated. Half the problems in his life could be ascribed to his very bad habit of giving in to reckless impulses.

Whatever lingering connection he had with Bella felt fragile. He refused to let himself sift what seeing her again had sparked in him.

Rather than knock and step inside as he would have done years before, he rapped gently and waited.

Bella opened the door on a frustrated huff, as if he'd interrupted. Her cheeks were flushed, her brow crinkled in a frown, and she held her coiffure in place with one hand. Whether he'd interrupted or not, her green-gold eyes widened at the sight of him.

"You don't look happy to see me."

"I thought you were the maid. Why are you up here?" She gripped the edge of his waistcoat, glanced both ways down the hall, and pulled him into her room. "You really are determined to start a scandal."

"Old habit," he told her as she let go of him and closed the door. "I always came upstairs to find you rather than waiting for you to come down."

She gave him a harried glance over her shoulder as she worked at winding her loose hair into artful pinned curls.

"I thought it best to decide on our plan of attack."

"The only plan is for you to be downstairs making

a grand entrance and all of our gentlemen guests nervous," she told him as she approached her vanity to rifle through a crystal dish.

Rhys swallowed hard and curled his hand into a fist.

Three buttons at the back of her gown were unfastened, exposing her lovely freckled skin. Long auburn waves of hair had fallen from her half-pinned coiffure, and he longed to reach out and sweep them aside. To see more of her.

Good God, what was wrong with him?

He'd seen Bella disheveled before. Covered in pond muck, rain soaked, even splashed with paint from the one occasion when they'd decided to try their hand at watercolors.

This was different.

He'd seen her as a friend then. A child. Now he saw only a woman. An inconveniently desirable woman. And he had taken the liberty of coming to her room, to her bedchamber. Uninvited.

He wasn't unused to entering ladies' bedchambers, but he only ever did so with an explicit invitation.

Casting his gaze away from her, he noticed a series of documents strung along the wall. They weren't art. He recognized Bella's handwriting and what appeared to be sketches of some of her puzzle games.

"What's all that?" He gestured toward the wall and started to move closer.

"A project I'm working on. Nothing I have time to talk about."

"Perhaps you'll tell me some other time." There was

a period in their lives when he knew everything she was up to, all her secrets and plans. He missed being privy to Arabella Prescott's projects.

Turning to him with an irritated look, Bella seemed to be suffering with none of the sentiments he felt.

"Does this look all right?" She'd put a bejeweled comb in her hair but it was crooked and only half in place. "It doesn't, does it? Would you ring the bell again?"

Rhys approached the mantel and gave a tug on the bellpull. Her frustration was palpable, and his impulse was to help, but all he knew about ladies' coiffures was how to take them down.

"I should be in the drawing room by now." She stuck two hairpins between her lips and a third into her hair so violently, she dislodged a few other curls. When another strand of hair became dislodged, she let out a little yelp of distress. "I'm making it worse."

"Sit down."

She snapped her gaze to his, eyes glittering with annoyance at his commanding tone. Then she seemed to realize what he intended and her expression softened.

Rhys felt something in him ease too. He approached her where she sat on her vanity bench. She straightened her shoulders and held out a palm full of hairpins.

"I take it the objective is to trap your curls with these." He drew his fingers along her palm and felt her tremble in response when he took one of the pins.

"Just these few strands that have fallen down. It

needn't be perfect. I'm not aiming to impress any of the gentlemen downstairs."

He looked into the mirror and their eyes met. She watched him, as if gauging his reaction.

"I'm sure you already have. That's why they're still here."

That seemed to embarrass her. She shifted her gaze to the wall in front of her and then down at her lap.

Rhys lifted one long curl and pinned it next to another. He did the same with two others, and did his damnedest to resist the urge to pull the whole thing down. Every time his fingers brushed her scalp or the back of her neck, her body gave a little jolt and he felt the movement all the way to his groin.

He had no idea why helping a lady pin her hair up was so arousing. His heart beat as hard as if he'd run all the way from Edgecombe. When he'd placed the final pin, he took the bejeweled comb and settled it among her auburn waves. The more he touched her hair, the more he sensed the tension begin to seep out of her body. Her shoulders rounded.

When he'd finished, he found he didn't know what to do with his hands. He didn't wish to stop touching her.

"That looks better," she said quietly. "Thank you."

He stepped back and turned to the long mirror in the corner of the room to check his tie and focus on anything other than her. But he was aware of her every movement. In the quiet of the room, he could hear that her breath had sped too. His gaze was drawn to her movements in the mirror. She touched the back of her hand to her cheek, then placed a hand at the base of her throat and swallowed hard.

Standing up from her vanity, she lifted both arms up and behind her head to try to reach the loose buttons on the back of her gown.

"May I help you?" he heard himself say.

Rather than answer, she turned her back to him. He walked the two steps toward her too quickly, and she glanced back.

"You should go down first," she told him matter-of-factly. Always practical. Always solving problems. But he'd known her long enough that he didn't miss the quaver in her voice.

His own hands trembled as he fastened her buttons and he bit his lip at the softness of her skin against the backs of his fingers. Good grief, he needed to stop touching her.

When he'd fastened the last button, he stepped away and started toward the door.

"Five minutes?" she said as he reached for the door latch.

Rhys closed his eyes, fought to steady his heartbeat, and looked back at her with his mask of bravado firmly in place. "Whenever you wish. It's your birthday. I am merely here for you to command."

"You've never let me command you in your life."

He chuckled and winked at her. "Consider it a birthday gift."

BELLA'S PLAN WASN'T going as expected.

Fanning herself with her hand dispelled a bit of the heat in the blue drawing room but not an ounce of the tension. The night had turned cool and servants had lit a fire, but the combination of overdressed bodies and the irritation Rhys's presence stoked made the room stifling.

She told herself tension was good. Unease was what she'd intended, and by inviting Rhys she'd definitely ruffled feathers.

Dinner had been miserable, with conversation rarely crossing the divide of candles and bowls of flowers at the center of the table. She'd been seated with Hammersley and Nix on one side, her parents at either end, and Louisa and Rhys on the opposite side. Lord Wentworth sat beside Louisa and was the only one who attempted to cross the battle line of the centerpiece by asking Bella about the quality of her roast and whether or not she liked autumn weather.

Now, in the drawing room, conversation remained at a low uncomfortable hum. The men darted glances toward Rhys, and she heard a few whispered condemnations. They weren't as quiet with their barbs as they probably thought they were, but they took care not to speak of their disdain too loudly. Rhys was a duke, after all.

Still, her ultimate goal seemed nowhere in sight. The gentlemen suitors may cast judgment on Rhys, but none of them seemed put off in their pursuit of her.

When everyone at the dinner table had offered her a birthday toast, Hammersley leaned so close, she'd feared he might kiss her on the cheek. He was deep in conversation with Mr. Nix now, but he continually cast glances her way, as if she might be the subject of their discussion.

If they were wagering on her again, she'd have her father send them all away.

Casting a glance around the room, she noticed that her father had slipped out at some point. Her mother didn't seem concerned at his absence, but Bella had an impulse to go and check on him nonetheless.

"Bella is excellent at riddles and puzzles of all kinds," Louisa said, raising her voice from the corner settee where she sat in conversation with Bella's mother and Lord Wentworth. "Someone pose her a riddle and I promise she'll solve it."

"Why doesn't Miss Prescott pose one of her own riddles, and we will try to solve it," Mr. Nix said with a tone that implied he was very certain *he* would solve it.

Rhys sat forward on the chair he occupied, elbows on his knees, hands clasped. He'd always liked her riddles and had even helped her devise a few. The first that came to mind was one they'd worked on together.

"There is one that has a head without an eye, and one that has an eye without a head." Bella enunciated each word carefully and more slowly than she'd normally speak. "You may find the answer if you try and when all is said, half the answer hangs upon a thread."

"Can you solve it, Mr. Nix?" Louisa asked pertly. Anyone looking at the man could tell he didn't have a clue.

"I fear," he said with a grimace, "Lord Hammersley and I were distracted with conversation." They weren't. Both had listened attentively, but Louisa allowed him the fib to save his pride.

"That is unfortunate," she told him with forced sweetness. "I wonder if the Duke of Claremont can unravel the words."

Bella snapped her gaze to Rhys's. Louisa had no notion that reading had once been his torment and that he often doubted his ability to think quickly. It was why he'd helped her construct her riddles. Together they'd discovered that he was actually quite skilled with words, as long as he didn't have to confront them on the page. Though in time, he'd gotten better at that too.

"I already know the answer," he said, his gaze still fixed on Bella. "I was there when Miss Prescott came up with this conundrum."

"You helped," Bella insisted.

"Very little." He grinned and then settled back in his chair, hands clasped over his waistcoat as if he was suddenly completely relaxed. "You've never really needed my help."

"That's nonsense." Bella scooted forward on the chair she occupied, prepared to argue with him. But then she noticed the hush in the room. Everyone had turned their attention to her exchange with Rhys.

"I think I may have it," Lord Wentworth said into the silence.

Louisa shot him a pleased look and nodded encouragingly. "Then tell us, my lord."

"Thread gives it away, does it not?" He looked around at the other gentlemen. Hammersley and Nix wore a matching frown. Bella's mother smiled knowingly. Perhaps she recalled this one too.

As soon as she and Rhys came up with a day's worth of riddles, they'd share it with her parents.

"Go on," Louisa urged Wentworth.

"Is it pin and needle? One has a head, the other does not, and only one goes on thread."

Louisa clapped and Bella joined in. It wasn't a terribly challenging riddle, but Wentworth had been quick. Hammersley and Nix grumbled individually and then leaned in to grouse to each other.

"Shall we have some music and dancing?" Bella's mother stood and approached a footman standing sentry near the door. "If you'd all be so good as to stand, we'll make a bit of room and I'll take a spot at the piano."

Louisa usually played when they had a musical evening, but everyone had agreed that leaving Bella alone to dance with each gentleman in attendance would be awkward, to say the least.

Everyone obeyed her mother's command and stood. Another footman appeared and the two young men quickly moved both settees to the sides of the room to create space to dance. In the flurry of activity, Bella didn't notice that Hammersley had ambled toward her.

"Miss Prescott, may I claim the first dance?" He was so earnest in his request, Bella was tempted to agree but before she could form a reply, Rhys approached as if summoned.

"I'm afraid that's already been claimed, Hammersley."

The older man's face reddened like dinner's wine and his jowls began to quiver like the aspic Rhys loathed. His mouth worked as if he wished to protest, but no words emerged. Just sounds of frustration.

Rhys reached his arm out in front of the viscount's chest and offered Bella his hand.

"Forgive me, Lord Hammersley. I will save you the second dance."

Rhys took her hand and led Bella to the center of the room while Louisa and Mr. Nix stepped into place beside them. Soon after, Bella's mother began playing to cue them that the dance would soon begin. Bella had requested a waltz. Her mother hadn't known at the time that Rhys would accompany her, but she looked distinctly unsurprised.

"You didn't have to promise him anything," Rhys told her as he rested his hand at the small of her back.

"There's no point in being impolite."

"Bella, you want him to leave your home because he's overcome with irritation and disdain." He didn't speak the words with any anger or judgment, just his usual good humor and enough of a smile that a dimple flashed at the corner of his mouth.

"Leaving must be his choice. My goal is to avoid

adding any more men to my list of refusals if I don't have to."

"Are our dancers ready?" Bella's mother didn't wait for an answer before beginning to play. The music started with an introductory trill and then the smooth insistent rhythm of a waltz emerged.

Rhys led without a moment's hesitation, as if he'd danced the waltz a thousand times. Bella had danced often, but she still counted the steps in her head. It calmed her and was the one way she could be certain her feet would obey. With Rhys so near, she needed all the calm she could muster. The warmth of his palm against hers and the grip of his hand at her back made her intensely aware that they were connected, moving as one. She had to trust him to lead and move them in sync.

"It bothers you what others say," he said while he swung her around in counterpoint to the movement of Mr. Nix and Louisa, who came toward the front of the room as they moved back.

"That I'm cold and heartless?" Bella started to stumble and gripped his shoulder tighter.

He pulled her an inch closer, keeping her steady. "You're not."

Of course she wasn't. He knew her too well to believe she was icy and uncaring. What he didn't seem to understand was that *he* was the reason she couldn't bear the thought of marrying another man.

When she said nothing, his cool blue gaze bored into hers and his brow twitched upward. It was the look he'd always given her when he was pressing her, waiting for her to answer.

"Why do you refuse them all?"

No, not that question. She wasn't prepared to offer him that answer tonight.

Suddenly, she wanted the dance to end. He held her too close, so near that his scent filled the air. His hands scorched her where he held her and the warmth building between them made her breathless. Even the movement of the dance made her dizzy. She tried focusing on his face but all she noticed was the room whirling by, the pale faces of Hammersley and Lord Wentworth in the background, and the figure of Louisa dancing gracefully in Mr. Nix's arms.

"Arry," Rhys spoke her nickname tenderly, his breath fanning against her cheek. "Speak to me."

He was taller than she was by just enough inches that she had to tip her head back when they were this close. She squeezed her hand reflexively and the muscles of his shoulders bunched and shifted.

"I need to concentrate when I dance. If I don't, I'll miss a step." She was breathless now, her skin heated from exertion and the tall, broad wall of Rhys's body moving in time with hers.

Rhys drew his hand up her back and leaned in to whisper. "I've got you. I won't let you fall."

But she had. She'd fallen so hard for Rhys that she feared she'd never be able to pick herself up again. She remembered every clawing, painful step of the climb.

And here she was. With the same man and the same feelings welling up inside her.

She couldn't let it happen. She'd learned her lesson. Never again would she allow herself to fall. Another rejection from him wouldn't hurt, it would crush her.

Chapter Eight

$\mathcal{B}$ella headed for the library, both because she thought it likely she'd find her father there and because she needed to escape. She couldn't breathe with Rhys so close. She couldn't think practical thoughts when he was near.

And, mercy, did she need her practical mindset back.

Lamps burned low along the hallway and she noticed a warm glow coming from the half-open door of her father's study. Drawing closer, she heard him coughing.

"Papa?"

"You've found me." He glanced back at her from his favorite wingback in front of the fireplace. "Why have you left your party?"

She stepped inside and reminded him, "In fairness, you were the first to depart."

"Shall I return?" He sounded distinctly hopeful she'd tell him not to. "Perhaps I should partner your mother for a dance."

Her mother would probably enjoy it, but he looked so cozy with his cup of tea and a blanket across his knees that Bella wasn't about to encourage him to return to the drawing room.

She took the chair next to his, tucking the crinoline skirts of her blue gown around her. "Are you unwell, Papa?"

He'd never admit as much to her. In their family, he was the encourager and Bella's mother was the worrier.

"I'm well enough, my girl. And you? How are you on the first day of the three and twentieth year of Arabella?" He took a sip of tea and cast her a slanting glance. "Interesting decision to invite the duke. Strategic, I'd say."

He'd always been able to see through her better than most. Sometimes even better than Rhys.

"I had a plan."

"You always do."

"I'm not sure it's working." Bella crossed her arms and tapped a finger against her lips. "I have no real notion of what I should do."

"That's not quite true, is it?" He smiled but kept his gaze fixed on the fire. "You've already decided to refuse them all."

Bella shot up from her chair and stepped away from the heat. Not that the warmth in her cheeks had anything to do with the coals in the grate. "No proposals have been made, Papa. No refusals have been given."

"But you don't want to marry any of them." He didn't sound angry or chastising. Just resigned. "Perhaps you still don't wish to marry at all."

"I want you and Mama to go to Greece. Please don't let me be the reason you don't." Bella approached and crouched next to his chair, placing a hand on his arm. "Could we not find a chaperone if you're worried about leaving me on my own?"

Her father patted her hand, set his blanket aside, and stood. She thought he might ignore her question. Was he truly that upset with her?

But he went to his desk, opened a polished wooden box on top, and pulled out a tiny silver chalice. He held it out to her, and Bella stood and stepped forward to take it. She thought at first it was a gift for her birthday, but he'd already presented her with new books.

"Note the inscription." He gestured toward the slightly tarnished silver cup.

Bella frowned. "Was this from the day you married Mama?"

"A souvenir of the best of days. All that's worth remembering in my life began on that day."

"So you believe I should marry, just as Mama does."

"We don't distrust you, Bella, or worry overmuch about the propriety of leaving our unmarried daughter on her own." He glanced toward a portrait of her mother that hung over the fireplace. "Perhaps that is your mother's concern, but mine is for your future. A man wishes to see his children—" Drawing in a long breath, he cast his glance away from Bella's before continuing. "A father wishes to see his only child settled. Content."

"I understand." Without an heir, the Yardley estate and title would go to a cousin who her father had been estranged from for years.

"When Edgar inherits . . ."

"Hillcrest will no longer be my home."

"So you must have another." Concern drew the skin above his brow into lines and his tone turned grim. "Worry for your future is what inspired this house party, my girl."

"But Mr. Nix thought of me so little that he was prepared to wager for my hand, and Lord Wentworth doesn't say much but spends most of his time looking at Louisa."

"Hammersley?" There was a hopeful tinge to his question.

In that moment, Bella realized he *was* hoping she'd accept one of them.

"I meant what I said, my girl. You needn't marry any of them."

"But you'd prefer that I marry, and sooner rather than later." Now, before she'd even finished her book let alone found publishing success.

"Would I prefer to see you merrily wed? Of course.

But that proviso shall always remain. Your choice must make you happy."

Happy. He spoke that word again and again, and yet Bella was no longer certain what it meant. She'd believed Rhys would make her happy. Of late, working on her book gave her satisfaction and she clung to the hope that she might prove herself by getting her ideas into print. But could marriage to someone like Hammersley produce happiness, whatever it meant?

Her heart, her body, everything in her resounded with an unwavering *no*.

"You're right, Papa. I've already decided about these men."

The nod he gave her was accompanied by the flicker of a smile. "Then the one who'll suit you must be out there still." He gestured toward the windows and then swept his hand around, as if encompassing the whole room. "Waiting for the day you meet."

This is where her father always lost her. He believed in fate, but she considered it nonsense. She'd once fancied that fate was why Rhys's estate bordered theirs. Fate was why they'd met one autumn day and taken an instant liking to each other. But if all of that was fate, then Rhys breaking her heart was meant to be too.

"As long as that day comes after I've published my book."

He offered her a tender smile. "That book is very important to you."

"It is, Papa. Before I get lost in the duties of marriage, I need to achieve something for myself."

"Tenacious girl."

"Mama would say stubborn."

"I say you possess the determination to have anything you set your heart on."

If only that were true.

"I should return to the party." Bella mustered a smile. "I promised a dance to Lord Hammersley."

He let her go. There was little more to say.

Out in the hallway, a shadow emerged from a darkened corner and she nearly jumped out of her boots.

"Bella?" Rhys approached hesitantly.

He wasn't at all sure she'd wish to speak to him. For all he knew Lord Yardley had directed her to see him out altogether, though he couldn't imagine that from a man who sometimes called him *son* as a sign of affection.

"You needn't sneak up on me." She'd jolted when he called her name, and now she glanced both ways down the hall, as if to ensure that none would see them speaking alone.

"Forgive me. I was waiting until you'd finished speaking to your father." He didn't bloody care who saw them. The party was over as far as he was concerned. "We need to talk."

Bella was miserable, and there was a great deal she wasn't telling him. He needed to know what schemes were spinning in her clever head.

She wouldn't look him in the eye. Even in the dim light of the hall lamps, he could see some mystery flickering in her gaze. She stared at his jaw, then her gaze trailed down. He'd already untied his cravat and the fabric hung loosely around his neck. His breathing hitched. Bella gazed at the bare skin at the base of his throat as if it fascinated her, and he was shocked to find that being the object of her intense scrutiny was intoxicating.

"I should return to the party," she said in the least convincing tone he'd ever heard. "Mama will send Louisa to drag me back if I don't return to the drawing room."

When he said nothing, she turned.

He reached for her arm. He couldn't let her walk away. "Bella, wait."

She glanced down at where he held her.

"Why are you doing this?" He knew he'd broken trust with her years before and might never get it back, but he needed to try.

"The party is in my honor—"

"That's not what I mean. Tell me why you're playing along with your mother's machinations." He still held her. He knew letting go was the proper choice. The wisest course. Yet he kept holding her. She was soft and warm, and being connected to her felt right and achingly familiar. "I know you've always been a dutiful daughter, but this is something more. You've refused many men and yet—"

"A few men. Not many." She tensed her jaw.

The names they called her, the things they'd said

about her, he'd known it wasn't true. But he hated that they'd hurt her.

"I trust you know your own mind and had a good reason every time. And yet now you can't see your way clear to simply telling your mother that this house party is a farce."

"Mama planned this for months."

Duty. She'd always bowed to it so much more easily than he had. He'd loved her moments of rebelliousness, the flashes of fire and boldness. But she had the same skill he had. The ability to pretend, to put on a facade of agreeableness or even joviality for the benefit of others.

"I appreciate that your mother put effort into the event, but these men are wasting their time, are they not?"

Bella blinked and her eyes widened in shock. Something snagged in the center of his chest, a flare of fear that she might actually be considering one of the men her mother chose to woo her.

"Your concern is for these men rather than me?"

"No." Rhys let out a breath that turned into a chuckle. "You know that's not true. But you're a young lady who speaks her mind. At least you used to with me. You said you promised your mother you'd try. I simply wish to know why."

She swallowed hard, started to speak, and then shook her head.

"Miss Prescott, I've come to claim our dance." Lord

Hammersley's voice echoed loudly as he approached from the opposite end of the hallway.

Rhys cast the man a glare that seemed to have no effect whatsoever.

"Claremont." Hammersley acknowledged him with a nod, then turned to Bella. "May I escort you back to the party, Miss Prescott?" He lifted his arm and wore a grin of smug certainty that she would agree.

"I am returning in a moment, my lord. Would you be so good as to go and tell my mother? She'll want to prepare her sheet music for the next dance."

The jolt of pleasure that rippled through Rhys wasn't just pettiness at seeing Hammersley's face fall. It was pride in Bella's self-assurance.

Hammersley blustered for a moment, as if on the verge of protesting. Bella stared him down, a cool smile on her face and her hands crossed in front of her.

The two conducted their standoff for what seemed long minutes and just when Rhys sensed Hammersley would relent and return to the drawing room ahead of Bella, the man turned and reached for her hand. Bella pulled back but not quickly enough. The viscount clutched her wrist.

Rhys's vision dimmed to a pinpoint focus on Hammersley's hand latched on to Bella so firmly she winced. He stepped forward and wrapped his own hand around the man's arm and squeezed. The viscount let out a yelp and released his hold on Bella.

"Don't touch her again. Ever." Rhys could barely get the words out past clenched teeth.

Hammersley yanked his arm free from Rhys's grip and glared at him. "You take an eager interest in Miss Prescott." He spared a scowl for Bella. "I don't know whether she welcomes such attention, but your reputation will ruin her before you ever have a chance to do so yourself." Hammersley looked at each of them in turn. "Unless you already have."

"How dare you." Bella's cheeks flamed and she clenched her hands into fists.

"Goodness, girl." Hammersley barked out an offended chortle. "I interrupt your tryst with a notorious blackguard and I am the one to give offense." All pretense fell away and Hammersley sneered at Bella. "They say you're clever, Miss Prescott, but I can find no evidence of it in your choice of suitors."

"Get out." The voice boomed to the high ceiling as Bella's father shuffled out of his study. "Leave my home as soon as you're able, Lord Hammersley. I won't have my child insulted."

"Never in my life—" the viscount started in an affronted tone.

"Go, man," Rhys told him. "Save your pride. Whatever's left of it."

The viscount pursed his mouth and puffed out his chest but said nothing more. He turned on his heel and shuffled toward the staircase. Midway down the hall, he turned back.

"Everyone in London will hear of this."

Without thought or plan, Rhys strode past Bella toward the viscount. The older man reeled back, but

Rhys caught him by the lapel and pushed him against the wall.

"No, they won't," he told Hammersley quietly. "The party ended early. Make up whatever story you like, but if you try to harm her, spread rumors, *I* will ruin *you*."

"Won't be necessary. Will it, Hammersley?" Bella's father's voice emerged raspy and hoarse, as if he'd been shouting, though his voice now was as calm as Bella's outward demeanor.

"Go, my lord." Bella approached until she stood side by side with Rhys. "You will find a suitable bride. I'm sure of it, but you probably knew we wouldn't suit from the day we met."

For a moment Hammersley gazed at her with an expression that was less than irate. Then he nodded.

Rhys released him and retreated a few steps to allow him to pass. The viscount made his way up the stairs without looking back again.

As they watched him, Bella's father stepped closer.

"Seems a long while since you two managed to get yourselves into this much trouble."

"Mother will be disappointed," Bella said worriedly.

"She will," her father admitted. "But mostly that a man she invited to our home dared insult our daughter."

"I made it worse." Rhys feared his threat would appear in some scandal rag in a few days' time.

"You convinced him to leave. That's what matters most." Bella stared at him a moment but said nothing more.

"Shall we all return to the drawing room and salvage this party?" Lord Yardley sounded almost jovial.

Rhys felt anything but. "Bella? Spare me one more moment."

Lord Yardley nodded at his daughter, patted her hand, and headed down the hall toward the drawing room.

Being left alone with her was exactly what he'd wanted, but everything he thought he wanted to say was gone. The only thought in his head was that she looked lovely and entirely unhappy. He missed the mischievous twinkle in her eye that he'd seen every day when they were young.

"You were about to tell me something before Hammersley interrupted." He yearned to reach for her, to somehow bridge the distance that had opened up between them over the years.

"The viscount is gone or soon will be. That hardly matters now."

She didn't trust him. Until this moment, he'd never realized how much he'd missed being someone that Bella Prescott entrusted with her private worries.

"I don't want to disappoint my mother," she said in her unconvincing I-must-do-my-duty tone that he'd never been able to master because he'd never given a whit about duty.

"We'll never talk easily again, will we? Like we used to."

For a moment, she looked at him with the same kind of openness as when they were young. Like a girl who liked him, trusted him, believed in him. Then it all shuttered and she turned as cool as the gossip rags claimed she was.

"No," she said in a soft firm voice. "I don't think we ever will."

Chapter Nine

$\mathcal{B}$ella shifted on her mattress, pushed at her pillow, and told herself for the hundredth time to go to sleep. She often struggled to quiet her mind before rest would come. Puzzles filled her head when she closed her eyes, and she'd see the end like the center of a maze and have to wend her way back to the start. Or she'd conceive an idea and have to work out every step.

Tonight there were no ideas. Just memories. Voices played over and over in her head. She heard Rhys asking in a raw tone if they'd ever confide in each other again. Hammersley blustering that she'd be ruined in the eyes of society for consorting with the infamous Duke of Claremont. Papa's voice echoed in her mind too. He spoke earnestly of happiness, urging it upon her with an eagerness that stirred a flutter of panic in her chest. Panic at the thought of being trapped in a loveless but practical marriage.

As an only child, she'd always felt her parents' desires for her keenly. She'd collected accomplishments and done her best to learn her lessons, and she'd always intended to fulfill their hope that she'd marry well.

But marriage was far different from a deft hand at watercolors or having a clever eye for embroidery.

Marriage was a contract binding two people. Forever.

Just the thought made her shiver. The only men who'd ever offered for her were the sort with whom she could never imagine spending every day of the rest of her life. Or every night.

She'd only entertained *those* thoughts about one man. He'd treated her as no one ever had, not as a child to be coddled and doted on but as if she was intelligent and capable. She'd imagined his affection for her might grow into deeper feelings, and it had, but only in her heart.

Never again would she be foolish enough to give her heart where her feelings weren't returned. If only she'd adopted her new practical mindset back then.

Slipping out from under the covers, she lit a lamp and went to the long table where she'd laid out page designs for her book. This was practical. This made sense. The way she'd organized the drawings and notations fit together like its own enormous puzzle and it soothed her. But still there was a nagging sense in the back of her mind, as if she'd left something important unfinished.

The house party had gone unlike any social event

her mother had ever coordinated. Bella couldn't deny her relief.

In the morning, Hammersley would depart. As Rhys had pointed out, it was the only way for the viscount to salvage his pride. Nix would go too. Which left only Lord Wentworth, and Bella suspected the awkwardness of being the only gentleman remaining would drive him back to London too.

And then?

What had she truly won? Her mother had mentioned another Season. Bella's stomach tumbled at the thought of more balls and dinners and whispers about her coldness.

One of the pages she'd designed and pinned to her sitting room wall caught her eye. A matching game with various ladies and gentlemen drawn in a grid of squares. She'd written a riddle to accompany the game. The answer to the puzzle was marriage.

Someone rapped softly at her bedchamber door. She crossed the room but before she could turn the latch Louisa slipped in and said quietly, "It's me, Bell."

"You're up far too late."

"Or far too early. Sun will be up soon, but I couldn't sleep. I heard you moving about and knew you couldn't either." Louisa took one of the stuffed chairs near the fireplace and tucked her feet underneath her, as if she planned to stay awhile.

Bella tugged a blanket from her bed, pulled a chair next to Louisa's, and spread the blanket between them. "What's keeping you awake?"

Louisa glanced at her and then shifted her gaze down, running her fingers over the crisscross design of the blanket as if its knitted pattern fascinated her. "You first," she finally said. "I'd think chasing Lord Hammersley away would put your mind at ease."

"Lord Wentworth is still here." Bella had her suspicions about the man and Louisa's interest in him, but the way she shifted uncomfortably on her chair told Bella her speculations weren't unfounded. "You like him."

"He likes me," Louisa said defensively. Then, less certain, "I think he does anyway."

"I'm sure he does. He's been very attentive to you."

"And you." Toying with the braid at her shoulder, Louisa shrugged. "He's said nothing certain, but he is rather quiet in general."

"Very quiet. Perhaps he's simply thoughtful and isn't one to bluster." Bella didn't dislike the man, and if he had an interest in Louisa, she could at least concede that he had good taste.

"You have no wish to marry him, then?" Louisa lifted one sandy blond brow, but the teasing twinkle in her eyes indicated she knew what Bella's answer would be.

"None at all." Bella stood and pressed her hands to the small of her back, stretching and wishing the sun had risen enough for her to take a walk across the fields. "I've no interest in any of them."

"What about the Duke of Claremont?" Louisa asked in a mock-serious tone.

Bella choked midway through a deep breath and coughed. She assessed her cousin with a narrowed gaze. Louisa was up to something. She was familiar enough with Rhys to call him by his given name, and she knew one other crucial fact too.

"I could never marry him."

"Why not?" Louisa's brows tented as if she was truly perplexed. "He's a duke. The finest catch in the county. And you did want to once, didn't you?"

Bella willed her cheeks not to redden but she couldn't find her tongue fast enough to reply before Louisa spoke again.

"Isn't it funny how time has turned everything around?"

Bella crossed her arms over her chest. "What mischief are you concocting, cousin?"

"Me?" She did that thing, eyes wide, shoulders back as if she was offended by the very notion that she'd ever put her clever mind to any sort of plotting. Bella knew the girl liked strategy almost as much as she did. "I recall that you were once infatuated with him. And now it's clear that he quite fancies you."

"That's absurd." Laughter built so quickly that Bella chortled and cupped a hand over her mouth to keep from more unladylike sounds erupting. "He came to Hillcrest to apologize."

Louisa's smile was irritatingly knowing. "That would explain the first visit."

"He came last evening as a favor."

"To make up for the falling-out you had years ago?"

"Not exactly." Bella rubbed at her temple. "We made an agreement. An exchange. He asked for my assistance with Lady Margaret's coming out and some other matters at Edgecombe. I asked him to visit Hillcrest in the hope of putting off Hammersley and the others."

Louisa had been plucking at the knitted blanket over her knees and stopped to stare at Bella, her mouth agape. "But that's a terrible agreement."

"Why? It worked."

"He's expecting a great deal of you and all you asked was for him to come to a fine meal and dance with you in the drawing room? Hardly onerous."

Bella crossed her arms. Louisa possibly had a point.

The idea of inviting Rhys to Hillcrest had been impulsive, and she'd known that even if every gentleman visitor departed, her one main dilemma still remained. Her parents wanted her to marry and sooner rather than later.

Wedlock was beginning to feel like a pursuer she could neither refuse nor avoid.

"There must be a great many ways your acquaintance with a duke could be helpful," Louisa said thoughtfully.

Bella's mind began buzzing in that way it did when a new idea bloomed. She started toward her wardrobe, and called back to Louisa, "Perhaps there *is* one thing I could ask of him."

MIST CURLED ALONG the ground and the soft gold of morning light gilded every dewy spike of field grass on the east side of Edgecombe. Rhys stood on the long veranda behind the house, surveying his ancestral lands. He drew in a deep lungful of country air and stifled a cough when he exhaled.

Bloody bales of endless fresh air. It smelled earthy and green. Unlike in London, he couldn't taste soot on his tongue or breathe in its dense fog. He rather missed both. And darkness. He squinted up at the sun-gilded clouds and thought for the umpteenth time that the countryside was far too bright.

He'd become nocturnal over the years, loving when dusk came and his day could truly begin. Indulging through the night and rising in the late afternoon. That was how he lived his life.

But for some cruel reason he couldn't fathom, his body betrayed him since he'd arrived at Edgecombe. Every morning, his eyes slid open at the cusp of sunrise and once he was awake, he found he couldn't bear to lie about being idle.

Upon waking, he craved heat in his muscles. Something to get his blood pumping.

Twisting the hilt of the fencing foil in his hand, he lifted the blade and pointed it toward the copse at the far edge of Claremont land. He longed for a proper fencing bout. Not that he'd ever been terribly good. His favorite fencing opponent had been formidable and she'd rarely let him come out the victor.

He lowered the foil and circled the veranda, his breath billowing in white puffs.

Bella. It always led back to her. Every thought since

he'd arrived was colored by memories of her. She'd been an essential part of every good thing about his life in Essex.

Now she came to mind for other reasons.

They'd made amends, but it wasn't enough. For so long, guilt had ridden him. An apology, he'd told himself, would salve the ache whenever he thought of her.

But the ache hadn't gone away. If anything, it was more acute now and it wasn't so much an ache as longing.

No relationship had ever come close to the trust and closeness they'd once had. Not even his friendship with Iverson and Tremayne compared. They were good men and God knew they believed in him when few others in society did. But nothing compared to confiding in Bella.

Rhys sliced the air with the foil, then again. He stepped forward, assumed en garde position, and imagined Bella standing before him on a fencing strip.

"You're out of practice."

For a moment, he wondered if he'd imagined her voice in his head. But then he heard her footsteps on the stone slabs of the veranda.

"I lack a partner to keep up my skills," he said, glancing at her over his shoulder.

Her bodice buttons were askew and the knot she'd pulled her hair into had begun to spill strands along her shoulders. She looked as if she'd dressed hurriedly and he could tell from the hem of her gown that she'd walked to Edgecombe. Pink infused her cheeks and her lush mouth.

She looked absolutely lovely.

After assessing his fencing stance a bit longer, she came up beside him and reached down to slip the foil from his hand. "May I?"

Her bare fingers were warm against his cool skin and he held on a moment longer just to savor her heat.

Testing the blade, she swiped it through the air and stretched as much as her skirt would allow into a better en garde position than he'd achieved.

He frowned. "Who have you practiced with since I've been gone?"

Ignoring him, Bella lunged forward and aimed high as if targeting the upper chest of an opponent. "Louisa," she said on the exhale that came with another thrust. "I usually best her too." The smile she shot him over her shoulder caused warmth to spill through his veins.

He'd missed her smiles. Especially the ones that held a bit of challenge.

"I know I've called quite early," she said as she lowered the foil and approached to hand it back to him.

"I'm as eager to start on the ledgers as you are. Meg wishes to venture to London, but sorting the accounts comes first."

"The ledgers. Of course." She bit her lower lip. "I need to speak with you first."

The urgency in her tone set him on edge. He imagined there had been ugliness with Hammersley or her mother. "Is something amiss?"

She shook her head. "Not at all. I have an idea."

That was not surprising. He'd never met anyone with such a fertile mind. "I'd like to hear it."

"Good." The smile that bloomed on her full pink lips was too brief. "But what I wish to say will require some explanation."

"Then let's do this inside." He gestured toward the conservatory door and she allowed him to lead her toward his father's study. He'd come to think of the room as the place where the dreaded ledgers were housed, and it had become such a frequent haunt he was almost prepared to think of it as his own.

When they were both inside the dark-paneled room, Rhys closed the door. Something told him that whatever she'd come to say wasn't meant for Meg or anyone else to hear.

"I can ring for tea or anything you might wish. Have you eaten?"

"No." She waved off the question as if it was the least of her concerns. "I couldn't." She began pacing the edge of the dark ivy-decorated carpet, behind the settees and tables, making her way around the room. "Maybe tea."

Rhys strode to the bellpull, tugged the fabric, and waited. Not for the servants, who would be up in minutes with tea and whatever scone had just emerged from the oven, but for Bella.

This ritual of being patient while she thought of how to phrase all that she wished to say was a familiar one. While he could ramble for an hour when an idea struck, Bella preferred to speak when she'd sorted out precisely what to say. She didn't like to make mistakes and was unforgiving toward herself when she did.

"You make deals in London." She didn't stop pacing but she turned her gaze his way expectantly.

"Yes."

"And you gamble?"

"Occasionally." He didn't wish to admit that he'd once been exactly the sort of nobleman who made an enterprise like Lyon's Gentlemen's Club profitable. Night after night, he'd find himself leaning on the green baize tables, throwing away money in the foolish hope he could make his pounds and promissory notes multiply into much more.

He was a lucky man, wasn't he? He'd never placed a bet without expecting to win.

Bella circled the room's settee and perched on the center cushion. "Will you sit with me?" She gestured to a chair as if she was the lady of the house and he was a visitor.

He kept his gaze fixed on her as he sat, settling back on the cushions. Not a single muscle in his body felt relaxed, but he did his best to feign ease.

"Whatever it is you've come to say," he urged her, "I'm willing to hear it." Eager was more like it.

"I want to make a deal with you." Her tone was confident, her voice clear, and yet Rhys was almost certain he'd misheard her.

"You mean a wager?"

When they were children, they'd place nominal bets on things like how far a frog could leap or who between them would win a foot race across the fields. He couldn't imagine what Bella would wish to wager on now.

"More of an exchange," she said a little too brightly.

"We already worked out our exchange, did we not?" He slept better knowing she'd agreed to assist him with Edgecombe's financial mystery, and he was willing to sit at her family's dinner table or hold her in his arms for as many waltzes as she wished.

"I'd like to change the terms."

Rhys couldn't repress a chuckle. "That's rarely allowed."

"Rarely means it sometimes is allowed." She leaned toward him. "Let this be one of those exceptions."

When she was determined on a course, Bella was the most immovable woman he'd ever known. He liked her determination. Except when he was the object in her way.

"Tell me what you have in mind." A great many images came to Rhys's mind. The same wayward thoughts that plagued him whenever she was near. Very little of it was appropriate.

She stared at him and little lines of worry pinched between her brows.

"Bella, just say it."

"You're the talk of the county."

"Am I? I haven't been here long enough to do anything dastardly."

"You're a duke. A bachelor. The highest-ranking unwed nobleman within a hundred miles."

The way she said it made him want to bolt the doors and cover the windows to stave off the army of marriage-minded mamas that were no doubt planning a march on Edgecombe.

"If you were engaged, it would keep the husband hunters away." She drew in a long breath. "I suggest we marry."

He heard the word *we* and then something that sounded vaguely like *marry* and after that his brain tripped over itself like a drunk at a ball. No matter how he pushed and pulled at the two concepts, they didn't fit together.

Nothing made sense.

"I don't understand." His tongue had gone as sluggish as his thoughts.

"Not a real marriage, of course," she said dismissively, waving the prospect away and acting as though what she'd said before hadn't changed everything. "We won't get that far. What I suggest is simply an engagement. A very public engagement."

Rhys opened his mouth and still no words emerged. He rose from the settee and began pacing the perimeter of the room. Speechlessness wasn't anything he was used to, nor the feeling that his mind had gone blank as a wiped slate. The idea was ludicrous.

"After my parents have departed for Europe, we could call off the engagement." She spoke as calmly as if she was describing one of her puzzles. "This idea benefits both—"

"Why are you sending your parents away?" What

she'd said finally began to sink into his brain. "And why in God's name would you want to marry a reprobate? A day ago you were horrified at the notion of me playing suitor to you and now it's your fondest wish?"

She stood and approached to join him where he'd stopped behind the settee. Her expression softened as she looked at him, and he found himself calmed by her amber-green gaze.

"I need your help," she said quietly. "You asked for my help giving Meg a proper Season and unraveling your ledgers." She gestured toward the enormous pile of maddening volumes stacked on his father's desk. "I'm asking you for this."

"The two are not equal. Sorting out a Season and ledgers versus marriage—"

"Not marriage. Just an engagement. Entirely temporary." She let out a shaky sigh, the first crack in the calm she'd exuded since arriving. "My parents have an opportunity that I don't want them to waste. A position for my father at a school in Greece. They'll only depart if I marry."

"But you said we wouldn't marry."

"Yes, but we'll tell them we plan to." Excitement flashed in her eyes. "It's practical, Rhys. You must see that. It will allow me to spend time here assisting Meg and taking a look at the estate's accounts as you requested. And it will keep you out of the sights of all the village families hoping to match you with their daughters. I'm sure you've received many invitations since arriving in Essex."

"I'm quite capable of refusing invitations." Unfortunately, Bella had always been harder to refuse.

He moved away from her and headed to the window. But staring out on Edgecombe's fields didn't allow him to escape her. Every inch of the estate's grounds reminded him of the years they'd spent traipsing them together.

"I have questions about this proposed arrangement," he said to her reflection in the window glass and then turned to face her. "But only one that's essential."

"Ask whatever you like." She nodded eagerly. "I'll do my best to answer."

"You realize what this will entail? Such a plan will require us to spend a great deal of time together."

Chapter Ten

$\mathcal{B}$ella stared into Rhys's clear blue gaze and felt heat rushing across her cheeks.

Before his question, her thoughts had been laid out as methodically as the pages of her puzzle book. Doubts had welled up as she'd walked to Edgecombe, but they'd faded as soon as she'd seen him. She knew how to rally arguments and he'd always been reasonable enough to listen.

All that lay before her was the challenge of convincing him her idea made sense. And with every word, she'd convinced herself too. This was practical. Her plan could work.

But now all her arguments and rationales scattered like dandelion fluff on the breeze.

Did he think she'd devised this scheme to get close to him again?

How could she admit that she'd come to him because

there was no one else? No other man would agree to such a scheme, and she couldn't imagine feigning an engagement with anyone but Rhys. He was, after all, the only man she'd ever considered marrying.

"I'm not trying to trap you in an engagement if that's what you fear." The heat in her cheeks spread down her neck and her pulse began to race.

"No." He shook his head. "That's not what I meant."

"Rhys, this could benefit both of us."

He stepped closer, limned in golden morning light. He looked achingly handsome with his windswept hair and bright blue eyes, but he also looked exhausted. He glanced back at the pile of ledgers, one brow arched. "You agreed to help me, so I should agree to help you?"

"It does seem a fair exchange."

He still had the foil in his hand and dragged the tip across a leaf in the study's carpet design. "Wentworth is still at Hillcrest, is he not?"

"I departed early this morning, but I suppose he is."

"He seems the most bearable of the lot. Would you not consider a real proposal from him?" He laid the foil down, balanced atop two ledgers. Turning to face her, he rested his backside against the desk's edge.

"I barely know him." Even from across the room, the intensity of his perusal made her warm. Her pulse sped. Tapping her foot against the carpet, she willed herself to face him. To maintain the same confidence she'd felt when she walked through Edgecombe's doors.

"He seems a decent sort of chap," Rhys retorted.

"I don't trust him."

His mouth curved. "But do you trust me?"

"Yes." The single syllable felt sharp and false on her tongue. Though she was proposing a deception, she hated lying. "No."

"No," he agreed. "Of course you don't. As you know too well, I'm not a trustworthy man."

There was such wounded bitterness in his tone that Bella felt an urge to reassure him, but she couldn't. She didn't trust him, at least not with her heart. But she could believe in him enough to enter into an agreement that benefited each of them.

"Isn't making deals the sort of thing you do in the Duke's Den?"

"No. Not like this."

"I know you well," she told him, trying to find a way to explain why it would have to be him and no one else. "We're familiar with each other."

His eyes glinted when she said the word *familiar* and his mouth tipped in a mischievous slant.

"We *were* friends once." He lifted off the desk and approached. "But you said you didn't think we could be again."

"I never said that. Not exactly in those words anyway." Parting from him last night had left her unsettled and miserable because she'd allowed that single glimpse of hurt to slip out.

"Ah yes, only the implication that we'd never share confidences." There was an aching wistfulness in his tone. "But if we do this, we'll share quite a big secret between us."

Bella clenched her teeth. He was making this far more difficult than she'd expected.

He stepped closer, arms braced across his chest. His gaze was intense, unrelenting. Somehow their positions had changed. She'd come to petition him and now all the questions were directed her way.

She blew out a breath and squared her shoulders. "My parents wish me to marry. I will not agree to that for expedience's sake to a man I barely know and who does not . . ." She'd been on the verge of confessing all the foolish notions that still filled her head when it came to love and romance. "A man who does not appeal to me."

"Ah." His eyes lit up. "So I appeal to you?"

"You did once," she admitted. "Not anymore." Never would she let herself tread that path again.

His low chuckle shocked her and her pulse pounded in her ears when he stepped closer.

"That almost sounds like a challenge, Bella."

"An impossibility, I promise you." If there was one man in England she would never trust with her heart, it was the handsome scoundrel watching her with a knowing smirk.

"You shouldn't underestimate me."

She barely resisted rolling her eyes. He wasn't simply bold. His confidence had reached epic proportions. Though he'd teased her plenty in the past, it had never been like this. With heat in his gaze.

He was too close. She could see the darker flecks of lapis blue in his eyes and the dusting of blond stubble along his jaw that glinted in the morning light.

This wouldn't do. She hadn't come to assess his masculine appeal. This was supposed to be a sensible agreement.

"My parents are familiar with you." The words tumbled out unbidden, as if her mind had dredged them up to save her from making an utter fool of herself.

"They are, and I admire them both. But what will they think of me after such a deception?"

"It's a very temporary fib. And for their own good. They needn't ever know it wasn't a real engagement, only that we changed our minds." The truth was that lying to her parents made Bella queasy. But this was necessary. There was no other way. "They worry ceaselessly about my happiness. They wish to see me settled."

Mention of her parents seemed to unnerve him. He nodded and ran a hand over his chin. A muscle in his jaw began to tick. "They dote on you."

"And expect a great deal of me."

He smiled at her again, but not with his usual wolfish charm. This grin was softer. Almost tender. "You've never had trouble living up to their expectations."

"My mother would disagree." Bella's mother had probably written a dozen poems about how her only daughter had disappointed her. "My four unsuccessful Seasons are glaring proof of how I've failed them."

"Knowing your own mind isn't failure."

No one had ever put it that way. No one had ever framed her refusals in a way that made her seem admirable for making the decision that resonated as the right one, the only one, in her heart and mind.

"Maybe I'm just stubborn," she confessed.

"You've always been stubborn, Arry. But I admire you for wishing to wait and choose wisely." He took another step closer, his gaze fixed on hers. "Which is why I would be the worst choice you could possibly make."

"It need only be—" Panic rushed up. He had to agree.

"Even temporarily." He ducked his head, but she sensed there was more he wished to say. "My reputation is well-earned and that will affect how others think of you."

"I don't care." A worse reputation than being icy and unfeeling? More dire rumors than that she was frigid and incapable of love? None of that frightened her.

"I do. It's bad enough that my past choices may affect Meg. I won't let them impact you."

Bella stepped away from him and headed for the desk where the estate ledgers were piled. Whatever the problem was he wished her to solve, going through the books could take several days. If the mismanagement had begun earlier, the search could take weeks.

She moved the foil from atop the ledgers and opened one. "We will need to spend time together anyway.

I'm willing to help you. If you wish to help me, this is the best way. I promise you that."

There had been a time when they'd asked each other for favors and assistance without a second thought. That was long ago, and they'd changed in the years they'd been apart. But Bella trusted that he could see the necessity of what she was asking.

He lifted a hand and squeezed his nape, staring out the window as if contemplating.

Bella willed him to nod or smile or give him some sign of agreement.

A knock sounded at the study door, and he turned immediately, as if eager for a distraction from giving her an answer.

The moment he twisted the latch, Meg bounded into the room.

"Miss Prescott, what a lovely surprise." She exuded eagerness like a sweet fragrance that filled the room. Bella found herself smiling despite the tension lingering between her and Rhys.

"You must call me Bella as you once did."

Meg placed a hand on Bella's arm. "I'd very much like that. And thank you, Bella, for agreeing to assist me with preparations for the Season. We spent time at finishing school speaking of the day when we'd be presented at court, but doing so seems an entirely different challenge."

"There is much to consider." Bella winced at the memory of her coming-out Season. So many gowns and fittings and decisions to be made. So much hope and a mountain of expectations.

"You have a great deal of experience, so I trust you to guide me." Her smiled faltered as soon as the words were out. "Oh, I didn't mean . . ."

"It's all right. Nothing you said is incorrect. I've had four Seasons, attended more balls than I can count, and was in London recently enough to remember what's in fashion."

"Wonderful." Lady Margaret clasped her hands and held them under her chin. She smiled and her eyes were much like her brother's, glinting with an eagerness that verged on mischief. "There is so much left to do. Would you join me for lunch next week? We could begin planning, if that suits you."

"Meg, perhaps you two can make arrangements another time," Rhys interrupted. His words were like a chill breeze when everything had been sunny a moment before.

Meg's face fell as she looked from her brother to Bella and back again. "Of course. I burst in and interrupted your conversation." She offered a sheepish smile and turned toward her brother. "I only came to remind you that we're due at the vicarage at noon. You do recall we agreed to visit?"

"I didn't," Rhys admitted. "But I appreciate the reminder."

Meg seemed to sense the dismissal in his tone and offered Bella a tiny nod and a smile before heading toward the study door. "I'll be in the drawing room if you wish to speak before you depart."

Bella couldn't help but turn her gaze on Rhys. His answer would determine everything, and yet she could see he didn't have one. Or that he knew she wouldn't like the one he planned to offer.

"If not, I'll send a note," Bella assured the girl.

"A note would be lovely," Meg told her. A moment later, she slipped out of the room and pulled the door shut.

"I don't honestly know how to avoid disappointing her," Rhys said after his sister departed. "I have no desire to disappoint you again either, but I cannot agree to this scheme."

"Please." Bella had rarely pleaded with him for anything. He'd always given her help freely, but she couldn't remember a time she ever needed his cooperation this much. "We could start looking at the accounts right now." Bella strode to the desk and picked up one of the leather-bound ledgers, hugging it to her chest. "If we start directly, I could be through half of this one by teatime."

She wasn't at all certain she could manage the feat, but she was more than willing to try.

Rhys shook his head in that stubborn way of his. "I wish I could make you understand. Inviting me to dinner one evening to put off a couple of pompous noblemen is worlds different from telling everyone you've agreed to marry me."

"You're the Duke of Claremont, for heaven's sake.

Many will say I've caught the most eligible bachelor in England."

"You mean the most incorrigible bachelor in England. I have few merits, Bella. I'm known as a man of terrible morals. A rogue and a reprobate. I can't even argue with those claims."

Bella wanted to argue with them. At least the bit about him having few merits. Whatever he'd become, she believed a few things were still true. Rhys had always been loyal and he'd always been kind.

"You have a much different reputation," he continued. "You're known as—"

"Cold."

"Clever," he insisted. "And no one would believe you're silly enough to choose me."

Suddenly his handsome face looked weary and his jaw tightened. There was no sign of the easy smile he usually wore. His gaze flickered over her face, tracing the curve of her cheeks, pausing on her lips, then dipping low to stare at her necklace. Her bodice buttoned all the way to her neck, but she'd lifted the daisy pendant out, as she often did.

"I'm sorry. You'll never know how much."

"Then there's nothing more to say." She'd heard the pain in his tone, but all she could feel was her own anger. "Good luck with your ledgers."

She was nearly to the door before he spoke again. "And what of Meg?"

Bella gazed at him over her shoulder, staring at his cravat, too angry to look him in the eyes. "There are others to advise her. Lady Bembridge or the Dowager Viscountess Cartwright."

He let out a sound of disgust. "They're petty, judgmental women who look down on my family despite rank."

"Please tell Meg I'm sorry." Bella sighed.

Thinking of Meg reminded her of all the nervousness she'd felt before her first Season. She would have liked to help the girl.

"If you're not willing to help me, I'll be departing for Greece. I won't be here to assist either of you." She looked at him and a potent wave of tenderness filled her, confused her. She was angry with him, and yet she could never stop caring. "Good-bye, Rhys."

BELLA'S PARTING WORDS echoed in his mind after she'd gone and Rhys sank into the chair behind his father's desk. He pushed at the ledgers until he'd created open space on the desk, lifted his booted feet onto the blotter, leaned back in the chair, and covered his eyes with his hand.

God, he needed a drink. Several of them. Unfortunately, it wasn't even midday and he didn't want Meg to find him sloshed at such an hour.

He heard her footsteps outside the door. He knew she'd be watching for Bella's departure and come to collect him for their visit to the vicar soon after.

She entered so quickly the door cracked against the wall.

"What have you done?"

"The list is long, little sister. How much time do you have?"

Meg sighed. Rhys scrubbed a hand over his face before meeting her irritated gaze.

"I'm referring to Miss Prescott. She stormed out the front door without a word, and she looked upset."

Pointlessly Rhys wondered if Bella was more upset with him this morning than she'd been that day at her garden party. He suspected both days were a pinnacle of disappointment.

He'd failed her. Again.

"She asked something of me that I couldn't give her."

Meg narrowed her gaze at him. "There was a time you would have done anything for Arabella Prescott."

"I did do something. Saying no was the best thing I could have done for her." Rhys pushed his chair back, stood, and started pacing again. He'd had enough sitting still in the last weeks in Essex to last him a bloody lifetime. "Believe me, I wanted to say yes."

"I don't understand." Meg perched her hands on her hips. Never a good sign. It meant he wasn't going to escape this conversation without answering a dozen questions. "Explain."

He grabbed the foil from the top of his father's desk as he made a circuit around the room. He whipped it sharply through the air as he approached the window. "Sometimes the best we can do for someone is to *not* give them what they want."

"That would only make sense if she asked for something outrageous."

"Yes."

"She's known as one of the most proper young ladies in the county. I can't believe she'd ask for anything improper." Meg's tone turned dubious and her brows lifted in curiosity. "Did she?"

"She needs a husband."

He couldn't resist turning to see his sister's reaction to that, and he wasn't disappointed. Meg's big blue eyes widened at the same moment her mouth dropped open.

"Marriage? She wishes to marry you?"

"No, that would be ludicrous." He let out a bitter chuckle. "It's complicated."

"She's famous for not wishing to marry anyone. Which seems strange," Meg said softly.

"She wishes to please Lord and Lady Yardley."

"But marriage would please them, and the right one might make her happy too." Meg bit her lip as if she'd given too much away.

He tried not to think about how eager Meg was to marry, how vulnerable she'd be to fortune hunters on the marriage mart. He wished she had even an ounce of Bella's hesitance about wedlock. It was why he'd been so keen on her advising Meg.

"Someday I'm sure she'll find a suitor that . . ." He paused, hating the taste of those words on his lips. "Suits her," he finished.

He tried to imagine the kind of nobleman who could deserve Bella and came up with nothing. She was a uniquely smart, maddeningly stubborn woman and it would take a man of far more intelligence and patience than he could imagine to make her happy.

"I take it she won't be coming back to visit if you don't assist her." Meg's worried tone spiked his own anxiety.

"I'll send a note to the Duchess of Tremayne. She's quite the popular hostess during the Season."

Meg wrapped a finger around a ribbon fluttering down from a bow at the front of her dress. "She's never had a Season herself though, has she?"

"No." Tremayne's wife was lovely and capable and could manage a household with an efficiency that verged on frightening, but she had been born the daughter of a land steward and never had a formal coming-out.

"Perhaps Miss Prescott, Bella, would still be willing to speak to me." She cast him a look tinged with accusation. "Unless she's too angry with you to have anything to do with our family."

"Her parents will be traveling to the Continent and she will most likely accompany them."

"When does she depart?"

"I don't know."

"Do you think she'd accept an invitation to luncheon before she leaves?"

"I don't know."

"Perhaps—"

"No more questions, Meg." He winced at her shocked expression. He rarely snapped at her. "I promise your Season will be a success. We'll find you some well-meaning lady who will shepherd you through the entire nonsensical round of balls and visits and parlor games."

She tsked irritably. "Preferably one who doesn't refer to it as nonsense."

"Preferably." He tried a grin and as always, she gave one in reply. Eventually. "Now go prepare for our visit to the vicarage and I'll do the same."

Rather than depart, she stared at him. "Are you certain?"

Rhys tipped his head. "Certain of?"

"Your refusal." She stepped toward him, hands out as if beseeching him. "She was once your dearest friend and then you parted ways but now you seem to have made amends. Why fall out again?"

Rhys strode to the study door. "Questions are closed for today. Except for whatever the vicar plans to ask. And I'll let you do the answering." He opened the door and gestured into the hallway. "Shall we depart?"

"Couldn't you help her? Whatever it is. She came to you, Rhys, rather than anyone else."

Without realizing it, he'd gripped the door handle so hard his knuckles began to ache.

Meg was right. Bella had come to him. And he'd failed her. Again.

"When do we meet the vicar?"

Meg's whole face brightened. "A little less than an hour."

"I should be back in time."

"You're going to help her?"

He still had doubts. He still feared what trouble their

connection might cause her. But the impulse to help her was too insistent for him to ignore. Bella needed him and despite all the reasons he should leave her to her own devices, he couldn't.

"I'm going to do my best."

Chapter Eleven

*B*ella stomped so hard through the field grass that her teeth rattled whenever her boot landed on a stony patch. She didn't care. She was already clenching her teeth and clutching her hands into fists, and the stomping was doing wonders for working out her frustration.

Infuriating man. What had ever possessed her to believe Rhys would help?

She wasn't asking for much. A few days of pretense. Perhaps a few weeks. Afterward, they could go back to being barely acquainted again. He could return to London and be a ne'er-do-well and she could focus on her book.

She understood his aversion to wedlock, but was he so terrified that he couldn't even agree to pretense for a few weeks?

"Bella."

She was so lost in her thoughts, the single shouted

word seemed unconnected to her. But then he shouted again, louder, more desperately. And that made her jerk to a stop. Rhys was far enough away that she could ignore him and it would be believable she hadn't heard him at all.

She started off again, stomping less and picking up her pace. She'd gone to him and pleaded with him. That was enough of the Duke of Claremont for one day.

"Bella, please wait."

It was the *please* that made her stop. But she couldn't bring herself to turn to face him. She took in deep gulps of air, willing her pulse to steady and her anger to subside. When he was close enough for her to hear the sound of his footsteps sweeping through the tall grass, she turned her head.

He was striding toward her, his blond hair tousled by the breeze and his black greatcoat billowing out behind him. As usual, he'd dispensed with his cravat and his shirt lay open at his throat, revealing the muscles of his neck and a dusting of darker hair at the base of his throat. He marched toward her with such determination it made her take a step back in retreat.

"I thought you'd decided against my *scheme*," Bella called when he was close enough she didn't need to shout.

"I think we should settle this the way we used to." Barely slowing his stride, he reached down and plucked one of the wild daisies dancing among the field grass. "I have a decider at the ready, as you see."

What she could see was how his embroidered dove gray waistcoat hugged his broad chest so tightly the fabric strained against the buttons' hold.

She tried not to stare at his chest, but it was nearly impossible to meet his gaze. Her emotions tipped and tumbled inside her. Perhaps he'd changed his mind. A sweet ribbon of relief started at her throat and ran all the way down to her toes.

But she was afraid to trust any of it. "You'll tell my parents we wish to marry?"

"We'll soon find out," he said as he stopped an arm's length away from her. He was breathing hard. The chill in the air had brought blood to his cheeks, a glint to his eyes. Sunlight lit them with a vibrant glow. "You first," he told her, lifting the daisy between them.

"We're not children anymore." And she couldn't risk her future and her parents' choices on the whimsy of a flower.

"All right, I'll go first." He plucked one petal.

Bella sighed and yanked another free.

He smiled as if she'd just offered him a compliment and pulled a second time. She did too. They continued on until only a single petal remained. One for her to pluck.

When she hesitated, his gaze grew serious. "Looks as if I'll be telling your parents I wish to marry you."

His agreement was precisely what she wanted to hear. Yet for the first time in all this scheming a warning bell sounded in her mind.

Perhaps she wanted this too much.

"That look of worry tells me you understand the pitfalls of this arrangement."

"Pitfalls?" Bella swallowed hard. She very much doubted he understood what she was thinking.

"We must make others believe we're sincere and yet we ourselves must not become . . ." He looked at her as if he expected her to finish the sentence for him, as they'd often done in the past. When she didn't, he added, "Entangled."

"Entangled?"

He chuckled. "The first rule is that you mustn't simply repeat every final word I say as a question."

Bella crossed her arms. "And the second rule?"

"We probably shouldn't do this in front of others." He waved a hand between them. "Bickering."

"We're discussing." In tight irritated tones, she had to admit. "Not arguing."

"Let's do it in private from now on. Nothing travels faster than gossip, and we wish those observing to believe we are enamored and in accord."

"Is there a third rule?"

He looked at her so long she wondered if he'd forgotten the question, then finally said, "You shouldn't defend me."

"Will there be a need?" Had the man been called out by some angry husband in London?

"Bella," he said slowly, carefully, "I haven't been a good man of late, and when the talkative ladies of

London society hear that I'm to wed a very upright young lady . . . There will be talk. You will likely learn more about me than you ever wished to." He swallowed as if there were something bitter on his tongue. "I don't want you to become caught up in that when we're among London society. So let them say what they will and never mind any of it."

"You needn't worry about me."

"If you're my fiancée, that will be my job."

Bella rolled her eyes. Twenty minutes ago the man couldn't fathom assisting her and now he was taking all of it far too seriously. "I won't be your fiancée in truth."

"Others must believe that you are and your connection with me, as you know from Lord Hammersley, may cause you trouble. Do you have any rules?"

As Bella stared at him, her gaze fell to his lips. Always. They were beautifully shaped, full and forever flickering into a grin or a smirk. She had a good excuse to look at them when he spoke but she found herself looking when she shouldn't.

"No kissing," she blurted.

He arched a brow. "Very well. No kissing, it is. Anything else?"

"No promises either of us cannot keep."

Both of his brows winged high at that.

"We will be clear with each other," he said in a low earnest tone. "Honest, in all matters." He stepped close enough for his greatcoat to rustle against her skirt. He shocked her by reaching out and tucking a strand of hair behind her ear, then letting his fingers linger there, a warm soft weight against her skin. "I won't fail you this time."

Goodness how were they going to do this if he could unsettle her with the brush of his fingers?

"Touching," Bella breathed. "We should only touch when necessary."

Rhys dropped his hand as if she'd scorched him. "Of course. Forgive me."

"Can you call tomorrow and speak to my parents?"

"Bloody hell, that's quick."

"There's no reason to delay now that we've decided. The sooner we tell them and set everything in motion, the sooner we can end the subterfuge."

"Tomorrow, then. I'll call in the afternoon."

"The morning? Father is in his office by ten."

"I'll arrive at quarter past."

Bella nodded and assumed he would offer her a leave-taking, but he didn't. He wore his usual air of confidence like a cloak atop his greatcoat, but there was a strange hesitation in the way he darted his gaze from her face out toward the open fields and back again.

"What is it?" she asked. They'd just agreed on honesty. Best to start immediately.

"Should I not acquire a ring? Are there any words we should exchange?"

"A ring isn't strictly necessary—"

"But it would be useful. Our subterfuge will be based on appearances. Those who see us together in society must get the impression that we are truly engaged."

"I appreciate that you wish to do this properly." Bella wasn't certain what propriety looked like when it came to false engagements. "But my parents come first, and I don't wish to delay for a ring."

"I understand." He nodded, almost solemnly. It was odd to see him somber. Seriousness didn't suit him.

Bella stepped away, eager to get back to Hillcrest. Eager for their plan to begin. "I'll see you in the morning?"

"You will."

Bella smiled back at him over her shoulder before setting off. She was relieved. This was exactly what she wanted. So why was she flushed and trembling? Why did the prospect of seeing him again tomorrow make her anxious?

"I WISH TO marry your daughter." Rhys exhaled a breath of relief as soon as the words were out.

He sounded believable and his stomach hadn't plummeted into his boots. He'd been waiting in the Yardleys' drawing room for what felt like days, though the clock indicated less than half an hour had passed. He'd tested the words on his lips a dozen times. Rephrasing. Practicing various intonations like an actor about to perform on the stage.

Rhys supposed he was a performer of sorts. He knew how to feign laughter, make others happy, and paste on a smile when he was bone weary. But no matter how many times he tested these words on his lips, hearing them echo in the empty drawing room sent a jolt of shock through his body.

"Lord Yardley," he said aloud, imagining the older man's kindly gaze on him. "I wish to make Bella my duchess."

Yes, better to make it personal. Though making it personal also made the subterfuge feel unsavory.

Footsteps sounded in the hallway and he turned toward the door. But no one came. A servant perhaps?

He'd tried sitting but couldn't remain still. He strode to the window, pushed the drapes aside, and lifted the frame. Some small insistent voice in his head told him to climb out and avoid this mad scheme.

Bloody hell. What had possessed him to agree to an engagement, even a false one? And to Bella of all the women in England. The one woman he didn't wish to harm or disappoint any more than he already had.

A flash of movement caught his eye and two servants emerged through Hillcrest's front doors, their arms loaded with luggage. Wentworth came next and cast a longing glance up at the house's facade before entering the carriage that awaited him.

Was the man looking with that yearning expression at Bella?

"Did you need air or are you considering an escape?"

Rhys smiled at the sound of her voice. There was a tinge of mischief in it that immediately eased his mind.

"You're ready for this?" he asked as he turned to

find her fussing with an enormous vase of flowers on a table near the door. She was dressed in a gold gown that clung to her curves and yet wasn't frivolous. Always practical Bella.

"I'm ready," she said, on a breathy whisper, glancing back toward the door as if her parents' arrival was imminent and she didn't wish them to hear. "I take it you are too."

"I am." Rhys slid a hand across his middle and straightened the buttons of his waistcoat.

"Here they come," Bella said before opening the drawing room door. "Mama, Papa, won't you sit?"

Lord Yardley's gaze narrowed the moment he spotted Rhys. "An early hour for a social call, Claremont."

"Some things can't be delayed, Lord Yardley."

Behind him Bella's mother beamed at him. Rhys knew that of the two of them the viscountess would take the least convincing.

"Shall we all have a seat?" A bit of nervousness had seeped into Bella's voice.

"You wish to marry, is that it?" The viscount scanned both their faces.

"Yes," Rhys answered in the same matter-of-fact tone Yardley asked.

"We do." Bella's words were spoken quietly.

Rhys was grateful she hadn't balked. It made him doubt what they were going to do a tiny bit less.

Her father would definitely take some convincing. The viscount assessed Bella with eyes narrowed behind his spectacles. "This is all very sudden, my girl."

"Is it?"

"Indeed, and rather convenient too." This time he lowered his spectacles down his nose and peered first at his daughter then Rhys over the brass rim.

"Seems rather inconvenient to me, Papa." Bella smiled, trying to put him at ease. "Rhys and I have always been friends. This is new and unexpected."

"Mmm." The viscount looked supremely dubious. His frown hadn't softened and he stroked his beard as he settled back in his chair.

Rhys took a seat across from him and offered a smile when Yardley shot a glance his way.

"I know you well, young man. Or I once did. I watched the two of you ramble through this countryside together for years and get into all manner of mischief." He worked his jaw as if contemplating and then added, "But you bickered too."

"We debated," Bella retorted.

"And she usually won," Rhys admitted without looking at her.

"Because I was usually right."

"Either that or I let you win."

Yardley nodded approvingly. "That is a good precedent, Claremont. Don't forget that principle." He grinned at his wife, who'd been uncharacteristically quiet.

"You'll make each other happy?" Lady Yardley asked the question as if there could be an easy answer.

Rhys was suddenly glad the engagement wasn't real. He couldn't make Bella happy. He wasn't sure he could make any lady happy, at least not for longer than a few evenings of pleasure.

"He could make me very happy," he heard Bella say, and couldn't quite believe his ears.

When he looked her way, she shot him a conspiratorial nod. Of course, this was all part of the ruse. Whatever her parents asked, they would reassure them.

"I will make it my mission to make Bella happy."

Her brows arched at that and he wondered if he'd laid the assurances on too thickly. But when her mother clasped her hands together and smiled, he and Bella both let out a breath of relief.

"Then we should begin planning a wedding." Lady Yardley stood and rang a little bell on a table next to her chair. "I think refreshments are in order. There is much to discuss."

"Mama—"

He'd worried about this. Her parents had been waiting so long for this news. It was no surprise that her mother would want to begin planning their nuptials immediately. The very same hour.

"Let me just get some paper and a pen so we may make some notes."

"I can speak to Vicar Eames. Securing the church before Christmas, especially for a Claremont, will be easy enough." Yardley turned to Rhys. "Unless you wish to marry in London. That might be a bit more of a challenge to schedule on short notice."

"There needn't be short notice," Bella said in a loud, clear voice. "Rhys and I wish to wait to marry."

"Wait?" Lady Yardley nearly tripped on the rug on her way back to her chair. "Whatever for?"

Bella swallowed hard and took a long breath. They'd discussed this and knew it would be the crux of her plan. Whether her parents would accept this farce or not relied on this single moment.

"Rhys hopes to put the estate in order and Lady Margaret must have her coming-out this year. There is a great deal to plan without adding a duke's nuptials to the list."

"This is most irregular, Bella."

They'd anticipated how much of a sticking point this would be for Lady Yardley. Rhys scooted forward in his chair, laced his fingers between his knees and summoned the kind of charm he'd employed to get him through most of the tight spots he'd encountered in life.

"Your enthusiasm is heartening, Lady Yardley," he told her as he stood and took a seat on the settee next to Bella. "The sooner we can be wed the better." He cast Bella a grin and for a moment she stared at him uncertainly, then her mouth curved too. "This delay is entirely my fault. I want to do right by my sister and give her the attention she needs."

"A duke's wedding will garner a great deal of notice," Bella added, seeming to understand his intent. "The last thing we wish is for Lady Margaret to feel her first Season has been overshadowed."

"That I can sympathize with," Lady Yardley said, and then let out a disappointed sigh. She approached her husband's chair and fussed with the doily atop the back. "A year isn't so long to wait."

"It will allow you and Papa to get settled in Greece before the wedding."

"Oh, but we must wait." The viscountess looked from her daughter to her husband and back again. "How will we help you plan from so far away?"

"Letters, Mama. You were planning to come home for a visit at some point, were you not? We'll simply marry during one of your visits."

"But—"

"My dear, they have agreed to marry. It is all we asked of Bella. A betrothal."

For the first time, Rhys wondered if Lord Yardley suspected the truth. The viscount was clearly determined to accept his post in Greece, but he seemed as determined to convince his wife to depart as they were.

"I know you're eager to be on our way." Lady Yardley gazed at her husband with a reticent smile. "So we should begin preparing, my dear."

"Excellent." Bella nearly bounced on the cushion beside him. "We'll keep you updated on the progress at Edgecombe and with Lady Margaret's Season."

When the servant arrived with a tea tray, Lady Yardley helped the girl arrange the dishes on the low table between settees.

Lord Yardley leaned forward, laid a hand on Bella's, and whispered to her, "Your mother is disappointed."

"Greece will soothe her," Bella whispered back.

"I hope you know what you're about, my girl."

Bella clasped her father's hand tightly. "I've waited years to make this choice, Papa. I've had the opportunity five other times and refused."

Lord Yardley patted her hand. "Then I trust you know your heart."

"I do, Papa."

Rhys realized he was holding his breath and his fingers ached because he'd clenched his hands into fists. This wasn't about Bella's heart. He wouldn't let it be. Once before, he'd been careless with her feelings. Never again.

He'd agreed to help her because he needed her help. Because he owed her and needed to know he'd done as right by her as he'd once done wrong. Their agreement would be mutually beneficial and then, when the time was right, it would be over.

With any luck, in a couple of months.

Rhys never made a deal he couldn't walk away from. This one would be no different.

Chapter Twelve

There must be some way I can be of use." Rhys sat on the edge of a wingback in his father's study, bootheel thumping against the carpet as he watched Bella peruse a ledger with care and patience. "Give me something to do."

How could she sit hunched over staring that long at a page without her eyes blurring? The lack of movement alone would have had him out of his chair and fencing shadows just to get some blood pumping in his veins.

She lifted her head and looked at him when he began tapping his heel against the carpet.

"You could take notes as I find things of interest." She gestured toward a piece of foolscap at her elbow. "I've started but it might work better if you assist."

Anything but sitting useless on his arse.

"Of course I will." He stood and dragged the wingback closer to the desk.

Bella pushed the notes she'd begun toward him, then the ink pot and a pen. Once he took a seat, she met his gaze a moment. He couldn't read her thoughts as easily as he once had, and there was some inscrutable emotion brewing in her pretty green-gold eyes.

"Ready?" she asked, returning her gaze to the columns of numbers and notations.

"Always." Rhys caught the flicker of her thick lashes as she glanced at him once more out of the corner of her eye.

"There was a significant purchase in June of last year," she told him. "A cottage called Tide's End at the seaside. Near Margate. Did you know anything about it?"

"Nothing at all. Father and I didn't keep in touch."

She shot him a curious frown. "Was there a falling-out?"

"You know how he felt about me." Rhys didn't need to explain. She'd seen enough. Heard the epithets his father tossed his way. "When I went to London, we stopped speaking. But a seaside cottage is far too whimsical for him. He never liked the seaside and he wasn't keen on spending money on anything but fashion and frivolity."

"He purchased property in London too." She flipped through the ledger's pages. "Back in October of last year. A town house in Gordon Square."

"That makes no sense." Rhys shook his head as he noted the fact on the foolscap. "My father owned Claremont House in Belgravia and a second town house in Grosvenor Square inherited from an uncle. He had no need of more London property."

"Perhaps he rented them for income." She tapped her finger against her lower lip. "Yet there are no notations indicating rent from either property." Her eyes widened as she continued scanning the page. "Here's another one. It's so strange."

Rhys leaned closer. "Another property?"

"No. One month after the purchase of both the seaside property and the London town house, there are a series of errors in the running total that subtracts nearly a thousand pounds. It's too obvious."

"So not errors?"

"I don't think so. Mr. Radley's mistakes are strategic. There's a pattern and the errors are always to the detriment of the dukedom's accounts. If it was by chance, you'd think he'd accidentally add funds on occasion."

"You almost sound as if you admire his boldness." Rhys didn't know why the prospect made him bristle.

"I could never admire a thief. He certainly isn't clever. Anyone looking at these ledgers would find his misdeeds."

Rhys didn't bother mentioning that he had in fact looked at them and had entirely missed the error she'd pointed out.

"There seems to be a missing ledger too." She flipped the pages of the one in her hands to show him the initial page. "Those at the corner of the desk are from the first two quarters of the year. This one is from the last quarter of the previous year. Where's the July, August, and September ledger?"

Rhys felt like an ill-informed fool. "I've no idea."

"Where did you get these?"

He pointed to a bookshelf behind her. "There are no others. These were easy enough to spy. They're overly large volumes and covered in a dark leather."

Bella scanned the bookshelves, her gaze sharp and intense. She stood up from the desk and made her way to one of the bookcases.

"I've searched them all, Bella."

"Are you certain?"

Rhys felt a flare of irritation. "I'm quite sure."

"Then what's that?" She glanced back at him with a triumphant grin.

Rhys followed the direction of her finger and noticed that far at the top of the third bookshelf, there was a dark corner with black-bound books. One was significantly taller and thicker than the others. Before he could admit she *might* be right, Bella was moving the rolling ladder attached to the wall of bookshelves to the spot where she'd noticed the book.

"It's high," he said, and approached to retrieve the ledger.

"I can get it," she told him with one foot already on the first rung of the ladder.

She'd always been stubborn, and she frustrated the hell out of him when she became determined on a course that would risk her own neck.

Her skirts belled out enough to get in her way, and

she swayed on the ladder as she tried to move them aside. Rhys approached and gripped the wooden frame to steady it. Instinctively, he placed a hand on the back of her skirt, pressing until he could feel the outline of her calf.

She inhaled sharply and let out a little gasp of shock. With a tip of her head, she looked back at him, her expression questioning and annoyed.

"This is necessary touching," he told her.

"I'm steady now. Thank you."

Rhys lifted his hand and tugged at the fabric of her skirt so it wasn't tangled around her ankles.

"Very well, but I'm not letting go of the ladder. Be careful, Bella."

But of course she was already reaching out, holding on to the ladder with one hand and stretching as far with her other arm as she could. Her fingertips grazed the edge of the volume and she hooked her thumb under the spine to nudge it out.

"Got it."

But she didn't. The ledger had moved out an inch but remained firmly wedged between its neighbors.

She glanced back at him and huffed out a sigh. He expected she might descend and let him go up and get the book. Most of the time, she was a logical woman and he was taller and his arms were longer.

"Hold the ladder steady?" She bit her lip when she looked back at him.

Rhys's gaze fixed on the place where her teeth sank into the soft, plump flesh of her lower lip and the rogue thought came that he wanted to kiss her right on that spot.

"Of course." Once again, he gripped the frame of the rolling ladder, but his fingers were an inch from the hem of her gown, and he wanted to touch her again. It was as if that brief contact of his hand on her body had unleashed every carnal impulse. He stifled the urge to slip his hand beneath her skirt and touch her stockinged leg. Or better yet, slip her stockings down and feel her flesh against his.

It wasn't as if he'd never seen her bare legs. They'd swam together in the mill pond many times. But this was different. They were different now, and his reactions to her were precisely what he should not be feeling. He wasn't the man she deserved.

"You've got me?" She sounded nervous.

All of his protective impulses welled up to dispel his lecherous thoughts.

"I won't let you fall."

She paused, as if contemplating that claim, and then edged an inch closer to the book, stretching and letting out a little groan of effort.

"I have it," she cried triumphantly. This time she did and the volume slid free. She grasped it firmly to her chest and started to descend, but her boot caught in the hem of her skirt and she lost her balance.

"Careful."

She tried to turn and free herself but leaned too far. Rhys reached up to catch her.

"Rhys." Eyes wide, hands out to break her fall, Bella

dropped the book at his toes and then came tumbling down.

Her body slammed into his and he landed on his back, his arms wrapped around her as she settled on top of him. She immediately scrambled to get up, her hands pressed to his chest, legs straddling his waist. When she squirmed against his groin to find her balance, Rhys instinctively grasped her hips.

She stilled. Breathing hard, she stared at him. She was still trembling from the shock of the fall.

"Are you all right?" he asked her softly.

Rather than answer, she gripped his shirtfront where her hand was pressed to his chest.

"Did you hurt yourself?" Rhys glanced down to see if her ankle was twisted or there was some other evidence of injury.

Her hand came up and she nudged his chin to bring his gaze back to hers.

If the press of her body against him hadn't already aroused him, the intensity in her gaze would have. She looked at him the way he'd been watching her the last few days. Hungrily. Heatedly.

"I'm not the girl I used to be," she said on a breathy whisper.

It seemed an odd time for her to tell him what was already apparent every time he was in her company but he nodded his agreement.

Yet she still didn't move. She remained astride him, one hand fisted in the fabric of his shirt, the other pressed to his chest. The weight and heat of her felt delicious. So good he had the wayward notion of bucking up to get her closer.

"What is it?" If she remained on top of him, she'd soon know exactly the direction of his thoughts. Was he misreading the look in her eyes for desire? He was more than prepared to remain pressed against her all day, but he knew the crinkle in her brow meant there was something she wished to say. "Tell me, Bella. What's wrong?"

Rather than speak, she acted. Her finger came down on his lower lip and that single touch sent a shiver of pleasure down his spine.

She was so soft, so warm. And she wanted him. There was nothing hidden in those expressive eyes of hers now. He'd promised himself he wouldn't do this with her. But he did want her, and he'd wished for her to look at him just like this for longer than he'd ever let himself admit.

He tightened his hold on her hips, but he wasn't certain if he was drawing her closer or holding her at bay.

This was Bella. Sweet, brilliant, proper Bella, and she deserved a hell of a lot better than a man who'd devoted himself to nothing but self-indulgence for the last half decade.

She pulled back as if she too had come to her senses. He felt a strange brew of frustration and relief.

He shifted to help her back onto her feet, but instead of getting up she bent closer. She slid her hands up his chest and planted one on the carpet next to his cheek. Then slowly, shockingly, she lowered her head and brushed her lips against his. Not quite a kiss, more like an experiment. One hot breathy too-quick press of her mouth and she pulled back, studying his lips as if they were one of her riddles to be solved. She lifted her hand and traced the outline of his mouth with the soft pad of her finger.

Rhys held his breath, wary of moving, though, God, how he wanted to. She was exploring, thinking, testing, and he never wanted her to stop. But he wanted more too. He knew exactly how easy it would be to tumble her onto her back, to slide her stockings down her legs and kiss every inch of skin he exposed. Images flashed in his mind.

His self-control had always been flimsy at best and it failed him now entirely. He slid one hand down to her thigh.

And all the delicious tender intimacy between them shattered.

Bella pushed away from him and began getting to her feet. She used his chest for leverage and he reached for her hand.

"Don't." He didn't want her to go back to hiding behind rules and propriety.

"We should get back to the ledgers."

She got to her feet next to him, dusting herself off and straightening her clothes. Rhys lifted onto his elbows and watched her.

They were locked in the same quiet study as they had been a moment before and yet everything had changed. He could feel it like the tremor of storm clouds in the air.

"Bella—"

"I was impulsive." She tucked the daisy pendant back into her bodice, then worked to push waves of hair back into pins.

"I like you when you're impulsive."

"I'm not sure I do."

Before he could say more, three short taps sounded at the study door.

Rhys growled out, "Come," as he got to his feet.

One of the footmen stood in the hallway. "Your Grace, you have a caller who says the matter is urgent."

"Did they mention why?" Villagers had been calling almost daily since his arrival, but aside from those Meg wished to entertain with tea and biscuits, he intended to put them off for as long as he could.

"He mentioned Mr. Radley."

"Send him up." Rhys cast a glance at Bella. She finished with her hair and stood behind the desk, ready to resume her study of the ledgers as if nothing had passed between them.

"The steward," he told her by way of explanation. "The man was supposed to call days ago but never appeared. I've made inquiries about him and his whereabouts. I hope perhaps this caller has answers."

She looked intrigued and far more composed than he felt. He could still taste her on his lips, smell her floral scent on his clothes.

The man rapped once on the study door and strode inside as if he was familiar with Edgecombe. He was short and burly and studied them both with searching black eyes.

"I presume you're the Duke of Claremont," he said to Rhys while taking him in from brow to boot.

"An accurate presumption."

The older man cast a glance at Bella. "May we speak alone, Your Grace?"

Rhys bristled at the man's tone. He had no intention of asking Bella to depart. He didn't have to look at her to know how curious she'd be to hear what the man knew, but he glanced back at her anyway, just to see the flush that still lingered on her cheeks and lips.

"Miss Prescott is my betrothed and will remain to hear whatever you have to say. Start by telling us who you are."

"The name is Macadams, Your Grace. Of Scotland Yard." He'd offered Rhys a nod and was smart enough to offer Bella the same courtesy. Then he got straight to business, removing a small journal and pencil stub from the pocket of his overcoat. "You employ a man named Radley?"

"Have you found him?" Rhys loved the notion that Macadams had the man trussed up in a carriage somewhere or clapped in irons in London.

"Ah, I see." The older man's shoulders slumped. "I take it you've no notion where he is either, Your Grace?"

Well, bullocks. Rhys repressed a groan.

"I don't. But I must speak to him, so you must find him." Rhys glanced at Bella.

Her eyes had widened with curiosity but now she looked as disappointed as Rhys felt. "As near as we can tell, he's drained the ducal accounts by thousands of pounds," she told the inspector. "Do you have no clues at all? What do you know of him, sir?"

Macadams's brows drew together in a frown. "I know his name isn't Radley, my lady. His last alias was Hayes." The man from the Yard squinted at his notepad. "His true given name is Roger Ellsworth. He's served as a clerk in London and a butler in Bristol for a time. In both cases, there were irregularities with the accounts."

"Wonderful." Rhys pinched the bridge of his nose. Some part of him had held on to hope that the errors in the ledger were just that. Perhaps overpayments to vendors that could be recovered or simple mismanagement that could be resolved by hiring a new steward. Now the odds of ever recovering what Radley—or Ellsworth or whatever his damned name was—had stolen seemed bleak.

"We'll find him eventually, Your Grace. The man won't always be a step ahead."

"But he is a step ahead now. Several of them. Do you have any idea where to look next?" Bella asked.

The inspector seemed shocked every time she spoke, as if he wasn't used to dealing with ladies during the course of his investigations. Especially ones who questioned him so mercilessly.

"We have reason to believe he is from Buckinghamshire, miss. I shall inquire there next."

Bella shook her head. "But it seems unlikely he'd return to family, particularly if he knows you've discovered his identity."

"We shall take our investigation wherever it leads, Miss Prescott." Macadams narrowed his bushy-browed eyes and his voice turned rough and blatantly offended.

Bella stared back unperturbed. Rhys was almost curious to see what would happen if he let them continue.

"I'm sure you'll be diligent in your search, Inspector," Rhys told the man by way of taking leave. "I'd be pleased to recover the monies he's taken."

"Of course, Your Grace. And if he should reappear, please inform us straightaway."

The man departed as hastily as he'd entered the study, and Rhys could feel the press of Bella's gaze before he turned to face her.

"With a pursuer as laissez-faire as Inspector Macadams on his trail, Radley will never be apprehended."

"You're a bit hard on the man, are you not?" Rhys asked playfully.

He trusted her judgment as much as he believed in his own gut instincts. She'd always been discerning. Except, perhaps, when she'd chosen him as a friend.

"I'm not. Do you think it's likely a man with thousands of pounds at his disposal and a good lead on evading the law would return to the place where he's best known?" She crossed her arms and stared at the closed study door. "If only people would employ logic."

Rhys knew it wasn't the time for laughter, but he fought the urge to break into a smile. Given half the chance, she'd probably have Radley in custody by now.

"You're right. Macadams won't find him in Buckinghamshire." Rhys tried to focus on the problem of Radley and worry about his thinned-out bank account, but all he could truly think about was Bella and the taste of her lips.

She caught him watching her. "I agreed to meet with Meg while I'm here. I should go down and find her."

"Bella—"

"I know what you're going to say." She stepped out from behind the desk and approached. "As I said, I was impulsive, and I'm aware that I broke one of our rules."

"So did I."

She cast a glance at the rolling ladder and bookshelf. "That touching was necessary. We agreed."

Rhys thought it best not to mention that touching her in general was beginning to feel very necessary. So much so that when she started for the door, he reached for her arm and drew his hand down to gently clasp her wrist.

"What would you do if it was up to you to find Mr. Radley?"

"I'd inspect the properties he acquired on your father's behalf. If I wished to disappear, I might go to the seaside. Or a quiet London square where I could blend in among others. I certainly wouldn't go to the countryside and face my family."

"Then let's inspect them." London. He needed to make a trip there. He'd promised Meg.

"Together? My mother will insist on a chaperone."

He liked that he detected interest in her tone, though he wasn't certain if it was the prospect of traveling as a pair or the thrill of the chase.

"We're engaged, and Meg will accompany us. Shouldn't we be seen together? Meg has been asking for a shopping trip to London. If you're advising her, she'll wish for you to come too."

He wanted her to come, and he realized he was rambling but he couldn't seem to temper his eagerness. He sounded like one of the inventors presenting before the Duke's Den.

He held his breath as she considered the prospect. Something troubled her. He sensed her hesitation.

"Can it wait until after Friday?" she finally asked.

"Why?"

"There is another opportunity to be seen together." She fussed with the chain of her necklace and pressed her lips together as if she wasn't looking forward to telling him the rest.

"Which is?"

"Mama has planned for us to formally announce our engagement to the local families. A small affair. Shouldn't take long."

"What does she have in mind?" Mention of her mother and planning made him nervous. He expected the Yardleys to have an announcement printed in *The Times*, but of course the viscountess would want to share the news among the county's notable families.

Bella frowned, clearly dreading whatever she was about to say next.

"She's planned a garden party. Tomorrow afternoon. At Hillcrest."

"There's no way out of it?"

"No. We knew there would be moments when we'd have to feign this engagement for the benefit of others. It will be all right." She sounded confident and that was almost enough to put him at ease. "We can be convincing for a couple of hours."

Convincing others that he desired Bella? Easy enough.

Persuading himself to keep his hands off her? Very likely impossible.

Chapter Thirteen

$\mathcal{A}$t least you've no speech to present this time."
Louisa stood at the window watching servants prepare
for the garden party. She loved parties almost as much
as Rhys and had been brimming with excited energy
all morning.

"That is a relief." Bella sat at the desk in her sitting
room feeling distinctly unrelieved and wondering if
there was any reasonable way she could call the whole
thing off.

Not just the party but the entire ruse of an engagement.

For the first time since she'd conceived the idea, she
was certain she'd made a mistake. Since the moment
Rhys walked into the billiard room, she wasn't feeling
like her new sensible self anymore. And rather than
avoid him as she should have done, there was a good
possibility she'd be spending part of every day with
him in the foreseeable future.

She imagined ways she could forestall what was about to happen. Rhys would no doubt be willing to end the charade, but her parents would be embarrassed and disappointed. Again.

"He seems very at ease with this plan of yours."

Bella didn't need to ask. Rhys might have hated the idea of the garden party, but he was the one person who was always at ease or could at least pretend to be better than anyone she'd ever known.

"I think he enjoys parties the way I like working on a new puzzle." Her wall of puzzles and plans beckoned her. *That* was where her focus should be.

"You two know each other well. It shouldn't be too hard to convince others that this engagement is in earnest." Louisa came away from the window and took a chair across from Bella.

Bella had confided everything to her cousin and Louisa had been more than happy to be included as coconspirator.

"We'll convince them."

The party didn't make her nervous. She'd helped her mother plan the event, knew who was coming, and had already decided what she would say when others questioned her about her decision to finally accept a proposal.

What Bella hadn't counted on was finding herself straddling Rhys in the middle of his study and being unable to stop herself from touching him. And it had been intoxicating, not just the heat and hardness of his body beneath hers, but for once being the one in control. She'd always been a fool for him, but yesterday he had allowed her to do as she wished.

For as long as she'd known him, Rhys had tempted her—into mischief, into fun, into breaking free of the rules she tried so hard to follow. Now he was a different sort of temptation and she had to find a way to shore up her defenses.

She couldn't deny the pull between them, but she had to be less impulsive.

"Shall we head down? Guests will begin arriving soon and it's probably best if you're with the duke when they do." Louisa offered Bella a shawl, holding it out so that she could turn and step into the outspread fabric.

"We should go down. There might be some last-minute tasks we can do to assist the preparations." She sorely needed something to do rather than worry.

"Aunt Gwendoline says you're not allowed to help," Louisa said with a soft smile. "This is all very exciting for her."

"I know."

Her mother had arranged everything with giddy enthusiasm. She'd been waiting for Bella to marry for so long.

"This will be a happy occasion."

"It only needs to be a successful one. After it's done, the next step will be to convince Mama and Papa to depart."

"Aunt Gwendoline has already spoken of preparations and I know how eager your father is to see the Grecian ruins. I don't think that step will be difficult."

Bella nodded. Louisa's cheerful demeanor made it hard to hold on to doubts and worries.

But her stubborn nature wanted to try.

"This could all go spectacularly wrong." Bella hated the quaver in her voice. She thought of Rhys and his unflappable bravado. If only he could lend her a bit.

Louisa stared at her, brow crimped in concern. "You're rarely this pessimistic about a well-thought-out plan, Bell."

"Yes, but none of my other plans involved the Duke of Claremont."

RHYS FLICKED HIS pocket watch from his waistcoat, caught it in his palm, and checked the time. Only quarter of an hour since he'd last looked. No one told him that engagement parties involved a great deal of accepting well-wishes from virtual strangers and not a single moment alone with one's betrothed.

He and Bella had stood together as Lord Yardley announced the engagement and they'd both smiled when a few guests immediately offered up murmurs of congratulations. But soon after they'd each been whisked away in opposite directions and he hadn't spoken to her since.

The news only seemed to come as a surprise to a few. Most in the intimate gathering of lords and ladies from the county's best families already seemed to know. News traveled fast in a small village and it was probably the only scandal-free bit of gossip a Claremont had generated in decades.

"You're not smiling as much as you should be." Meg approached the spot where he stood a few feet away from the other guests. She wore a cheerful smile and offered him a crystal cup filled with punch. "You look restless. Thought perhaps you could use some refreshment."

"Unless that's been spiked with whiskey, no thank you." He'd already had enough of the sickly sweet concoction to turn his stomach.

"Is there a reason you're hovering here on the periphery? You usually love parties." Her smile faded as she moved to stand beside him. "Is something amiss?"

"Honestly, I was hoping to steal a moment with Bella."

Together they looked out on the gathering to find her. Bella stood in a cluster of ladies, where she'd been stuck for over half an hour. The conversation seemed jovial enough, filled with bursts of laughter and chatter that drifted all the way to where he stood near the hedges.

"The ladies are understandably curious about where she'll obtain her dress, when the nuptials will be held and where." Meg glanced at him. "She says none of those decisions have been made. I understand why you're waiting. A wedding requires so much preparation."

"As does a Season." He winked at her.

Meg's eyes widened. "Good heavens, tell me I'm not the reason you're postponing the wedding until next year."

"You're not. Though it's better if Bella has time to help you prepare for the Season."

"She already has." Meg turned to him, almost breathlessly eager. "We've decided on everything I'll need and we've prepared lists of tasks to accomplish and she knows exactly which shops I should visit."

"Sounds as if it's time for a trip to London. I say we depart tomorrow. Stay a few days at Claremont House."

Rhys expected a smile. Maybe even a shout of glee. Instead, Meg cast her gaze toward Bella and then shot him a worried look.

"Tomorrow may be too soon."

"Why?"

She darted a glance toward the guests again. "I should consult with Bella. She's inquired for me with a milliner and modiste in Knightsbridge. We don't yet know when they could accommodate a fitting."

"Very well." Rhys focused on Bella too. She was smiling, but it was a tight uncomfortable smile. "We shall consult her first."

"I'll go and rescue her," Meg said, echoing his thoughts.

"She's my fiancée. I rather think that's my job."

His sister giggled. "Oh it is. But in this case, I'll

have an easier time getting her away and distracting the others while you two have a moment on your own."

"Very well." He glanced behind him at the hedge-rows and his stomach clenched at the memory of what had happened there. "Tell her I'll be waiting at the temple."

Lord Yardley had indulged his love of ancient architecture by having a Grecian-style folly constructed on the grounds of Hillcrest. Rhys recalled every moment he and Bella spent playing in and around the circular temple with fondness.

Meg nodded and headed into the gathering of women. Rhys started off toward the folly. Before he'd even made it halfway, Bella called to him.

He turned to find her a few feet away, her cheeks flushed and her pale yellow gown flecked with bits of grass. She looked so much like the girl who he'd romped through the fields with barefoot that he couldn't help but grin.

"Did you run to catch up?"

"Mother would never approve of running." She glanced over her shoulder to where her mother mingled with guests on Hillcrest's veranda, and then turned back to him. "But I did sprint a bit when I felt certain I was out of sight."

Her voice was playful, full of relief, and suddenly he felt lighter too.

"The party seemed to go well." He hadn't participated as much as he should have, but Bella had spoken to nearly every guest.

"Extremely well. I've rarely seen Mama so happy. Papa withdrew to his study soon after it started, but I think he's pleased too." She came a step closer. "Why did you retreat?"

"I didn't *retreat*. I was friendly for quite a long time. The conversation waned and I stepped away," Rhys protested. "I don't think I gave anyone cause to suspect—"

"That we're lying to everyone we know?"

Rhys clenched his teeth. Guilt gnawed at him. He didn't want to tell her that he'd stepped away to avoid the whispers and looks of disdain. He'd expected them. By reputation, he'd earned them, and normally that didn't warrant his notice. But he wasn't Bella's fiancé then.

"You have a very good reason for this scheme. It's born out of love for your parents, and this plan won't harm them. We've already agreed on all of that."

"Yes, I know."

Her doubts were understandable. He didn't like the deception either and he still worried for her reputation. But most of all he hated that she no longer seemed at ease.

"Shall we make our way to the folly?" He began walking backward, keeping his gaze on her, offering her a smile to entice her to join him. He was prepared to do anything to make her forget her worries and guilt. "I haven't been there in years."

She hadn't budged from where she stood near the entrance to the hedge garden. "We could just find a bench here if you wish to talk."

Rhys swallowed down his own dose of guilt. There was challenge in her gaze. As much as he wanted to avoid reliving that day, she seemed to want to do so in equal measure.

"As you wish." Stalking past her, he headed down one row and turned. When he spotted the bench where she'd confronted him years before, he turned back and waited.

He wasn't a terribly honorable man. He'd wagered recklessly, poured most of his energy into revelry, and sought and found pleasure more often than any man should. Looking back on the last five years, he had little but his involvement with the Duke's Den to be proud of, but that particular instance of thoughtlessness haunted him like nothing else he'd ever done.

Because no one in his life had ever thought so highly of him as Bella.

When she turned the corner to join him, it wasn't the confident mature Bella he saw standing in front of him now. He saw a girl, young and sweet and innocent. A girl who'd trusted him entirely and idealized him too much.

"This is where I found you," she said matter-of-factly. "Why did you do it?"

"The usual reason." That's what she wanted? For him to confess he was a libido-driven wretch? All of London knew that. He could provide her with a dozen scandal rags from the past months that documented his exploits.

"I don't know what that means." She truly looked confused, and he realized this wasn't just a ploy to force him to humiliate himself and relive his misdeed. In true Bella fashion, she wanted to understand how he worked. If he was a clock, she'd take him apart to figure out what made him tick.

"I think you know what it means." Rhys circled around her so she was sheltered from the view of anyone who might be taking a stroll through the gardens.

She backed up until the bench was pressed against her legs. "You mean desire."

"No." He had not truly desired that lovely widow. Desire was deeper. A longing for someone. Not just wanting their body but their nearness, to hear their voice and smell their scent in the air. "Merely indulgence. Giving in to an urge."

"You wanted to . . ." Bella swallowed hard. ". . . bed her."

"I responded to an impulse."

"Without any thought or consideration of what you being there meant to me?"

"None at all. I was selfish." He wouldn't defend himself, but he also didn't bother adding that he was still selfish most of the time. It was something he needed to change. Her selfless desire to make her family happy was an example he wished to follow with Meg. "I was cruel."

"You were never cruel."

Rhys laughed. "Still defending me, I see. You are aware that's not allowed. It breaks one of our rules."

"It doesn't. The rule implied defending you to someone else and we're alone."

"We are." Rhys moved a step closer.

He heard her breath catch.

"Will you ever trust me again?" The words came out less as a question than a plea. Of all the commodities he'd traded, all the inventions he'd invested in, nothing was more precious than winning back her faith in him.

He took her hand and held it lightly. Then he pressed her palm flat against his body, much as it had been when she'd arched above him in the study.

Before she could answer, he added, "I'd change it if I could. There's nothing I'd like more."

She paused, taking a moment to consider her reply. "Emotions are inconvenient at times, and we can't always control what we feel."

It wasn't an answer and he sensed she wasn't just referring to his stupidity years ago.

"Like yesterday?"

"Yes." She spoke the word like a confession, laced with guilt and a touch of embarrassment.

Rhys couldn't bear her feeling either. But he also wanted to know, needed to know, why she'd done it. "Just an impulse? Or was it more?"

"More?"

He took a step closer and told himself not to give in to *his* impulse to put his arms around her. Those rules of theirs were going out the window quickly, but he couldn't bring himself to care.

"Impulse or desire?" he asked softly.

Bella's hesitation to answer made him wish he hadn't pushed her. Her answer mattered to him a great deal, and yet he had no right to what he wanted.

"How would you define each?"

"Impulse is simple. Shallow. Fleeting."

She ducked her head and took a deep breath. "And desire?"

Reaching up, he laid a finger against her daisy pendant. The metal was warm from the heat of her skin and he almost envied the circle of gold. He slid his finger under her chin.

She lifted her head and looked at him. First at his lips, then his eyes, then at his lips.

The memory of her kiss was still fresh. But not nearly fresh enough.

"This is desire." He bent his head and took her mouth. Gently. Tenderly. She responded, opening to him, letting him deepen the kiss.

A moment later she took the lead, tipping her head and pressing her lips to the edge of his mouth. Then she offered him a long, lingering kiss that made him greedy for more. She gripped his lapel but then slid her hand underneath, burrowing under his waistcoat until he could feel the heat of her palm against his chest.

Rhys pulled her closer, sliding his hand up, grazing the edge of her breast.

She let out a little hiss at that and he pulled back reluctantly, wary of expecting too much. Everything between them felt fragile and he didn't want to break it again.

"Rhys."

He always liked the way she said his name, lingering on the sibilant end, especially when she was cross with him.

"What you felt in the study yesterday?" he whispered against her lips. "That was desire."

She didn't let go of him. He loved that she kept her hand pressed against his chest. It made him bold. He wrapped a hand around her waist and drew her closer, until their bodies were as flush and connected as they'd been the day before.

For the first time, he saw trepidation in her gaze.

"We mustn't do this," she said with a quiet certainty that cut straight across his longing. "There were rules we agreed to."

"You know I've never been very good at following rules."

"But I am. Rules are what keep me from giving in to impulse anytime I wish." The bite in her tone was new, but he couldn't tell if she was angry with him or herself.

"I told you, Arry. This isn't impulse."

"No." Bella shook her head and stepped away from him as if she meant to depart and leave him standing in the spot where he'd once nearly destroyed their friendship. "Whatever it is, I can't let myself give in to it. Not this time."

With that, she turned her back on him and headed toward the party.

For the briefest moment, he felt the desolation he had that day. The fear that he'd never see her again.

Chapter Fourteen

$\mathcal{I}$t will all go well." Bella huffed out an irritated sigh as she pushed clothing aside in what was beginning to feel like a futile search for her black traveling gloves. "It's to be a short trip. What could go wrong?"

"Are you trying to reassure me or yourself?" Louisa sat at the window seat and sipped tea as Bella gathered the last few items she needed for the trip to London.

"Perhaps both of us."

"Are you sure you shouldn't simply tell Claremont what you have planned?"

"No." Bella pulled out another wardrobe drawer and sifted through a pile of scarves. "If it goes well, believe me I'll be happy to let everyone know."

Tomorrow she had an appointment with a publisher and while she was confident about what she'd say at the meeting, the prospect of slipping away without raising Rhys's suspicions had her on edge. The plan had seemed entirely workable when she'd discussed it privately with his sister.

Now anxiety gnawed at her.

Meg had been encouraging and promised Bella that she'd cover for her absence however she was able. And somehow, she'd intuitively understood why Bella couldn't tell Rhys.

In some ways, he still viewed her as her parents did. A dutiful girl, and the only future he could imagine for her was marriage. But he'd also been protective in the past. If she told him, he'd wish to help her, and she wanted none of that.

"I thought perhaps Aunt Gwendoline would ask me to accompany you."

Bella didn't miss the wistfulness in her cousin's tone. Any other time, she would have enjoyed her company in the city. But this trip was to be brief and full of activity. Meg had appointments with a modiste and milliner, and they intended to shop for shoes and other accoutrements she'd need for her first Season.

"You'll be returning to Hampstead soon to prepare for your own Season, and I think Mama is satisfied that Meg's presence will serve the role of chaperone well enough."

Despite Rhys's terrible reputation, they seemed to persist in seeing him as the young man he'd once been. A man they'd often trusted to spend time with their daughter alone.

"We are engaged. That affords a little more freedom to be seen in each other's company. And the Duke and

Duchess of Tremayne have agreed to host me while we're in London, so I won't be lodging at Claremont House."

"True, but this will be the first time you're seen together in London society. Heads will turn."

"It will be fine." Bella didn't know if it was true. The idea of being toe to toe in a carriage with Rhys for hours had been on her mind all morning. But she had to salvage whatever calm she could.

A noise beyond the window caused Louisa to stand and peer down onto the front drive. "It's the Claremont carriage."

Bella's breath hitched, but she ignored the flutter in her chest and gathered her scarf, then slid her hands into the traveling gloves she'd found at the bottom of the drawer.

"Enjoy the trip." Louisa drew close enough to give Bella a peck on the cheek. "And best of luck with your book."

"Thank you, my dear." Bella smiled and scooped up the small portmanteau she'd chosen to transport her manuscript. Hugging the case to her chest, she willed her pulse to steady. "I can do this."

Louisa giggled. "I don't have a single doubt."

Bella made her way downstairs and was relieved to see that the staff had already placed her luggage on the carriage. She'd said her good-byes to her parents earlier.

Meg clambered down and rushed toward her. "I'm so excited for our trip."

Before Bella could answer, the girl wrapped her in a hug. She vibrated with enthusiasm and smelled like springtime, and a bit of Bella's tension eased.

Then she glanced over Meg's shoulder as Rhys stepped down from the carriage.

For a tall man with such broad shoulders, he maneuvered out with surprising grace. Bella got distracted watching the way he moved and when she looked up, she found his gaze fixed on hers.

When Meg released her, he stepped forward and reached for her hand.

"What are you doing?" There wasn't supposed to be any touching. They'd already broken that rule far too many times.

"Helping you with your bag." Glancing down, she realized he was trying to grasp the handle of her portmanteau. His hands were so much larger that his fingers covered hers. She felt the heat of him even through the fabric of her gloves. "It's heavy. Have you adopted your father's habit of taking books with you wherever you go?"

"Yes, but I've got it." Bella pulled away from him, grasping the handle of her case tighter, and climbed into the carriage after Meg.

Her heart was beating too fast and they hadn't even started their journey. She claimed the center of her bench, and Rhys seemed to take her cue and settled next to his sister.

The spot right in front of Bella, where every gray-suited, ruby-waistcoated inch of him was an unavoidable distraction. And, of course, when she looked up, he was watching her.

A slow smile lifted the edges of his mouth, and she didn't know whether he was looking forward to the trip or knew precisely how much being in such close confines with him unnerved her.

"WOULD YOU MIND sitting next to me?"

Bella lost her grip on the book she'd been holding as a shield between them.

Rhys reached out and caught the volume.

"Pardon?" she asked, her brow crumpled in a frown.

Rhys handed her the book and then lifted a finger to his lips. "Ssh." He glanced beside him where Meg was leaning against the wall of the carriage. A soft whistling snore escaped her lips.

"Oh." Bella's expression softened.

"I thought," Rhys whispered, "I'd let her stretch out and join you on yours."

"Of course." Bella scooted immediately toward the edge of her bench, gathering the voluminous fabric of her skirt and petticoats snug against her legs.

Rhys put an arm around Meg and pulled her gently until she was lying across the seat, her head resting on the balled-up overcoat he'd removed.

Then he moved to Bella's bench.

He heard her breath hitch when he placed his hand near hers and brushed the edge of her fingers. She'd removed her gloves. He rarely wore any. Her skin was soft and deliciously warm.

But he removed his hand. She'd made herself clear. Whatever she felt for him, she was determined not to surrender to it. And she was right.

She deserved a better man than he could ever be.

He stared out his carriage window, listening to the rhythm of her breathing, enjoying her violet scent, and wondering what thoughts were churning in her clever mind.

She stared out her own window, fingers tapping on the book in her lap that she hadn't yet resumed reading.

"Other than shopping and inspecting your father's property in Gordon Square, do you have plans while we're in London?" she asked quietly without looking his way.

"I should visit the club."

"The Duke's Den?" She glanced his way and he liked the tone of interest in her voice.

"Yes, though I doubt I'll have time to sit for any presentations."

"I quite like the notion of investing in ideas." She laid her hand on the brown leather portmanteau as she spoke.

"Perhaps you'd care to visit the club." He turned to look at her. They were so close, he could see the flecks of darker emerald green that glittered in her eyes.

"Perhaps I would."

Rhys smiled. "We could go tomorrow."

"Not tomorrow." She swallowed hard, and Rhys sensed there was something she held back. "I have a few matters I must attend to, as well."

"Should I accompany you?" They were engaged, after all.

"No," she said quickly. Too quickly. "Most of our time will be spent assisting Meg."

That explained nothing about the other matters she wished to attend to in London, but Rhys decided it was best not to pry. She wouldn't confide in him as she once had.

For long minutes they said nothing more to each other and the only sound in the carriage was Meg's soft rhythmic snore.

Rhys scrutinized the portmanteau Bella had pressed between her side and the carriage wall. "Did you bring any other novels with you?"

Her eyes widened at the question and she gripped the latch on her case. Looking down, she scooped up the book in her lap and offered it to him.

"You can have this one."

"What will you read?"

"I'll take Meg's lead and rest."

Rhys flipped open the book and got as far as reading the title page of *Jane Eyre* by a Mr. Currer Bell when Bella shifted on the bench.

He watched out of the corner of his eye as she settled back against the squabs and reached up to loosen the scarf around her neck. Her scent wafted off the fabric and filled the air. A moment later she unfastened the top button of her bodice, and Rhys licked his lips as she stroked the skin of her neck as if to ease tension.

There was no hope of concentrating on the damned book and all the words determined to confound him when Bella was inches away, her body relaxing against the cushions as she began to doze.

Once her breathing slowed and he was sure her eyes were closed, he set the book aside and allowed himself one long look at her. She looked peaceful and lovely. When she was awake, there was always a sense of urgency about her, as if all the ideas in her head were impatient to get out. But in repose, her face softened and she wore the tiniest of smiles, as if whatever she was thinking of in slumber pleased her.

He wondered if he ever featured in her dreams.

For a while, he simply enjoyed her nearness. Then he leaned his own head back and tried to clear his mind of the yearning he'd felt since the moment he saw her again. He'd agreed to help her. He had no right to all his other wayward desires.

Bella's hand landed on his thigh and his eyes shot open. She'd moved so that her head leaned against the carriage window and her arm had fallen slack at her side.

Rhys laid his hand on hers gently and realized how much he relished the simplicity of touching her. But there were rules, and Bella's resolve, and he couldn't deny that he wanted far more than to hold her hand.

With tender care, he placed her arm back against her body, letting her hand rest on the stretch of seat between them.

He couldn't turn back time and undo the past, but

he owed her the most honorable behavior he could muster now.

Glancing at her, he noticed the pulse dancing at the base of her throat and could only think of how much he wanted to kiss her there.

"Damn it," he mumbled under his breath. This wasn't going to be bloody easy.

Chapter Fifteen

The next morning Bella sat in the dress shop of one of London's most touted modistes and glanced at the clock on the wall, wondering when she could reasonably slip away.

Rhys seemed nervous too and eager to escape, if his fingers tapping insistently against his thigh were any indication.

When Lady Margaret and the dressmaker settled down on a settee to peruse a catalog of possible dress designs, Bella clutched the portmanteau she'd brought containing the pages of her manuscript. A few minutes later, she eased out of her chair, hoping to quietly depart.

But Rhys beat her to it. "Ladies, do you mind if I leave you to order what you wish? I'll return in an hour."

Meg cast a glance Bella's way and Bella nodded at

the girl. Perhaps it was best if Rhys left first. Her appointment wouldn't take as long as an hour, and Meg would be well occupied with the modiste and her assistants. When Rhys returned, he'd be none the wiser.

"Perfect," Meg told him. "I have Bella to help me and I'm certain we'll still be here in an hour." She offered Bella a surreptitious wink.

"Excellent," he said, though the look on his face was anything but pleased.

He was nervous and unsettled and had been all morning. During the latter part of carriage ride, rather than engaging in conversation with his usual enthusiasm, he'd kept watch out the carriage window or napped as Meg chattered on about the shops they'd visit and items that needed to be purchased.

Rhys offered Bella a nod and then started for the shop's front door, but at the threshold he turned and beckoned her to join him.

"You seem troubled," he said quietly. "Is it about Mr. Radley?"

Radley. Of course, they still had the address in London to visit. "No, I'm just anxious for things to go well today."

She didn't want to tell him about her appointment. Not until she could report success rather than failure. Even if he would encourage her, and she suspected he would, this was something she needed to do on her own.

"Don't worry. You've helped immensely, and once we meet with the Tremaynes and the duchess meets

Meg, all the burden of assisting her won't be solely on your shoulders."

"I don't mind."

"Good." The smile he offered her was full of the kind of ease they'd once shared, and she felt guilty for not telling him of her other purpose for coming to London. "I'll see you in an hour."

Once he'd gone, she retrieved her bag and told Meg, "I'll be back as soon as I can. The office isn't far."

The girl stood immediately, nearly toppling two bolts of fabric on the settee next to her. "Good luck." She kissed Bella softly on the cheek. "I don't know much about your puzzles but Rhys always said you were the most intelligent girl he'd ever known."

"Did he?" He'd complimented her occasionally in the past but she'd never dreamed he'd shared those opinions with others.

"Always. He still thinks so. It's why he asked for your help with the ledgers."

"I know."

"Who knew it would lead to such a quick engagement?" Meg's smile was full of genuine warmth. "I'm glad we'll be sisters."

Bella couldn't meet her gaze. Guilt had been her constant companion since they'd begun their charade.

"I should go." She gave the girl's hands an encouraging squeeze. "If there's anything you need help with, hold the modiste off a bit and I'll be back before you know it."

As Bella exited the shop, she considered whether to

take a hansom or an omnibus, debating which would be quicker. Looking over her shoulder, she scanned for empty cabs looking to take on passengers.

"Bella?"

Rhys approached along the row of shops.

Damn it. An explanation would delay her and the chances of making her appointment on time were fading minute by minute. "I thought you weren't returning for an hour."

He looked wounded at her tone. "I came back. For you. I'm headed to my club and wondered if you'd care to see it."

"I thought ladies weren't allowed." She *was* curious about what went on at gentlemen's clubs. Just not at this precise moment.

He grinned. "I'm a co-owner and prepared to smuggle you inside."

Bella glanced back to the cab stand.

"Where were you off to?" He stared down at the bulky case in her arms. "Did you leave Meg on her own?"

"I'll only be gone a short while." Bella raised her arm but the empty passing hansom didn't stop. "I'm sorry but I'm late."

His frown went from confused to irritated. "Where exactly are you going?"

Bella ignored his question and stepped toward the curb. Another cab was coming their way and she hoped to catch it.

Rhys approached, bristling with palpable frustration. "Shouldn't you tell me? I am your fiancé, after all?"

Any other time they'd spoken of the ruse, there had been an almost playful tone in his voice. There was none of that now. His question felt like a demand.

"You're *not* actually my fiancé and this is something I must do." After a sigh of frustration, she lifted her bag. "My puzzles and cryptograms. I've arranged them into a manuscript. I'm meeting with a publisher and now I'm going to be late."

"No." After that single emphatic syllable, he turned and headed to the pavement's edge, then stepped onto the cobblestones. He raised a hand and whistled for the next cab passing by. The driver responded immediately, drawing up the reins so that the horse stopped in front of them. "You're not going to be late, Bella. I won't let you be."

Even now, she hesitated. The trust he so desperately wanted from her wouldn't be easy to regain.

Finally, she sprinted forward, placed her hand in his, and let him help her into the cab. When he settled beside her, she called up an address near Green Park, and the driver immediately urged the horse on its way.

"Thank you," she said without glancing at him.

The quarters were close. Thigh to thigh. Arm to arm. The nearness was tempting. Unnerving. He loved it. She didn't seem as pleased.

She vibrated with anxious energy and he had no idea how to soothe her nerves.

"I'm sure it will go well." He glanced at her lush mouth and searched his mind for any way he might ease her nervous trembling. Her hazel eyes, lightened to the color of whiskey in the sun, were focused forward as if she could see her goal ahead and refused to shift her attention to anything else.

Bella had always been lovely, but lately he couldn't help noticing all the things that made her beautiful. It wasn't just that Bella was pretty, she exuded a determined energy that made her breathtaking.

"He'll like your book. Your ideas."

She eased her intense focus long enough to glance at him. "You cannot know that at all."

"I have a good feeling."

"This has nothing to do with emotion." She still wouldn't look at him but she was doing nothing to hide her irritation. "If he likes my book, it will be because he thinks he can sell it. It's business. Nothing more."

"I do know a bit about business." He still wanted to show her the club. It was the only place he'd ever truly made a success of himself. A place where he'd made choices that made him proud rather than regretful.

"You've never even seen my book," she said quietly. "This could be an endeavor in futility."

"Hardly futile."

That earned him another glance and one auburn brow arched high. "Why?"

"Because you've gotten to this point." He tapped his finger against the square outline of the portmanteau she clutched against her lap as if it was long-lost treasure. "You produced all these words and ideas and organized them into a manuscript. It's not something I could do."

"That's nonsense. I've never seen you fail at anything you set your mind to."

Her compliments always came when he least expected them, slipping in past his defenses. Before he could reject her claim or offer words of gratitude, the hansom rolled to a stop.

Bella jumped down without his help and scanned the street. "You needn't wait for me," she called as she started off. "I shouldn't be long and will return to Meg as soon as I'm done."

"Good luck." He shouted the words so enthusiastically, a lady passing on the street shot him a curious glance.

All that mattered was that Bella heard him, and he knew she had when she offered him a tentative smile before ascending the steps of a town house two doors down.

He headed back to the cab but couldn't bring himself to depart. After paying the driver, he took up a post on the opposite side of the street, waiting, watching. He might have had moments of undeserved luck in his life, but now he wished he could transfer all of it to Bella.

When she hadn't emerged after quarter of an hour, worry set in. When she hadn't appeared after half an hour, he contemplated going in after her.

Just when he was about to burst into the publisher's office and make an utter fool of himself, the front door swung open and Bella stepped out.

He didn't require an explanation to read her expression.

"Not at all interested," she said grimly. "Perhaps I was mistaken. Maybe the entire project is nonsense." She stared down at her case as if she was considering whether to heave the whole thing into the Thames.

"Arry, there are other publishers in London. Many of them. We'll simply find one that wants your book."

"We? I told you I'm doing this alone."

"I know. Of course, it's your work. Your creativity. But I still wish to help, and you should let me."

She twisted her mouth, a gesture that usually indicated she was weighing her options.

"That's the whole point of this arrangement, is it not?" he asked. "We help each other."

Rhys knew the moment when she let go of her frustration. The edge of her jaw softened, she closed her eyes for the briefest of moments, and then she nodded decisively. Straightening her shoulders, she drew in a deep breath, as if already set on some new course.

"Very well," she told him. "Then it's time I help you. We should visit the town house your father purchased."

The change of topic made him frown. He much preferred helping her, but she was right. As usual. "We could go now. The address isn't more than walking distance away."

"Then let's go. Another task off the list."

"Meg will be all right, don't you think?" He didn't want her to feel they'd forgotten her.

"She will. Your sister is much more self-reliant than I think any of us give her credit for. We haven't yet been gone an hour."

They proceeded side by side on the pavement, and he found himself smiling. Her companionship was familiar and yet also new. Everything they accomplished together felt as if he was earning back a bit of what had been lost between them. And, of course, now he wanted more.

After several minutes of silence, she turned her head. "Thank you."

When had those two words gained the power to kick his heartbeat into a gallop? "For?"

"Your encouragement." She hefted her satchel up onto her shoulder. "I could show you a few pages of my manuscript if you're interested."

"When have I not been interested in your puzzles?"

The only response to that was a slow smile.

By the time they reached the town house, Rhys's thoughts were as far from finding Radley as possible. One image kept playing over in his mind. Bella's body over his, the hunger in her eyes. He didn't know if she'd ever look at him that way again, but longing for it was becoming an enormous distraction.

They stopped on the pavement across the street from the address they'd found in the ledger. Rhys had brought a few keys he'd discovered in his father's desk drawer, unmarked, hoping one might fit the lock. He dug in his pocket to retrieve them.

"Someone is in residence," Bella whispered. "I can see someone moving about inside."

Rhys moved to get a closer look, but Bella gripped his arm and pulled him back.

"What if it's Mr. Radley? What if he's armed?"

"I hardly think he'll be armed," Rhys told her, trying to reassure both of them. "And he's definitely not expecting us."

"Most likely, but the man stole thousands of pounds from a duke. Not to mention what he's filched from others. Even if he returns what he took, he could very well hang for his crimes." She got that determined look in her eyes and stared at the house. "I should go."

This time he grasped her arm to stop her.

"Bella, no. I count on you to make more sense than I do, and right now you're making none." He stepped closer so she'd look up at him. "If the man is dangerous, I should go."

"Trust me on this." As if she knew precisely the power she had over him, she placed a hand on his chest. "I'll be less threatening. As you said, he's not expecting us. He's definitely not expecting me. You, on the other hand, have met him."

"Briefly. Years ago. He may not remember."

"You're very hard to forget."

He wasn't often speechless, but Bella's comment froze his tongue and filled his chest with a pleasant warmth. If she was trying to charm him into agreement, it was bloody well working.

"Trust me," she said in that quiet but fierce tone that told him she would not be dissuaded.

"I'll be watching. If I see even the merest hint of trouble, I'm coming in after you."

"I'd expect nothing less," she said with a cheeky smile.

For the second time in less than an hour, he watched her walk away from him and liked it even less than the first.

She rapped on the door and someone answered, but he couldn't see whether it was a man or a woman. They stood back, shadowed in the dark of the foyer. Whoever they were, Bella spoke to them for several minutes in what seemed to be a series of questions asked and answered.

A chill of warning slid down his back when she nodded. They had no reason to trust anyone inside that town house.

Bella's name was on the tip of his tongue and it took every ounce of restraint not to call out to her.

As if sensing his agitation, she glanced at him.

He let out a relieved breath, but then she turned back toward the door, took a step across the threshold, and disappeared inside the house.

Rhys rushed across the street and caught a glimpse of someone moving in the front window. He pounded the door with enough force to make the lion's head knocker jangle. When no one answered, he pounded harder.

Finally, the front door swung open and Bella stood on the threshold.

He stepped inside and cupped her cheek against his palm. "You're all right?"

There was something worrying in her gaze. Uncertainty that wasn't like her at all. And another emotion he did recognize. Concern. For him.

"Bella, what is it?"

She slipped her hand inside the one he'd been holding against her cheek and led him deeper into the house. They stopped at the open door of a well-furnished drawing room.

Bella squeezed his hand and looked up at him. "This will be difficult."

"Bella, what is going on?" He peered through the cracked door of the room and glimpsed a woman inside. "Who—"

"Her name is Mrs. Belinda Turner. I don't think she intended any wrongdoing, and I think perhaps you should help her if you can."

Rhys understood the minute he stepped into the drawing room who the woman was and why his father had purchased the property in Gordon Square. A brooding portrait of the duke dominated the wall above the mantel and the petite blonde perching on an overstuffed chintz chair told the story.

"I take it you never knew about me, Your Grace?" she asked.

"No, Mrs. Turner." Rhys had never known about her specifically, but he knew his father kept mistresses. Even, unfortunately, while his mother was alive.

"Then I take it he left me nothing. He truly never spoke of me?" Sadness seemed to weigh her down.

Rhys shook his head. "My father and I rarely spoke in recent years."

Bella cleared her throat and gave him one of her raised-brow stares. A look that had always felt equal parts encouragement and challenge.

"I can provide you with some funds in the short term." His voice sounded more clipped and angry than he intended. He didn't know if Mrs. Turner had entered his father's life after his mother had died. Based on how recently the property was purchased, he suspected she had.

His real frustration wasn't with her, or even his father. All the disgust he felt was directed inward.

He'd kept a mistress and had his share of lovers set up in much the manner his father had treated this woman. Marriage had never crossed his mind. He'd never given much consideration to what would happen to the women when he tired of their company. And he always did.

"Do I get to keep the house?" There was a quaver in her voice, but her gaze was pure steel.

"For now." He didn't have the heart to ask the woman to decamp. She considered the town house her home and for the time being he would let it remain so.

"Until when?"

"I don't know." Meeting his father's mistress was like holding up a mirror on all his own offenses over the last five years. He didn't have answers. He couldn't fathom how to fix it. All he truly wanted to do was escape.

"You have enough for now?" Bella asked.

"My current funds will sustain me for the next several months." Mrs. Turner's gaze darted warily toward Rhys.

"I'll see to sending you more," Rhys told her. He wanted to help the woman as Bella has advised him to do, but he also wanted to be done with all of it.

"Thank you, Your Grace." When the lady nodded, Rhys offered her a slight bow.

"We bid you good day, Mrs. Turner."

"Wait." Bella reached for his sleeve as he stalked past her. "There's something I didn't ask her yet."

"What is it, Miss Prescott?" The lady rose from her chair and pulled her wrap tighter around her shoulders.

"Are you acquainted with a Mr. Radley?"

Leave it to Bella to have the good sense he forever seemed to lack.

"Yes, of course, though only through correspondence. He's the one who arranged for the purchase of the house and the funds the duke used to send to me."

"And when was the last time you corresponded with him?" Rhys asked. The man was proving damnably elusive.

A pained looked crossed her face before Mrs.

Turner said quietly, "A few weeks before your father's passing."

Rhys swallowed down the guilt that welled up like bile in his throat. The woman's grief was sincere. He wasn't certain he could say the same about his feelings regarding his father's passing.

"Thank you for your time, Mrs. Turner. We bid you good day." Bella shocked him by slipping her arm through his and leading him toward the front door.

When they were out on the pavement, he loosened himself from her hold and strode across the square toward the green.

He drew in gulps of autumn air and told himself to stop acting like a fool.

"I feared it would upset you."

"It doesn't. Not in the way you think. I bear no ill will toward Mrs. Turner."

"Toward your father, then?"

"How can I? Don't you see? The way he treated that woman. Making her promises and keeping none of them. It's no different from how I've conducted my affairs."

She couldn't look at him. For a moment she shifted her gaze to the pavement, and he waited for the condemnations he richly deserved.

"Do you have a mistress now?" she finally asked.

The question surprised him. They'd always been matter-of-fact with each other but never about love. Never about carnal pleasure. The last time he'd seen her she was still a girl.

"I do not."

"But if you married, you'd keep one?"

"No." That wasn't true. He'd always intended that marriage would be practical and pleasure would be separate. Now he wasn't sure of anything. Except that he didn't want Bella to look at him with that disappointment he saw in her eyes now.

He'd wanted her to look at him like she used to and he wanted her trust.

No, he wanted much more. Now, at the worst possible moment, he wanted to kiss her again. He needed her close. He craved the comfort of having her in his arms, even now when he'd just been reminded of why he didn't deserve it.

"Well, at least we know Radley isn't here and never was." She changed the subject as if it was a natural progression of their awkward conversation, but she betrayed her unease by tugging at her gloves that were already perfectly in place on her hands.

He didn't blame her for wishing to move away from the topic of mistresses and men who couldn't be trusted. It wasn't a discussion he was terribly eager to have either.

"The man is probably on the Continent dining at the finest restaurant in Paris and laughing at us all."

"Or he's in Margate looking out at the sea," she countered. "We should visit the cottage there."

Ah, a plan. That was Bella through and through.

"Miss Prescott, your tenacity is quite impressive." He tested a teasing tone with her. She might stick to her rules and appreciate orderliness above all things, but she rarely repressed her sense of humor.

"A mystery is a bit like a puzzle." Her eyes flashed with determination. It was a magnetic pull that never failed to draw him in. "I think we can solve this one."

"Will you take up detection professionally after this?"

"Maybe." He could live off the memory of the saucy smile she gave him for several days. "Might as well put my skills to practical use.

"So," she asked with a self-satisfied grin, "when do we leave for the seaside?"

Chapter Sixteen

$\mathcal{B}$ella kept her eyes closed a moment longer and nuzzled into the warmth against her cheek as she awakened. Fabric slid softly against her skin, though what was underneath was decidedly firm. It also smelled delicious. Like fresh air and sandalwood cologne.

And Rhys Forester.

She opened her eyes and immediately shielded them from the sun. Then she leaned as far as she could toward the opposite side of the carriage bench.

"We're here," he told her.

"I fell asleep."

"Just a short nap."

"On you." She smelled of his shaving soap and could feel the imprint of his overcoat against her cheek.

His eyes widened, then his mouth flickered into a mischievous smile. "Only on my shoulder, unfortunately. Necessary touching. You needed a pillow. I was willing to oblige."

Though his tone was teasing, his steady gaze stoked a pulsing warmth inside her that had nothing to do with the heat of the afternoon sun.

Bella turned her attention out the carriage window to get her first glimpse of the sea. But there was no cottage or water's edge in sight, though she could smell the sea in the air. The coach they'd hired had stopped at what looked to be an old weathered coaching inn.

"Thought we'd inquire here first," Rhys told her by way of explanation. "I've asked the coachman to wait for us so we can return to London before nightfall."

They'd been vague when departing in the morning, but Bella bid Meg good luck on her shopping expedition with the Duchess of Tremayne. She'd assured Rhys's sister that she would see her at dinner that evening.

"That all sounds very sensible." Now if only she felt that way.

She struggled to look him in the eye. They'd arm wrestled as children. She'd fallen on him body to body a few days ago. Yet something about the intimacy of napping against his shoulder, and enjoying it, unnerved her. Her attraction to him seemed to grow every time they touched.

He laughed as he exited the carriage and then turned back to help her down. "From you, Bella, that is an extraordinary compliment."

The inn was sparsely occupied and Rhys seemed to be scanning the few patrons around tables for Mr. Radley. He'd described the older man as gray-haired, bespectacled, and obsequious. Most of the men tipping back tankards were gray-haired, including their coachman, though none wore spectacles.

Rhys approached the bar and spoke to the wiry old man behind it. "Do I have the luck of speaking to the innkeeper by any chance?"

"You do." The older man assessed Rhys from head to toe and offered Bella a skimming glance. "What can I do for you, my lord?"

"What do you know of Tide's End?"

The crown coin Rhys slid across the table seemed to interest the innkeeper.

"A well-built cottage right near the seashore. Follow the lane outside toward the east and you'll find it yourself."

"Is it let?" Rhys asked with that easy way he had of making it seem as if the answer didn't matter to him at all.

"Indeed, Lord Radley seems to love the cottage, he does."

"*Lord* Radley?"

"Aye, my lord. Older gentleman. New to the village. I take it he rented the cottage quite recently. Comes to the inn for his repast now and then. Haven't seen him in a few days, come to think of it."

Bella stepped forward. "But you did see him as recently as a couple of days ago?" They were close and Radley might not have gotten too far away.

"Aye, miss." The old man frowned and stared at the bar as if searching his memory. "Four days past.

Come to think of it, he appeared as if he were ready to travel. Had bags with him and hired a coach."

"Where did he go?" For the first time Rhys's eagerness seemed to give the old man pause. His eyes narrowed under bushy gray brows.

"Couldn't rightly say, my lord. He comes and goes as he pleases."

"Whichever coachman took him, is that man here?" Rhys scanned the patrons seated at tables once more.

The innkeeper shook his head warily. "Never seen him before or since, my lord."

"Thank you, sir," Bella told the old man. "You've been most helpful."

Rhys lifted one blond brow to indicate he didn't quite agree but he followed her out of the inn nonetheless.

"This is a good thing. We can examine the cottage and see if he's left anything behind that might tell us where he's gone."

"Agreed." He looked over her head down the lane toward the seashore. "I'm not sure if I'm hoping he truly has departed or that he's still there and we can haul him back to London."

"There's only one way to find out."

They walked so quickly toward the cottage, Bella feared anyone noticing them might be alarmed or alert Radley to their presence if he was still in the village. But she understood Rhys's anxiousness and felt the same.

Nestled against a natural grassy embankment, its whitewash weathered away by sea breezes, Tide's End was the prettiest cottage Bella had ever seen.

"It's lovely."

Rhys looked at her quizzically. "Do you think so?"

"It's not Edgecombe, of course, or as fine as Claremont House, but it seems . . ." She shaded her eyes from the sun and looked up at him. "Cozy."

He gazed toward the cottage again and his expression softened. "Perhaps it is. Now all we need to do is discover whether it's still inhabited by a thief or we need to break in."

Ten minutes later, after peeking through windows and determining the cottage had been abandoned, Bella was shocked to find the front latch unlocked.

She slid the door open tentatively and offered a loud clear "Hello" in case Radley was lurking in the shadows. Rhys moved in front of her to enter first. He'd always been protective and apparently that aspect of their relationship hadn't changed.

"It is cozy," he said, grinning at her over his shoulder.

Every piece of furniture appeared to be new and as fine as what her mother might select for Hillcrest. The settee and matching chairs before the fireplace were covered in the same green damask and the dark wood furnishings were polished to a high sheen. Bella found the cottage's single bedroom to be equally well equipped.

"We know where he spent at least some of what he took."

Rhys shook his head. "I don't know. This is all very much my father's style. Perhaps he did intend this as a seaside retreat and never got the chance to enjoy it."

"Look at this." Bella had found a desk in the corner and a few bits of writing paper crumpled and discarded on top and on the floor beneath. She flatted one of the balled-up pieces of paper.

"Seems he was as bad at writing letters as I am." Rhys scooped up another one of the letters and unfolded it to begin reading. "He says he's headed to Bristol."

Bella reached for his sheet and handed her his. "This one says he's headed to Ireland."

The third letter they unwrinkled indicated that Radley was thinking of setting out for France.

"He's tooling with us," Bella told Rhys. "Or whomever might stumble on this hideout. I suspect if we find anything here, it will only be because he wished us to."

After gathering the rest of the pieces of paper into her arms, Bella dropped onto the settee and began straightening all of them, just for the satisfaction of leaving none in rumpled balls.

"I'm sorry. This doesn't make sense," she said after she'd examined all the scraps of paper and found nothing but an attempt to send them on a chase in a dozen different directions. "We should try harder to find the coachman he hired. If the publican doesn't know him, perhaps one of the other coachmen will."

Rhys had crossed his arms and was staring at her

intently. He looked thoughtful but the muscle ticking in his jaw indicated frustration.

"No," he finally said. "We're at the seaside. We're going to the beach."

"Rhys, we didn't come here for a jaunt. Meg—"

"Is enjoying a visit with the Duchess of Tremayne and will be perfectly fine until we return."

He shrugged out of his overcoat, then his suit jacket. Eyes fixed on hers, he rolled up his shirtsleeves, then untied his cravat.

Bella couldn't hold his gaze, mostly because she wanted to look at the rest of him. The way his waist-coat hugged his body, the way his trousers fit tight enough to outline his thighs. Even the dark gold hair on his forearms seemed worthy of study.

"The best sort of fun is the kind that isn't planned." He reached out and waited for her to take his hand. "Spontaneity, Bella. We were quite good at it once."

His fingers were deliciously warm against hers and his palm even warmer. "You have always been good at spontaneity."

He chuckled. "One of my few merits. Let me show you."

RHYS KEPT HOLD of her hand all the way to the beach and even once they'd reached the sand, he didn't want to let go.

"We should remove our boots," he told her with mock seriousness.

"Should we?"

"It's the only way to feel the water on your toes."

"We'll be cold," she said, rallying practical arguments. The sun had been out all day, but the breeze was brisk.

Rhys stared out at the horizon and imagined returning to the cozy cottage with her and getting warm. "There's a fireplace in the cottage. We can use Radley's letters as kindling."

Laughter burst from her lips, genuine and terribly unladylike.

Rhys smiled proudly. Letting go of her rules and control didn't come easily, but he liked it whenever she tried.

"Who goes first?"

"You're the expert in frivolity," she quipped.

"Very well." He strode toward a rocky outcropping near the beach's edge and sat on one of the sandy rocks. After toeing off his boots, he bent to roll off his socks and patted the stretch of stone beside him, beckoning her to join him.

Bella let out a little gasp when she sat down. The stones had been warmed by the sun but they were still cold against one's backside. She bent to unlace her boots at the same moment Rhys leaned forward to roll up his pant legs.

Their arms brushed, then their gazes met. Or rather she looked over at him. He found himself focused entirely on her legs. She'd lifted her dress to get at her boots and the sight of her ankles and calves wrapped in delicate white stockings made his throat dry.

"May I help you?" God how he wanted to.

"I've been removing my boots on my own for years," Bella told him as she tugged at her laces.

He forced himself to stop staring, but out of the corner of his eye he caught her examining him as she had at the cottage. Her gaze flickering to his arms, his thighs, his bare feet.

"I suppose you could help." She sat up, kept her skirt raised, and waited for him.

Rhys knelt in front of her and tugged at her laces. She bit her lip when he slipped his fingers inside to slide each boot off. The flowers embroidered at the edge of her ankle marched in a line along the outside of her leg, and he traced them with his fingertips up and up until Bella stopped him by placing her hands on his.

Rather than push him away as he expected, she lifted the bunched fabric of her skirt and let him slide his fingers higher. He licked his lips and wished he was tasting all the soft warm skin he was exploring with his hands but couldn't see. At the top edge of her stocking, he stilled, stroking her thigh, savoring her heat and softness.

"Take them off," she whispered.

Rhys's body responded as if she'd just asked him to remove the last stitch of clothing on her body. He wanted to, and he wanted her to ask him exactly the way she was now. Her mouth slightly open in anticipation and wonder, her breath coming quick.

He rolled one stocking down, taking his time, dragging his fingertips gently along her leg. Then he did the same with the other. By the time her feet were bare, both of them were drawing in sharp breaths and he was hard and aching and wished they were back at the cottage.

"Will it be very cold?" She stood up from the rock and looked out at the waves lapping at the beach.

"Let's find out." He strode toward the shore and she followed at his side.

Before they could reach the water's edge, a low wave built and rushed up to meet them.

"It's freezing," Bella said on a gasp that turned into a giggle.

"Arctic." Rhys jolted at the icy cold rush of seawater against his ankles. Whose bloody idea had this been?

Bella let out a yelp and he turned a worried look her way, only to discover it was a shout of joy.

A few feet away from him she splashed along the water's edge, kicking the seawater high enough to dampen the skirt of her dress, though she held the fabric bunched up above her knees.

This part of the beach was protected by a natural embankment and so they had this little slice of the English seashore all to themselves.

Rhys braced himself and waded a bit deeper into the water, as Bella had. He felt the current tugging at his ankles. "Take care with the waves."

She squealed and burst into laughter when a low wave built higher. "It's invigorating."

"Yes." Of course he wasn't talking about the icy seawater but about Bella. Her joy and delight were infectious.

Bending at the waist, she scooped an object from the sand, and held it up in triumph. As he approached, it glinted in the sun.

"Sea glass," she told him, holding the shard of bottle green glass up to catch the light. Its edges had been rubbed smooth. "Do you think it's from a shipwreck?"

"Possibly." Rhys thought it more likely from refuse someone had dumped in the sea, but he rather liked Bella being more fanciful than he was.

"Look!" She ran toward a spot on the beach where he could see something sticking out of the sand. She bent again and came up with a beautiful shell, spiraled and striped with a reddish color.

"If I'd known you were this lucky, I would have brought you with me to a gambling den long ago," he teased when she placed the delicate shell in his palm.

"Do you take ladies to gambling dens often?" Her fingers were cold when she retrieved the shell and her lips trembled as she waited for his answer.

"No." It was true depending on how one defined the word *often*. "You're shivering. Should we go back and get warm?"

She scanned the beach and looked out on the sea as if reluctant to depart but then offered him a decisive nod. "I'd like that."

RHYS'S JOKE ABOUT burning the letters Radley had left behind to throw them off his trail proved truer than he'd expected. They'd found a pile of wood stacked inside the cottage, but the paper was all they had in the way of kindling.

When he turned back to collect the bundles, he was struck by the sight of Bella removing her soaked petticoats. She let the fabric pool at her feet.

"Do you need help?" she asked when she noticed him watching her.

"No, I think I can manage." He wasn't used to building his own fires, but he suspected he could manage it far better than he could temper his raging libido.

He turned back to the fireplace and tried not to think about what the sounds of shifting fabric behind him meant. The grate was full of ash and he used the small shovel near the fireplace to collect a pile.

"Wait." Bella stopped him with a hand on his shoulder. "What is that?"

He looked closer at the debris he'd collected. "Bits of paper. More letters, perhaps."

Bella leaned across his shoulder and began collecting the larger pieces. Once she'd pushed aside some of the ash with her fingers, unburnt pieces emerged. They were layered as if they'd been thrown in together, perhaps torn from a journal. Or a ledger.

After a few moments, Bella had collected about twenty pieces that were still intact enough to detect writing. She carried them to a table near the window and began laying them out one by one.

"We don't know what's been burned. All the essential pieces might be missing."

"I'd still like to try."

"I'll collect the rest and get the fire going."

Once he had a good blaze, Rhys turned to offer Bella a spot closer to the warmth and found her hunched over the pieces in that entirely absorbed way of hers that made him wonder if she realized he was still in the room.

"I've found something." Her tone was shocked, her gaze wide as he approached.

"Just another ruse, do you think?"

"No, I believe this was from a journal." She pointed to three jagged pieces that seemed to only connect along a row of two lines, most of which were missing. "This doesn't sound like a letter. It's part of a list." She drew in a sharp breath. "I think it's an address."

Rhys placed a hand on the back of her chair and leaned closer. "I recognize a *B*. Two of them. Can you make out the rest?"

"Brine or Byrne, perhaps. A street name. And then this is unmistakable." She ran her fingers over a word that was missing a few letters where a hole had been burned in the paper. "It's Bishopsgate. I'm certain of it."

"You've very clever." Her dress was wet with seawater, her hair windblown and coming out of nearly every pin, and her fingers were dirty with soot. She was also the most desirable woman he'd ever seen.

Her cheeks reddened and he watched her swallow hard, as if struggling to accept his words. She'd always been terrible with compliments.

"Thank you," she finally said quietly. "I'm sorry but it appears we've come to the seaside just days after he headed to London."

"But we wouldn't know that unless we'd come to the seaside."

A little smile played at the edges of her mouth that warmed his insides far more effectively than the fire blazing in the corner of the small cottage.

"Come closer to the fire. You're still trembling," he told her. "And your skirt is still soaked."

"I should clean up." She held out her blackened fingers.

"Let me." Rhys retrieved a towel he'd found in the cottage's kitchen and knelt next to the chair by the fire where Bella had finally seated herself. He knelt in front of her very much as he had at the seaside. He took her fingers one at a time and scrubbed at them with the towel.

Her gaze on him was focused and intense.

He took care with her final finger, lingering because in truth he had no desire to stop touching her. When he finally finished, he lifted her hands up and kissed the back of each softly in turn.

Bella shocked him by turning her hand so that she could stroke his face, running her finger along the edge of his jaw, his chin, and then tracing the curve of his lower lip.

"Will you—"

"Yes," he told her because whatever she asked of him he'd do. Eagerly.

She let out a trill of throaty laughter. "You don't know what I'm going to ask."

"I am yours to command."

"Kiss me again."

He stood in front of her and her gaze took him in from head to toe, lingering on his waist, his neck, his mouth. He let her look her fill before reaching for her hand and pulling her to her feet.

Cupping her face, he stroked the petal soft skin of her cheeks and looked into her eyes. Everything he saw reflected his own feelings. Desire. Attraction. Hunger. And something more he dared not name.

As he lowered his mouth to hers, her eyes fluttered closed. He told himself to go slow, but it didn't work. He kissed her softly but then slid his tongue against her lips. He felt her jolt in response. When she opened to him, he tasted her again and again.

Her hands came up, clutching at his shoulders. He wrapped an arm around her waist and brought her body flush against his. Though he could feel her warmth beneath the fabric of her clothing, he wanted every stitch of it gone.

As if she read his mind, she whispered against his mouth, "Maybe we should get out of these wet clothes."

Chapter Seventeen

*B*ella couldn't pinpoint the moment she'd decided.

Perhaps it had been when he'd knelt before her and rolled down her stockings with a kind of tender reverence. Or when he'd said he thought her clever and she could hear in his voice and see in his gaze that he meant it. Maybe it was when he'd gently cleaned the soot from her fingers and then kissed the back of her hand more sweetly than any man ever had.

All she knew for certain was that she wanted him. She had for so long. But not like this. At eighteen, she'd been smitten. Blind to his faults, enamored with his masculine beauty, and charmed by the vulnerability he showed only to her.

Now her desire was something else. The intensity was new but so was the way she admired him. Not because she believed him to be perfect but because she knew he wished to be better.

"Have I shocked you?" she asked quietly. A tiny inner voice of doubt told her she'd misread everything.

He stroked a hand down her back. "Not at all. I only have one fear."

"What is it?"

Lowering his head, he brushed his lips against her cheek before whispering in her ear. "That you'll change your mind."

He loosened his hold then, taking a step back, keeping just one hand at her waist. His gaze held warmth, desire, but she knew he was leaving this choice to her.

Rather than answer with words, Bella reached back and freed the buttons at the nape of her gown. She pulled at her bodice until it slid off of her shoulders.

For a while Rhys simply watched her hungrily, and Bella found she didn't mind having his gaze on her. She was watching him too, gauging his reaction.

"May I help?" he asked softly.

Though she'd gotten most of the buttons on her own, she wanted his hands on her.

"Would you?" Turning her back to him, she reached up to expose her nape, then glanced at him over her shoulder. "There should only be a couple more buttons."

"You've no idea how much I wish there were more buttons."

Bella let out a shocked chuckle. "You could unbutton these few slowly."

She wanted him with an eagerness that made her body tremble, but she wanted to go slow too. To savor every moment.

He didn't attack the buttons. First, he simply laid his hands on her back. Then his mouth came down in a searing single kiss at the base of her neck. Just as she suspected he intended, a chill chased down her spine.

"You smell like flowers and taste like salty sea air."

Bella laughed. "Like a violet-scented sailor?"

"You would make for a fearsome lady pirate," he whispered against her skin.

"Perhaps we should go into the bedroom?"

"We should."

Yet he didn't make any move toward the small room off of the cottage's main living area.

"It's that way," Bella said, glancing toward the open door.

"Oh, I know where it is. I want you to lead the way. I can't bear for you to have any regrets."

She didn't. She wouldn't. Even if this day, this moment, were the only one they'd have free of rules and what was expected of them, she would not regret her choice.

Slipping her hand into his, she led him through the low doorway.

"You'll show me?"

"Anything you like."

"I have some idea but I don't know—"

He stopped her with a kiss, and then he slid a hand around her nape, drawing her closer and stroking her hair as she moaned against his lips.

"You just feel, Bella," he whispered before taking her mouth again. "No rules. No propriety. No duty.

Just pleasure." He stroked his hand across her shoulder and down the length of her back, a delicious trail of sensation and warmth that made her body pulse with need.

Why had she wished to take this slow?

She worked the buttons of his waistcoat free as she kissed him. He reached around and slipped the hooks on her skirt. Together, they made quick work of each layer of clothing. Only when there was nothing but his trousers and her chemise and drawers between them did she place a hand on his chest to catch her breath.

"We can stop—" The words emerged from his lips breathless and ragged.

"No." Bella realized he misunderstood.

As difficult as she found it to speak of what she felt, in this moment she needed to. There could be no uncertainty between them, at least for today.

"I want this. I want you."

"And I want you," he said huskily, and then let out a hiss when she reached to unbutton his trousers.

She marveled at the way he reacted to her. Reveled in it. He might like her eagerness, but he waited patiently while she tugged at the fastenings and ran her fingers over the muscled ridges of his stomach. Then she dipped her hand lower. He was burning hot and hard and felt extraordinary under her fingers.

Though she'd never seen a living man unclothed, she'd seen pictures in books, sculptures in museums.

Rhys's body was made with a different mold. His chest was broad and muscular, his thighs too.

"You may explore to your heart's content, but let me get out of these first." He slid his trousers off and reached for the hem of her chemise.

He paused, as if waiting for permission. Bella nodded and he drew the fabric up, skimming his fingers against the bare skin of her hip and stomach and breast. When she was free of the garment, he retraced the path. But more attentively.

He stroked her nipple and her tautened skin was so sensitive she let out a little moan. As if to soothe her, he lowered his head and took the peak into his mouth.

Bella gasped and clutched at his shoulders. "That's quite . . ."

"Mm?" He glanced up, brow creased in concern.

"Extraordinary."

He smiled and slipped his hand down to grasp hers. "There's more, sweetheart. A great deal more."

After settling on the bed, Bella remembered why she wished to take this slow. This was real. Years of dreaming of this moment paled in comparison. Rhys knelt over her as she lay back, then swept his gaze over her body from head to toe.

"You're beautiful, Bella." When he placed a hand on her leg, she realized he was trembling. "I'll try to go slow."

With deliberation and care, he stroked his fingers up the length of her leg, leaving a trail of warmth wherever he touched. At the top of her thigh, he nudged her legs open.

Bella bit her lower lip as he slid a finger along her body. She was wet and every ounce of need inside her converged on the spot where he touched her. When he slid a finger inside, she bucked instinctively and then gasped. The movement drew him deeper.

"I love your eagerness." He looked up at her, eyes glittering with hunger and need. "And that you trust me, at least for now."

"I do." She did. The past and future couldn't touch them in this moment. She'd wanted this too long. Waited for so many years, dreaming that she might have this with him.

Her admission seemed to embolden him. He grinned wolfishly and then lowered his head to kiss her, slipping his tongue inside and stroking at her very center. Pleasure like she'd never known drew a deep erotic moan from her and she arched to get him closer.

"Oh, Rhys." Bella stroked a hand through his hair.

He stilled and lifted his head, one brow arched in question.

"Please don't stop."

He couldn't stop if he wanted to.

Over the years, he'd mastered self-control in the bedroom. He could pleasure a lady for hours before seeking his own release.

But with Bella, he was trembling as if she was the first woman he'd ever touched.

This mattered because she mattered as no one else ever had.

She was too sweet against his tongue. Too soft under his fingertips. He couldn't get enough of her.

She clutched at his hair, his shoulders, digging her fingertips into his skin. He sensed when she drew close to her release, the way her body tensed, the way her breath tangled in her throat.

"Let yourself have it," he whispered against her thigh.

She did and quivered against his mouth, crying his name so sweetly the sound sent a ripple of pleasure straight to his groin.

He lifted onto his knees and stared down at her, flushed and glistening and sated. She was the loveliest thing he'd ever seen. Then she looked up at him, squinting her eyes and smiling as if emerging from a pleasant dream.

"Show me the rest," she said on a husky whisper.

The chuckle that rumbled in his throat was a kind of joy he hadn't felt in so long it felt new.

"Oh, I intend to." He braced himself over her, and she opened her legs, letting him nestle against her. They fit together as if their bodies had been waiting for this moment.

He knew he should take his time. Savor every second.

She bucked up against him, drawing him inside and gasped when he settled against her.

"We'll go slow," he said, and then took her mouth. He kissed her deeply, taking his time as he built a rhythm between them.

But when she moaned against his mouth and angled her hips, his control slipped. He bent his head and kissed her neck, nipping at her skin with his teeth. Then she arched against him, raking her fingernails along his shoulder.

"More," she whispered against his cheek.

He quickened his pace, reaching down to shift her body so that he could thrust deeper. She lifted her head to kiss him and he groaned against her lips. He rasped out her name and he lost any semblance of control.

This was Bella. Never had it felt like this. Right. Necessary. He couldn't get close enough to her and he hated the thought of never being this close to her again.

"Please," she rasped.

Her body told him she was as close to falling over the edge as he was.

"What do you want, love? Tell me."

"Just you."

Rhys looked down at her and the look she returned tore something inside of him free and mended it all at once.

He bent his head, took her nipple into his mouth, and thrust deep until he felt her body tense and then melt beneath him.

His own release drew him under and pleasure washed over him. When he could breathe again, she was kissing him. Stroking his face with her fingers.

Rhys rolled onto his back and drew her with him, holding her near and trying not to think of the moment when he'd have to let her go. He'd felt sated before, but never like this. The satisfaction wasn't just a physical release. Something else had changed inside of him.

After they lay together, warm, quiet, catching their breaths, Bella lifted her head. "You asked what I wanted. It's always been you."

"Bella—" Protests filled his mind. He didn't deserve her desire, but, mercy, how he wanted it. So much.

As if she sensed his conflict, she laid a finger across his lips and then replaced it with a kiss. "We'll always have this moment."

"Yes." He didn't want to think about what that meant. That she might regret this later. That they might never make love again. He didn't want to ask any questions, because he feared all the answers.

So he kissed her again.

RHYS'S EYES FLICKERED open and Bella's scent tickled his nose. He studied the ceiling above his head and realized where he was. Not his own bed back in London, nor the one he'd begun sleeping in since returning to Essex.

The seaside. The cottage. Bella.

He reached for her and his hand closed around warm sheets and an empty space. She couldn't have been gone long.

Sitting up, he noticed the light filtering through the curtains was still bright. Not too many hours could have passed since he'd dozed off.

After donning his shirt and trousers, he explored the

cottage, but he could sense immediately that she wasn't there. The vibrant energy she exuded was missing.

He slipped his boots on and ventured outside.

She stood near the beach, not at the water's edge, but further back, where she could remain dry but look out onto the sea. Her hair was down. He'd removed every single pin. The breeze whipped her skirt around her legs and swept long red-gold waves of her hair off her shoulders.

"I woke and you were gone," he said gently as he approached, wary of disturbing her reverie despite how much he wanted to coax her back into the cottage. Back into his arms.

She glanced back at him and offered him a soft smile. "Not gone. Just here, looking at the sea."

It wasn't any sort of invitation, but Rhys stepped beside her, close enough that his arm brushed hers. He needed to be connected to her again. It took control not to simply haul her into his arms, but he sensed she'd stepped away somehow. Not just from the cottage, but from the intimacy they'd shared.

"Regrets?" He was terrified of her answer, but he had to know.

Bella smiled and swept a strand of hair from her face before turning toward him. "No regret." Stepping closer, she slid a hand around his waist.

Rhys wrapped both arms around her and let out a sigh as he rested his chin against her hair.

"I will never forget our time here." She tipped her head up to look at him.

The look in her eyes didn't match the contentment he felt.

"We could come back anytime you like." Rhys offered her a smile.

"I almost prefer that it remain special. Unique." She pulled away from him a bit and Rhys loosened his hold. "We should return to London. Meg will begin to wonder where we've gone."

"And then?"

"We'll carry on with our plan," she told him matter-of-factly. "And see if we can't find Mr. Radley in Bishopsgate."

"I meant us."

"I think . . ." She lifted onto her toes and kissed him softly. "This will be a separate piece."

Despite the heat of the sun, a chill swept down his neck. "What does that mean?"

"Like a puzzle piece. One part of our relationship that is important but separate from the rest."

"An exception to the rules." Rhys loosened his hold on her and tried not to let the bitterness welling inside him sweep away all the contentment he'd felt an hour before.

"A wonderful exception. But yes." Bella stepped away. "Shall we collect our things and head back to town?"

The longer he looked at her, the deeper he saw behind the cool confident facade she was projecting. Her lips trembled as she gazed at him, and she held her shoulders with a stiffness that belied unease.

It was fear.

"You needn't worry, Bella. Whatever you wish, I'll agree to it." Could she really be worried he'd speak of these private perfect moments to anyone else? "Trust me."

"What I wish is to return to London." She took one step forward and reached down to clasp his hand. "I wish for us to remember this day fondly but realize it is a moment apart."

They walked back to the cottage hand in hand. Rhys stroked his thumb against her skin, savoring every moment of contact.

She hadn't told him he'd never get to touch her so freely again, but he sensed it. He feared it. Somehow, when they went back to London, he was supposed to put all of this aside.

He agreed to let her take the lead.

But he had no idea how to stop wanting her, especially now that he knew how perfect it felt when she was in his arms.

Chapter Eighteen

Rhys swung with his left fist again and felt a satisfying burn in the muscles of his shoulder and arm.

He was striking at the air, but he imagined punching the heavy leather bags suspended from the ceiling at the boxing salon he frequented in London.

Two more quick jabs, one with his left fist, one with his right, and he turned to the desk behind him. Taking up the letter lying there, he squinted at the words again. He'd made three attempts, in between shadow boxing, to make sense of the whole damned thing.

It wasn't that the words weren't written clearly. Iverson's penmanship was impeccable. What Rhys lacked was focus, but one thing was clear. The letter brought good tidings.

Iverson informed him that a recent investment had paid dividends, far more than expected. His bank account had grown to the point that he wouldn't worry overmuch about paying milliners and modistes for all the fripperies Meg had purchased in the last weeks.

But money and Radley and stolen ducal funds weren't what occupied his mind.

There was only a single thought in his head. Or rather every thought for the last several days had been about one woman. A lady who'd been in his head so long he couldn't recall a day when she hadn't crossed his mind. But this was different. Now he knew what she tasted like. How she sounded when she lost herself in the rapture of release. What her body felt like next to his when there was nothing but heat between them.

He'd chastised himself from the moment he awoke. As completely and utterly ridiculous as it was, he missed her. And that in itself was strange. He rarely missed anyone, let alone a woman he'd bedded once.

But of course she wasn't any woman. She was the one who he'd thought about every day. And now he feared the new memories they'd made would haunt him after their scheme was finished.

He had no regrets. *Enjoy all. Regret nothing.* The problem was that he could never be satisfied with returning to how they'd once been. Friendship was well and good, but now they'd shared more. And he wanted more still.

Unfortunately, as far as he could tell, Bella wasn't suffering any of the same worries. They'd been back from the seaside for three days and hadn't exchanged a word. He'd considered sending a note. The previous day he'd walked halfway across the field between Edgecombe and Hillcrest before turning back.

He'd vowed to himself that he'd accede to Bella's wishes.

Lately, he hated himself for that vow. Pursuit was his instinct. Yet she deserved better than a man with his tendency to act on every impulse.

At the edge of the conservatory, he leaned his forehead against the cool glass and stared out toward Hillcrest. They were engaged, for bloody sake. He could at least pay her a visit.

"What do you think?" Meg stood on the other side of the conservatory in a gown of deep purple with a row of satin flowers at the neckline and beads sparkling along the hem. "It's a ball gown."

"Quite a ball gown." Rhys smiled at her excitement. She was practically bouncing while standing in place.

"You don't think it's too much?"

"You look lovely." And far too innocent. For the first time, he felt real trepidation about the sort of men she might encounter on the marriage mart. He was prepared to offer a generous dowry, but she was so eager to fall in love, he feared she'd be easy prey for fortune hunters.

"For a gambler, you certainly have a difficult time concealing what you're thinking."

"Do I?" He must be slipping. His unflappable facade had been honed with years of practice.

"You're worrying. Mama used to wear that same frown when she fretted." She stepped toward him, drawing her beaded train behind her. "She fretted a great deal."

"Father gave her plenty of reasons." Rhys thought of Mrs. Turner and his stomach twisted.

"Please don't fret about me before I've been to my first ball." She offered him a mischievous smile. "Bella has prepared me better than you can imagine."

Just the mention of her made his mouth water. "Oh did she? How's that, then?" He flicked his shirtsleeves down and buttoned the cuffs, trying for as much non-chalance as he could muster.

"She says there are ways to discern a gentleman's motives, even if he wishes to hide them from you."

"Quite a skill to impart." Rhys swallowed hard. He had no doubt he was the reason for Bella's distrust of men's intentions. "How does one discern a man's true intentions?"

Meg blinked. "I'm not sure I'm supposed to confide them to a gentleman."

"I'm your brother." And a wastrel by the standards of London good society. "You're probably right. Perhaps it's best if you ladies kept these secrets among yourselves."

"Do you mind if I show you one of the other dresses? It's one I may wear to our visit to the Duke and Duchess of Tremayne."

"Which visit?"

"Did I not tell you they've invited us to dinner next week? You and me and Bella. I assumed you'd wish to go and I told them we'd attend. Is that all right?"

"Yes, of course." A chance to see Bella was exactly what he wanted. "When Bella was imparting advice, did she divulge anything you can share?" Anything about him, in other words.

"She did tell me how to politely decline an offer of marriage and the reasons one should."

"I expect you will receive proposals."

Meg dipped her head and looked up at him through gold-brown lashes. "I do hope so. But you needn't worry. With Bella's help I'm sure I'll make the right choice. As she said, there are ways to know when you've met a man you wish to marry."

His heartbeat clattered in his chest so loudly he wondered if Meg could hear. "What ways?"

"Once I've discerned that a gentleman's intentions are honorable, I should consider whether he makes me laugh."

Rhys sifted his memories for times he'd made Bella laugh. There were plenty to choose from.

"Whether his looks please me and reflect a kindness of spirit."

He was kind. Wasn't he?

"Oh, and also whether he is well-read and well-spoken and is someone I could imagine conversing with every day for the rest of my days. But most important is that he treats me with respect and thinks highly of me."

"Funny, because those will be my requirements for any gentleman who wishes to offer for you too."

Meg giggled. "I promise I'll choose a good man."

A good man. Meg deserved no less. Bella too.

Could he ever be a good man? He'd been lucky. Popular. Successful in accumulating wealth. But good was something he'd never quite managed.

He could imagine himself approaching it. Mending his worst habits. Striving to be the kind of man he'd often wished he could be.

He knew he shouldn't expect Bella to wait for that. She deserved the best, now and always.

The problem was that he wanted her as he'd never wanted any woman.

"You are planning to leave some of your books here?" Bella retrieved two more volumes from the shelf her father indicated and added them to a pile they'd built on the top of his desk.

He stared at her with his nose turned down, eyes looking up from over the rim of his spectacles. Then he looked at the pile. "Of course I am. But I do take your point. Those two won't be necessary. They will likely have books at the school."

"They'll have a library certainly."

"They do. I inquired and they assured me they've established a respectable library and would like my input as they add to the collection." He pointed to a letter in the center of his desk blotter. "The school is rather fledgling, you see."

"Then they definitely need you." Bella approached and took the books he'd collected into his arms and seemed to have forgotten he was holding. "Mama too. She's quite good at organizing."

"As are you." He indicated the book piles on the desk. "Arranged by topic, publication date, and then author?"

"Of course. Is there any other way?" Bella smiled at him. Her insistence on helping him organize his collection pleased him and had since she was a child.

"May I interrupt?" Louisa pushed the study door open but didn't enter the room.

"Of course," Bella's father told her. "The more the merrier."

"Actually, I was hoping for a word with Bella. I'll return her to you as soon as I can."

The wariness in her cousin's eyes made Bella nervous. "I'll be back," she told her father before following her cousin into the hallway.

"We should go to your sitting room."

Bella wanted to ask. Anxiousness was rolling off Louisa like smoke and she was usually as clearheaded as Bella. When they reached the sitting room, Bella closed the door behind her and leaned against it.

"Tell me what's wrong. You look miserable."

"I'm not," Louisa insisted. "Please don't worry. It's just a challenge that must be overcome."

"What is?"

For the first time she noticed that Louisa had something clutched in her hands. An envelope with Bella's name and address written on the front.

"I have bad news and good. Which do you prefer first?"

"Good." The practical choice was to hear the bad news first and comfort herself with the good, but she wasn't feeling practical.

Louisa smiled conspiratorially and slipped her the envelope as if it was a secret missive she'd need to burn after reading. "It's from a publisher in London. Mr. Peabody."

Bella frowned and took the letter gingerly. "I've already met with him. He rejected me."

"What does it say?" Louisa sat in one of the chairs near the window and leaned forward eagerly.

The man had been unequivocal and curt the day she'd met with him. He'd made her feel as if she was wasting his time by even visiting his office.

"Perhaps this is just a formal written rejection." Bella slid her fingernail along the letter's closure and pulled the note free. She read the formal salutation with a sigh and then gasped.

"Is it good news?" Louisa leaned closer, attempting to peek over the letter's edge.

"He says he would like to see the full manuscript and invites me to visit next week or at my earliest convenience." Even as Bella heard her own words and reread the note, she couldn't quite believe the man's change of tone. "It makes very little sense."

"People change their minds, Bella. Did you leave any of your manuscript with him? Perhaps he took a closer look and reconsidered."

"I didn't though. He had a cursory glance at a few pages and told me no. Very firmly."

"Then this truly is good news." Louisa beamed proudly. "He's changed his mind and wishes to give you a second chance. You deserve more consideration than a few moments and a few pages."

Bella had a feeling she knew what had led to Mr. Peabody's reversal. Only one person other than Meg knew of her plan to meet with the publisher in London. And only Rhys knew the precise address of the man's office. She was torn between gratitude for his wish to help her and frustration that he didn't heed her insistence on finding publishing success entirely on her own.

"Do you want to hear the rest?"

"Yes, of course." She'd almost forgotten there was bad news too.

"I've been helping Aunt Gwendoline sort through which clothes she wishes to take to Greece and had one of the footmen bring a traveling trunk from out of storage."

"Good. I promised I'd help her this afternoon too."

"She refuses to actually pack the trunk." Louisa drew in a breath and said, "I believe she's going to try to convince you to hold the ceremony before they depart."

Bella shook her head. "That's not what they agreed. We told them that we wish to wait until next year." Good heavens, she was speaking as if it was going to happen at all. "If they'd only go, I know they'll love it and even after I've told them the engagement is broken they'll see out Papa's term."

"And what if she insists on a wedding before they'll depart?"

"Planning a wedding would take too long. Papa is expected next month. The school year begins in late September. They must go now."

Louisa cast Bella a look that reflected all of her own worry.

"What will you do?"

Bella tapped her fingers against her lap and weighed the very few options she could imagine. Only one seemed both simple and effective. "I'll have to negotiate with her again. Urge her to go and accept that the wedding won't even be planned until next year."

Louisa crossed her arms and pursed her brow in a worried look. "I'm not sure that will work. She's not content to let it wait. She feels that arrangement still leaves you unsettled."

"Then I'll have to give her part of what she wants."

"How can you?"

Bella lifted her hand to the high-buttoned collar of her day dress, fingers searching for the reassuring feel of the pendant underneath the fabric. "It will require the duke's help. Now, let's just hope he agrees."

"I BEG YOU, Your Grace."

As Bella approached the ballroom where the housemaid told her she'd find Rhys, she heard Mrs. Chalmers's voice. The way she petitioned him with such earnest desperation made Bella quicken her step. What in heaven's name was he putting his faithful housekeeper through?

Crossing the threshold, she found Rhys, Mrs. Chalmers, and Meg in the center of the room.

"Miss Prescott, I hope you've come to save me." The older woman blotted her flushed perspiring face with a handkerchief. "Not certain of all these steps to the dance, but I am certain my old body wasn't made for such frolicking."

Bella looked from the harried housekeeper to Meg and then to Rhys.

"We were giving Meg a little dance lesson," Rhys told her by way of explanation.

"I know how to dance," Meg protested with a sheepish glance at the young footman. "Finishing school did include dance lessons," she told her brother. "But the quadrille has always confused me."

"It's far too vigorous for my taste. I'm winded. May I get on with my other duties, Your Grace?" Mrs. Chalmers asked, still breathing hard. "Miss Prescott must be far more adept than I am. Aren't you, miss?"

"I've danced my share of quadrilles," Bella told her to offer reassurance.

None of the memories were particularly pleasant ones but she didn't dare divulge those details. Most of her ballroom experiences had been less than pleasant.

"Actually, we're moving on from the quadrille." Meg caught her brother's eye and then smiled at Bella.

"There is only one dance in which I truly need instruction. We were never taught it at finishing school because it was considered too scandalous."

"The waltz," Rhys said. "I have personal knowledge of Miss Prescott's skill with that dance."

He'd been gazing at her since she'd stepped into the room, and she realized she hadn't offered him any greeting.

"Would you mind showing me?" Meg asked with a suspiciously innocent tone. "I'm sure if I saw you and Rhys performing the steps, especially if you went slowly, I could remember them."

"There's no music." It was the first reasonable protest Bella could muster.

"I can hum a waltz," Meg assured her with a cheeky grin. "I recently taught myself how to play one on the piano and I remember the tempo."

"Wonderful," Bella told her drily.

The misery of it was that she wanted to be in Rhys's arms, but the prospect of being so close to him in front of Meg made her pulse jump in her throat. Certainly, her feelings for him were written all over her face.

He knew exactly how she felt, if the look on his face was any indication. As he approached, his mouth curved gently and his gaze filled with mischief. "Shall we? Waltzing together can't be a scandal if we're betrothed."

"We danced the waltz *before* we were betrothed."

He laughed as he took her hand. "Then we'll be even better this time."

Bella went into his arms, one palm locked against his, and her body began to vibrate the moment he slid a hand around her waist.

"Meg, let's have some music," he said, never taking his eyes off of Bella's.

Meg began humming and tapped her slippered foot on the parquet ballroom floor to indicate the tempo of the waltz.

Rhys led her into the first steps of the dance, but he was closer than any ballroom matron in London would have allowed, his chest brushing hers, their hips bumping together when they turned.

"It's funny," he whispered as he stepped her back and then to the side.

"What is?" Bella clasped his hand tighter. If he meant to distract her with conversation, he might end up with crushed toes.

"How long a few days can feel," he said, his voice low.

Bella stumbled and then forgot what step they were on, so when he moved forward, she failed to step back and pulled him off-balance too.

He hugged her tight to keep them both on their feet.

"I've got you," he told her, his mouth against her ear.

Meg had stopped humming and a tense silence fell over the ballroom. "Are you two all right? Shall I start again?"

"No," Bella said before Rhys could reply. "I need to speak to you," she told him. "Alone."

"We'll have to resume the lessons later, Meg." He glanced at his sister and she nodded.

A moment later she left the ballroom and Bella stepped out of Rhys's arms.

"Is it bad news?" he asked, his voice lowered in concern. "Are your parents all right?"

"Yes, thank you. Papa is busy packing books, but Mama is a different story." Bella considered her next words. How she might phrase her request. In what manner she might convince him. Then all that faded and she blurted, "We have to set a date for the wedding."

She watched emotions shift on his face—from shock to confusion to something else. He drew in a breath and looked almost eager.

"You're not suggesting that we actually—"

"Oh, not at all. I'm not asking to change the terms of our arrangement. This isn't about what happened at the seaside." She was talking fast and took a breath. "We only need to tell her a date, and I think that may satisfy her enough for them to depart. She wants something to look forward to, to plan toward."

"Then what do you suggest?" His voice had gone chilly, and she knew there was more he wished to say.

"Next spring or even the summer?"

"Do you have a date in mind?"

Bella was relieved that he was agreeing to this extra step, but he sounded angry and some part of her understood. They'd set the terms of this arrangement and now she was changing them again. He had his own life to get on with.

"I know this deception is inconvenient, but it's only for a little bit longer."

"Shall I go with you to tell your mother?"

"There's no need. Now that we agree, it's just a matter of telling them. Mama will be pleased. I'm sure of it. Thank you."

There was more she wished to say. They hadn't truly spoken since they'd parted after their trip to Margate. The problem was Bella wasn't sure what to say, or even precisely what she felt.

"You're welcome." He didn't look entirely pleased but he tried for a grin. "Would you like to travel to London with us? Meg says you will have received an invitation for dinner at the Tremaynes."

"I did." What she hadn't decided was whether to accept. Though now, with the letter from Mr. Peabody in hand, she had even more reason to visit London.

"We should be seen together." He approached until they were almost toe to toe. So close, the heat of his body was pure temptation. "Isn't that what you said when we agreed on this arrangement?"

This arrangement. That's all it was. A ruse that would soon come to an end.

The past few days had been difficult for her too. Concentrating on anything but the memory of their lovemaking had proven impossible. And that was exactly why it needed to end soon. She couldn't go back to being the girl who thought of nothing but Rhys Forester. She was more than a fawning lovesick girl now.

"Bella, I hope you don't wish we had not—"

"I don't. I told you. That moment was my choice, and I regret nothing."

He winced and she bit her lip, knowing she wasn't being clear.

She hadn't meant to hurt him by using the words of his motto. For those hours in Margate she'd chosen to embrace every word.

"What happened at the seaside has nothing to do with our arrangement. I know how to keep them separate."

When he said no more, she turned and made her way out. She needed to speak to her mother. But as she stepped across the threshold, she heard Rhys's voice.

Softly, as if to himself, he said, "I don't know if I do."

Chapter Nineteen

 don't know why I should be surprised." Nick Tremayne swirled golden whiskey in his tumbler as he assessed Rhys.

"I'm thrilled if I have surprised you," Rhys quipped. "I suspect you could use someone overturning your expectations once in a while."

"So that's why you became betrothed within a week of heading to the countryside? To surprise me."

"Did it work?" Rhys chuckled and struggled to inject any genuine mirth into the sound.

"Perhaps I simply underestimated you."

"People often do."

"So . . . how did this happen? She's a beauty. I'll give you that. But she seems far too clever to be as impulsive as you are."

"She is. As to how, I have known Bella since we were children."

"And what? She's been waiting for you in the countryside all these years?"

"Not waiting for me." Hating him was more likely. "She's had four Seasons out and knows her way around London society better than most. What matters to her now is her book. She's been working on a collection of puzzles. Mental conundrums." Rhys didn't know how best to describe them, but he suddenly wished he had a few pages to show his friend. He'd be just the sort to enjoy the challenge.

"*Clever* doesn't do her justice, then, does it? Innovative too. And ambitious."

"All those things," Rhys agreed, and drained the tiny glass of sherry he'd poured himself.

Nick assessed Rhys for several silent minutes.

Rhys stood and poured himself another drink, opting for whiskey this time. Even with his back to Nick, he could feel the man's persistent gaze.

"The engagement is a sham." He let out a long breath after the confession and his shoulders felt like a weight had fallen away.

But when he turned to face Nick again, all the tension returned with a vengeance.

"You don't intend to marry this woman." His glower managed to combine disappointment and anger in a single glare.

"She doesn't intend to marry me either." That admission made him feel hollow inside. "It's a scheme to satisfy her parents. They gave her an ultimatum, and Bella isn't the sort to be forced into anything she doesn't wish to do."

Nick tipped his head. His glower had become a frown. "But she wished to pretend to be betrothed. To you."

"I was convenient, and I owed her."

Nick stood and refilled his glass too. "Now that's intriguing."

"Not money. I disappointed her many years ago."

"Disappointed?" Nick's brows arched high. "Well, obviously she's forgiven you."

"I hope so." An image came to Rhys, so sharp and sweet it stole his breath. Bella beneath him, staring up at him with a look in her eyes that filled the emptiness inside him as nothing ever had. "Yes, I believe she has forgiven me."

"So when does your ruse come crashing down?"

"I don't know." It was the question Rhys asked himself often. The answer to which he'd come to dread. "When her parents are satisfied, I suppose."

"And then you can go back to your parties and pleasure." Nick said the words lightly, almost playfully, and then lifted his glass as if offering a toast. "I imagine that will be a relief."

Rhys felt his mouth tilt in a smirk. "Pleasure is practically my middle name."

"Why don't I believe you?" Nick leaned his backside against the edge of his enormous desk. "You don't want the ruse to end."

"Nonsense. The sooner we desist with the farce, the

quicker I can get back to Claremont House and behaving exactly as I wish."

"You're falling in love with her." Nick ran a hand across his face and tipped his head again as if he could see straight through Rhys. "Or perhaps you have always loved her."

"Stop being fanciful, Tremayne. Just because you're entirely smitten with your bride, it doesn't mean we've all succumbed." Rhys turned his back on his friend and took a long swig of whiskey. He focused on the burn rather than the persistent needling of Nick's examination.

"True," Nick said lightly. "And you say she's been out for some time and is still unwed. It seems such a clever beauty would be more of an enticement."

"Bella is nothing but enticement." Rhys swung around and snapped defensively, "A man would be a fool not to love her."

"Indeed." Nick nodded and shifted his gaze to the carpet. "With her beauty and intelligence, she's quite the catch. And yet she's of an age to marry and has not. Any idea why?"

"There have been proposals." Rhys shrugged. "She's refused them all."

"Until now."

Rhys's irritation turned to amusement at his friend's foolishness. "I did not propose to her."

"Perhaps you should."

"Stop." His shout echoed in the room, filling up the quiet between them with angry tension.

After two long deep breaths, Rhys set his glass down and approached his friend. He needed to make Nick understand.

"Don't play matchmaker. Bella will marry when she wishes to, and it will be to a man far better than me."

Nick lifted off his desk, forcing Rhys to step back. He worked his jaw as if chewing on whatever he wished to say.

Then to Rhys's shock, Nick reached for him, bracing a hand on his shoulder.

"You are a good man."

When Rhys opened his mouth to protest, Nick cut him off.

"We should get back to the ladies before they realize how much more fun they can have without us."

"Nick, say nothing of this to anyone. Not even Mina."

He gave one curt nod. "You have my word."

They started out of the study and Rhys followed his friend toward the door, but Nick stopped short.

"Answer one question?"

Something told Rhys he was going to hate the question, but he nodded in agreement.

"Do you love Miss Prescott?"

"Of course." That was possibly the easiest answer he'd ever given in his life.

Nick waved his hand in the air. "No, not as a girl you've known since you were a child. You know what I mean. Are you beguiled by her?"

That answer was plain too. Of late, he thought of

little beyond the moments they'd shared together and when he might see her again.

"Never mind," Nick said with a grin. "I knew the answer from the way you speak of her."

"I haven't gambled in too long. I'm losing my ability to bluff."

"Love has a way of getting past our defenses."

Rhys tugged at his cravat. The last thing he wanted was a bloody lecture about romance.

"A bit of advice?" Nick asked. "You did the same for me once, if you recall."

"Vaguely."

"You must tell her."

"No." Rhys shook his head. On this point, he would not waver. "I've been a self-serving bastard for years, but even I have my limits. Bella deserves better."

Nick narrowed his gaze but seemed to finally relent. "Very well. Suit yourself. But remember one incontrovertible truth."

"What's that?"

"Women always discover the truth." Nick opened the library door and headed into the hallway, calling back, "Especially the clever ones."

"THE MINISTER'S CAT is an adorable, beautiful, coy, delightful, elegant, frisky cat," Meg said with a triumphant smile, pleased that she'd been able to remember all the other adjectives that had come before.

The parlor game was a simple test of memory, and Bella's mind immediately filled with fresh ideas for more challenging memory tests that she could add to her book. She could even add an explanation of how one could employ strategies to aid with memory.

"Your turn, Miss Prescott," the Duchess of Tremayne called to her.

Unfortunately, she hadn't heard the last word that had been added to the description. Something that started with *g*.

Meg cupped a hand around her mouth and with a very bad attempt at subtlety mouthed, *Gregarious*.

Bella sat up straight on the settee and steadily recited the familiar sentence, including all of the adjectives that had come before while her mind considered what she might add.

As she finished Rhys stepped into the drawing room and everything seemed more vibrant. "Handsome," she blurted, then corrected, "Handsome cat."

His grin made her heart tumble in her chest.

"What are we playing and is it too late to join?" the duke asked his wife.

"Minister's Cat," she told him as she stood to reach for the bellpull. "But we were just at the point when it becomes tedious. A bit of refreshment and conversation seems far preferable now that you two have rejoined us."

Rhys glanced at the empty spot on the settee beside Bella, and she scooted closer to the edge to make room for him. The cushions dipped when he dropped down next to her, tipping her toward him. Their bodies came together, his arm against hers and their thighs pressed together. He made no move to pull away. Neither did she.

"Having fun?" he asked quietly.

"I am. The duchess seems very intelligent and kind."

"Then you have much in common."

Bella glanced at him and tried not to let the compliment set her cheeks aflame. She was already feeling exponentially warmer because he was next to her and his body was like a furnace. She'd remembered that from Margate. Other than the waltz dance lesson for Meg, their bodies hadn't been this close since that day.

Rhys seemed to be thinking the same. His breath quickened and he licked his lips.

"Bella—"

"Will you go first?" Meg appeared in front of them and Bella had missed whatever she'd said before her question to her brother. "You've very good at charades and I've nominated you to go first."

"Meg, you've always been better at the game and you know it." He glanced toward the duchess. "I forfeit my nomination and pass it to my sister."

Meg giggled and reached for the first prompt that the Duchess of Tremayne had written on a slip of paper. "Oh goodness," she said when she read whatever was written there. A moment later she moved to the center of the room and held up three fingers, indicating the number of words in the answer.

"We should talk," Rhys whispered, and sat forward

on the settee, as if intrigued by his sister's performance. "You've been avoiding me, and I don't like it."

"I haven't. Not entirely," Bella whispered back, her eyes fixed on Meg. "But I agree we should talk."

"Tonight. Alone."

"That's impossible. You know I'm lodging with the Tremaynes." Bella laughed at Meg's antics. "Is it love?" she said when the girl made the shape of a heart with her fingers.

Meg nodded excitedly.

"I could feign illness," Bella told him under her breath.

Rhys chuckled. "Falsehood is becoming far too easy for you, Miss Prescott. You needn't lie. I'll just tell them I want you to see Claremont House and that I'll return you soon. We are betrothed and are allowed certain liberties."

"Labour," the Duke of Tremayne called out.

"*Love's Labour's Lost*," Rhys said before Meg could move on to the third word.

"Yes, that's it." With a look around the room, she added, "Did I not tell you my brother was good at charades?"

"Perhaps too good. It's unfair to everyone else," Rhys said with a hint of his usual bravado. "Rather than stay and ruin the game for everyone, I'm going to steal my fiancée away for a few minutes."

"Absconding with my guests isn't allowed, Your Grace." Bella couldn't discern whether the duchess's tone was serious or amused. "Where exactly are you taking her?"

Rhys stood and reached behind him, offering Bella his hand. "Home."

He said the word at the same moment her fingers laced with his, and both the sentiment and his touch sent a shiver down her arm.

"If Bella is to live at Claremont House for even part of the year, she should make it her own. I thought a visit was in order."

He tugged and Bella got to her feet.

"I'm sorry to depart so abruptly, Your Grace," she told the duchess.

"Well, according to the Duke of Claremont, he'll return you soon, so I'll allow it." She winked and took a sip of her sherry as Rhys led Bella toward the town house's front door.

"I fear we were rude," Bella told him, though he didn't slow down and neither did she.

"Honestly, Bella, if I don't get you alone and to myself soon, I would have been more than rude."

Rhys handed Bella up the carriage step and onto a bench.

She wanted him to sit beside her. Instead he took the opposite bench. In the darkness, his expression was unreadable. He said nothing and that alone was so unlike him that she feared he was cross with her or wished to call off their engagement before her parents had even departed.

He was right in some respects. She had been avoiding him, but it wasn't because she hadn't wished to see him. It was because she wanted to too much.

Lifting a hand, she twisted her finger around her necklace chain. Perhaps he was angry because unlike simply telling her parents and a few villagers in Essex, the news had spread to London now and tonight he'd had to live out a lie in front of people he knew well.

"I'm sorry you have to deceive your friends."

He'd been looking out the carriage window and snapped his head toward her. "We agreed we'd do this together. And I didn't lie to Tremayne. I told him the truth, but you needn't worry. Nick is a man who knows how to keep secrets."

"You told him this is a ruse?" Bella was incredulous. He knew she'd confided in Louisa but they'd both agreed that no one else should know.

"He knows me better than most. I couldn't hide anything from him." He leaned toward her, inching toward the edge of his seat. "I've made him vow not to tell anyone, even the duchess. We can trust him."

Before Bella could voice her worries, the very short drive to Claremont House was over. Rhys exited the carriage and helped her down. Saying nothing, he led her toward the front door and dismissed the young maid who admitted them.

"Promise we won't divulge this secret to anyone else," she said quietly in case any other servants might be nearby.

He turned to her, backed her up against the door, and stroked his fingers against her cheek. Then he dipped his head and kissed her.

It was against the rules they'd made. They'd vowed not to do this anymore. She'd promised herself she wouldn't lose herself in Rhys Forester ever again.

Yet all things she knew had nothing to do with what she felt.

He was what she felt, the firm heated length of his body against hers. And she wanted more of him. She wanted to make him cry her name because of the way she touched him, and she wanted him to use his fingers and tongue to make her unravel again.

"Yes," she told him, and the word came out more breath than sound. Yes, to another kiss. Yes, to more lovemaking. Yes, to breaking their rules. She'd thought of little else for days.

With utmost care, he cupped her face in his hands and swept his thumbs across her cheeks. "You're so soft. Like warm satin under my fingers."

Bella tipped her mouth up to his, waiting for his kiss. She thought she knew now what kissing Rhys again would be, but when his lips came down on hers this was different.

The kiss began tender, a gentle exploration, sweet and familiar. But when she reached for his waistcoat and worked the buttons free so that she could flatten her palm against his chest, he deepened the kiss. He stroked her with his tongue, slid his hand back to wrap his fingers around her nape.

He kissed her hungrily, possessively.

Bella opened to him. She wanted him. She always had, and she reveled in how much he wanted her too. She felt it in every stroke of his tongue and in the way he tugged at her clothes as he leaned his body into hers.

"Do you have any idea," he said against her lips, "how impossible it is." He kissed the side of her mouth, then traced the edge of her lower lip with his tongue. "Bella," he whispered with a desperation that made her center melt with need. "It's impossible to be close to you and not do this. Not think about this."

"Rhys," Bella hissed when he licked the spot behind her ear.

"I know. We should stop."

"Yes," she told him, as she worked the knotted fabric of his cravat loose. "But only so that you can take me upstairs."

He stilled, one hand gripping her hip, the other tangled in her freshly mussed chignon.

"What is it?" she asked him.

"When you say things like that and I'm in the state I am, I have to take a moment and make certain I'm not dreaming."

Bella tugged his cravat until the fabric slid from his neck, baring more of his skin to her view. She couldn't resist stretching up onto her toes and pressing a kiss at the base of his throat. She was rewarded with a moan and the rapid beat of his pulse against her lips.

"I can't be the only woman who's asked you to take her to your bed," she said teasingly.

For a moment, a bit of fire went out of his gaze. Then he reached for her hand, opened two buttons at the top of his shirt and pressed her palm against his bare chest.

"Feel that? Only you make this happen."

His heart pounded erratically under her hand. Hard and wild.

"This isn't just impulse," he rasped when Bella reached up with her free hand to release more of his shirt buttons. "This is desire."

Yes, desire, hunger, need. And something more. Feelings she couldn't yet name and knew he feared too. Words that might destroy this moment.

Bella swept his shirt aside and explored the muscled ridges of his chest, then dragged her fingertip over his nipple. "If you don't want to take me upstairs—"

He stopped with one deep breath-stealing kiss that left her knees quivering.

"I do." He stroked a hand down her neck. "Shall we race? For old times' sake."

Rather than answer, Bella ducked under his arm, lifted her skirt to keep it from tangling around her ankles, and bolted for the staircase.

Chapter Twenty

*H*e let her win. In the hallway at the top of the stairs, she stopped and swung to face him. She was breathing hard, her eyes sparkling, and she swiped some of the long strands of wavy auburn hair behind her ear.

"I don't know which room is yours."

For a moment he had the impulse to direct her to a guest room. He'd decorated his own room lavishly, thinking only of his own taste and being excessive and making every inch of the chamber look decadent. Now, for the first time, he cared how someone else might perceive what he'd done.

But he didn't want any pretense between them. Bella knew him better than anyone. She knew secrets he'd confided to no other. He wasn't going to start pretending now.

"On your left."

She immediately twisted the latch and stepped inside. He heard a gasp before he reached the threshold.

Perhaps he had gone a bit overboard with ostentation.

He watched her from the doorway. She worked pins from her hair as she explored, running her fingers along the statue of the Egyptian goddess Hathor. In front of the medieval tapestry, she tilted her head to take in the details. The Chinese vase atop a tall carved cherrywood stand seemed to fascinate her, and she reached out and then pulled back as if afraid to topple it.

"You may touch anything you like." His body responded the minute the words were out, because there were several aching parts of him craving her touch.

She smiled at his words and lifted onto her toes to stroke her hands along the fronds of the potted palm in the corner.

Mercy, how he wanted those hands on him.

"It's very—"

"Overdone. A mishmash. You see what I do when left to my own devices. I need someone with better taste in decoration to advise me."

Her. He realized all at once that he wanted Bella to be the one to take the room and make it her own. Theirs. The thought made a shiver slide down his spine.

She wouldn't ever be his that way. There would be no wedding. This wasn't ever going to be their home.

After circling the room, she came to stand in front of him. "I love it. There's beauty and history in every corner, and you have excellent taste."

Before he could offer any reply, she turned her back to him.

"Undo my buttons?" With one hand, she swept her hair off of her neck. The other came down on his thigh as she pressed her backside against his groin.

Rhys inhaled sharply but he didn't want her to stop.

"You did say I could touch whatever I want."

"Oh, you can." He made quick work of her buttons and spread the edges of her gown to run his hands down her back.

She let out a little ah of pleasure and then shifted her hand. With a gentle, tentative touch, she drew her fingers down the length of him, shaping her hand around him.

He told himself to let her explore, but he couldn't stop from bucking against her when she stroked her hand up and then down again.

"That feels perfect but—"

"I know," she whispered before letting him go.

He bent and kissed her shoulder, swept her chemise aside, and kissed the side of her neck. Without intending to, he seemed to have found a ticklish spot.

She stepped out of his arms and headed for the bed, working at the clasps of her corset on the way. By the time she reached the dais on which the bed stood, she'd shed her corset, and as she headed toward the bed, she stepped out of her petticoat.

Like a temptress, she watched him while she tugged at the single ribbon closure of her chemise and then let the garment fall from her shoulders.

Desire hit him like the tide at Margate, sneaking in and threatening to pull him under. There was pure physical need to have her body under his, over his, to be inside her. But there was more with Bella. Always more. Tenderness. Affection.

Love.

Allowing himself to acknowledge the feeling made his heart thrash with fear.

Biting her lip, she loosed the ribbon on her drawers and pulled them wide as if to let them fall too but she didn't let go of the fabric. She watched him and inched the fabric down as if to tease him.

He approached and stood below her. With Bella on the raised platform, they were almost equal in height. He stroked a hand along her stomach, then up between her breasts. She shivered and her perfect nipples pebbled under his fingertips. He bent to take one into his mouth. Bella stroked her hand through his hair, pulling him close.

"Rhys," she said, almost as a plea.

He lifted his head, then bent to taste her again, treating the other nipple to the same languorous licks and suckling. Sliding his hand around her waist, he pushed at the fabric of her drawers until he could cup her backside in his hands and the garment slid down her legs.

"You're the loveliest woman I've ever seen."

For the first time, she looked shy, uncertain.

He wrapped an arm around her waist and the warmth

of her bare skin against him seemed the best gift he'd ever been given. Holding her like this was becoming all that he wanted. She shifted and his body was so sensitive and aching for her, he groaned. Apparently, holding wasn't *all* that he wanted.

"You're wearing an impractical amount of clothing," she told him when she reached for the fastening of his trousers.

Rhys grinned. He imagined that being impractical was the worst character flaw Bella could imagine of anyone.

He slid his trousers and drawers off as she settled onto the bed. His throat went dry when she slid back and lifted onto her elbows to watch him.

"You're quite lovely too," she whispered.

He climbed onto the bed, holding her gaze. "I'm glad you think so."

"Everyone thinks so." She hissed out the last word because he'd begun to draw his fingers up her leg, all the way to her inner thigh.

"But you see," he told her as he stroked a finger into the damp heated curls at her center, "I only care that you think so."

When he slid a finger inside her heat, she arched against him and let her head fall back. There was such trust in the movement that something inside him melted.

He bent his head and replaced his fingers with his mouth, kissing and licking until she bucked against him. He loved the taste of her on his tongue, the way her body trembled and arched against him. She scraped her fingers along his shoulder, then sank them into his hair.

"Rhys," she said softly, lovingly. Then again with more need.

He knew the moment she was close. Already, he knew her body and her sounds well enough to know, and he loved every second of feeling her body go taut.

"Let go, love," he whispered against her. "I've got you."

When she did, Rhys lifted up to watch her face. To watch the moment she let control slip away and gave in to her release. When her breathing steadied, she reached for him, pulling at his shoulders, and he settled between her legs.

"I need you," she whispered on a shaky breath.

The words slipped inside him, soothed over pain, filled hollow spaces.

"I need you," he said as he eased into her and told himself to go slow, to savor every second.

But Bella refused to let him take her slowly. She set the pace, moving against him, wrapping her arms around his shoulders and lifting up to kiss him. Her kiss was deep and hungry and when she nipped his lower lip, he couldn't hold back any longer.

He wanted her desperately, not just to please her but to get closer to her, past all of the defenses she'd built up against him. Past all the rules and propriety that she believed she needed in order to keep others at bay.

Before he tipped over the edge, she whispered against his skin. The same words she'd spoken at the cottage in Margate. "It's always been you."

He kissed her and then said against her lips, "I love you, Arry." The words came unbidden because he couldn't resist them anymore.

She stroked his hair, his back, nuzzled against him as he settled beside her.

That was enough. He told himself that having her in his arms was enough. But, God, did he want her to give those words back to him.

BELLA WOKE WITH a start and squinted in the darkness. Not her room. Realization came and brought a wave of relief. Rhys's home. His bedroom.

She slid her hand slowly across the sheet and encountered the hot firm stretch of his body next to her. From his slow steady breathing, she knew he was asleep. She waited for her eyes to adjust and leaned closer so she could get a better look at him.

Good heavens he was a gorgeous man. Even his profile made her yearn to touch him, kiss him. She was sorely tempted to lie back down, wrap her arms around him, and go back to sleep.

She didn't want to wake him yet, but she couldn't bear to leave without brushing a kiss against his shoulder.

On the way to the door, she gathered her chemise and gown. Before stepping into the hall, she donned both and buttoned herself in as well as she was able.

Her thoughts were a jumble. Her feelings were a muddle. She needed to think.

I love you.

How long had she yearned to hear those words? How long had she ached to hear *him* say those three words? Yes, it had been at the pinnacle of his passion, at a moment when his body was in fact loving hers. But she couldn't convince herself it was just hyperbole born of a heated moment.

Bella headed down the stairs, but she had no idea where she might find a conservatory or a room where she could surreptitiously open a window. Stepping out of the front door was likely the best option but with her luck she'd end up locked out and on the darkened streets of Belgravia in nothing but an unbuttoned gown and a chemise.

Servants approached, chatting to each other as they walked side by side, and Bella panicked. She pushed open the door of the closest room and looked around curiously. It seemed to be a study or library, almost as well stocked as her father's.

Though the servants passed quickly, Bella lingered in the room.

While Rhys had quite eclectic tastes in decor, this room was far more reflective of his father. Stern, unwelcoming, and a bit too cluttered to be truly appealing. She found she missed feeling a sense of Rhys in the room.

One thing was for certain. Rhys's father had been as fascinated with maps as her own. There were no landscapes or framed portraits on the walls. Only maps.

One of Essex and the county where Edgecombe sat, one that encompassed all of the British Isles and Ireland, and several London maps.

She drew closer to the largest London map that took up most of one wall. The image was very focused in, showing streets and squares and a few landmarks. Bella traced her finger down roads and found Belgravia, Buckingham Palace, Hyde Park, and then she looked closer and began searching.

Bishopsgate.

Recalling the scrap of paper they'd found in the fireplace in Margate, she searched for any street name that started with a *B*. It had to be Bury Street. Mr. Radley would likely be there. Unless, of course, Rhys was right and he'd hied off to France.

"I woke and you were gone."

Bella turned to find Rhys in the doorway wearing only trousers and his unbuttoned shirt.

"I didn't want to disturb you. I thought I'd explore."

"And what did you find?" He still hovered at the doorway, and she hated the wariness in his tone.

"The street where Mr. Radley might be residing, I think. Remember the scrap of paper? We have the house number, unless there was a part missing." She pointed to the map. "And this must be the street."

He approached until they were shoulder to shoulder and stared at the point near her finger.

"Bury Street. I'll send a note to Inspector Macadams."

"No." Bella hadn't meant to shout but didn't regret emphasizing her protest.

"We started the search for him together. That clue we found at Margate, we found together. Contact Inspector Macadams if you like, but I think we should finish it together."

"You're determined."

"I am."

"Then we'll go," he told her, and covered her hand on his arm with his own. "We should go back to the Tremaynes' too. They'll be worried about you."

Bella leaned closer to him. "They needn't be. I'm in good hands."

There was an uncertainty in his gaze that she wanted to soothe, but she couldn't bring herself to say the words he wished to hear. It wasn't that she didn't feel them. Of course she did. She always had. But they terrified her now.

"Bella—" He frowned as he watched her and that often indicated that he was seeing something she hadn't meant to reveal. Over the years, she'd become quite certain Rhys could read her thoughts.

"Tomorrow?" she asked him to keep them from treading old ground. She couldn't give him what he yearned to hear from her.

"That will be fine. I'll have a servant take a note around to Scotland Yard."

"Excellent." She smiled and then lifted onto her toes to kiss him. "We can resolve this once and for all."

Her pulse quickened but it wasn't because of the way Rhys kissed her back. That was delicious and warmed her blood. No, the fluttering pulse at her neck came because of fear.

Tomorrow they might very well find Mr. Radley. The matter of the ducal accounts might be resolved. She'd helped Meg prepare for her Season and now the Duchess of Tremayne had stepped in to assist with that task. If all went as planned, her parents would soon be on their way to Greece.

Then what?

Soon there would no longer be any point in their ruse. No reasons to be seen in each other's company or slip away to Claremont House to make love.

Rhys would go back to his life and she would resume hers.

What frightened her was that she couldn't imagine that independent life she'd so longed for anymore.

She couldn't imagine any future that didn't include him, and she feared giving in to that yearning too.

Chapter Twenty-One

*R*hys had never seen Bella so anxious. She sat opposite him in his carriage but she hadn't cast him a glance in a quarter of an hour. Her gaze was fixed out the window at a house a few doors down the street.

"Macadams knows what time we intended to be here?" she asked, her voice an octave higher and revealing every ounce of her irritation.

"He'll be here. I'm certain. We were early, Bella."

"To thwart a thief, one should be a step ahead, don't you think?" She glanced at him but far too briefly.

"Since this is my first foray into criminal hunting, I really couldn't say."

That seemed to deflate a bit of her anxiousness. She let out a sigh and turned to face him.

"You're right, of course. I'm no detective inspector from Scotland Yard."

"Not yet anyway."

She grinned at that and he felt lighter for the first time all morning. But the ease between them faded because a moment later she was staring out the window again, chewing at her bottom lip nervously.

"Perhaps I should knock on the door and see if he's even there."

"Mostly definitely not."

"I don't fear him."

"If we go up to that door, we're doing it together."

She huffed out a sigh. "We did this at Mrs. Turner's. You've met him. If he sees you, he'll know the jig is up and bolt."

Rhys laughed. "The jig is up? Have you been spending time with Macadams that I'm not aware of?"

"No, I read it in a detective novel." She cast him an odd look. "I'm going in." Even before the words were out, she'd opened the door of the carriage and stepped down onto the pavement.

"Bella, stop."

But she didn't.

Rhys was out of the carriage almost as quick as she was, but before he could make it down the pavement to catch up, she was knocking at the door.

He waited to see if anyone answered. As he did, he heard a carriage rattle to a stop behind him. A moment later, footsteps approached.

"Your Grace, I didn't expect to find you here." Macadams was breathless and cast a harried look at Rhys.

The note Rhys had sent the man had been short, as all his written correspondence was, only laying out the details of what they'd found. He'd made no mention of him and Bella being present when Macadams investigated the address.

"My fiancée is a very determined woman." Rhys kept his gaze fixed on Bella as she rapped again on the front door.

"My God, is that the lady?" Macadams stared at her in horror. "She can't simply strut up to the man's door. Is she mad?"

Macadams started barreling toward her, but Rhys stopped him with an arm across the man's chest.

"Watch your tongue, Inspector, when you speak of my future duchess." Rhys spared the man one quick glower. "She's not mad. Simply stubborn as hell and damnably curious."

"Do you allow her to rush into danger often, Your Grace?"

Rhys ignored the man and turned back toward Bella.

"We should let Macadams do this," he told her.

"He isn't the one who found this address," she whispered while giving the Scotland Yard detective a single glance of acknowledgment. "We did."

"And if Radley is armed?"

"You should listen to the duke, Miss Prescott." Macadams had shuffled up beside them and assessed the building through narrowed eyes.

"I listen to him often, Mr. Macadams." Bella stared

at Rhys pointedly. "And he trusts my judgment. Don't you?"

"I—" Rhys was saved from answering, because at that precise moment the dark green door of number 32 creaked open and a man's head emerged and then retreated. A moment later the door slammed shut.

In his periphery, Rhys saw a flash of black and then Macadams rushed past him toward the front door. He knocked firmly with the edge of his fist.

"Come out. We know you're in there."

Beside Rhys, Bella sighed heavily and approached Macadams.

"Let me try, Detective?"

The man cast a one-arched-brow glance at Rhys and then stepped back, grumbling under his breath the whole time.

Bella rapped on the door with her knuckles. "Pardon me, sir. Might we have a few words with you?" Her voice was firm but pleasant, the opposite of Macadams's gruff shout.

Rhys feared they'd have to pry the door open or that the man was devising an escape out the back while they lingered in front.

Then the door latch twisted, shocking all of them. The door slid open slowly and a man emerged, stopping just at the threshold.

Rhys could only truly see his profile as he looked down and assessed Bella. He hated that she was in the middle of this and that the man stood ogling her, but he only needed one glimpse to know. He'd discarded his spectacles and wore his hair longer but Rhys recognized him without a doubt.

Turning, he offered Macadams a nod. "It's him."

Rhys spoke the words quietly, but they seemed to draw Radley's notice. He frowned at the sight of Rhys and then his expression turned to rage when he spotted Macadams.

The detective held out his hands, palms up. "Easy now, Radley."

Radley offered them a smug smirk, and Rhys wanted to clap the man in irons himself. He strode forward to confront him.

Radley grabbed Bella's arm, yanked her inside, and slammed the door shut.

Rhys broke into a run to beat Macadams to the door. He twisted the latch but the door had been locked. He pounded hard enough to rattle the ground floor windows.

"Open up, Radley."

"Let me, Your Grace."

With far more patience than Rhys could ever muster, Macadams removed two implements from his coat and bent to inspect the door's lock. He stuck one long needle-like implement inside and slid the other in beside it.

"Hurry, man." Rhys couldn't hear any voices coming from the house. His blood pounded so loudly in his ears, he wasn't sure he could hear anything else. The thought of Bella alone with the man made his stomach turn.

"Got it," Macadams said.

Rhys reached above him and slammed the door open wide.

He couldn't see anything. The hall before him was pitch-dark and he scanned every inch for her.

"Bella?" His heart was in his throat as he strode in, pushing open doors. "Bella!"

Desperation clawed at him as he shouted her name. He didn't give a damn about Radley anymore. Only she mattered.

He heard her cry out and his blood froze in his veins. He kicked the next door open and it slammed against the wall. Inside, Radley stood with Bella, his hand gripping her arm.

Rhys raised a fist and stepped forward to strike the man. All he could see was red and the fear in Bella's eyes.

"It's all right," she said, lifting a hand as if to stall Rhys. "He says he needs to explain."

But Radley didn't look interested in explanations. His face was twisted in anger and he seemed to reserve most of it for Rhys.

"There he is," the man spat. "The infamous Duke of Claremont."

"Take your hands off of her. Now."

Bella twisted out of the man's grasp and Radley had enough sense to release her.

"What is it you have to say, Radley?" Rhys moved closer to Bella.

"Stop right there, Your Grace." Radley reached for Bella's wrist again.

She winced in pain and Rhys advanced on the man, striking him with one sharp jab. Bella twisted out of his hold the minute Radley covered his bloody nose with both hands.

Drawing her to the far corner of the room, Rhys wrapped an arm around Bella's shoulders.

"Are you all right?" He cupped her face in his hands and only breathed easy again when she nodded.

"You see what he did to me, copper?" Radley shouted. "Assaulted in my own home."

Macadams stepped into the room, glowering like a headmaster come to chastise rowdy students. "That will be enough, gentlemen. You'll be coming with me, Mr. Radley."

Rhys wanted to leave the rest to Macadams. Let him put the man in irons. They could ask Radley questions at Scotland Yard. But when he turned to leave, Bella stopped him.

"Wait," she told Rhys, then turned to Radley. "Why did you take Claremont money?" Bella started to approach the man again.

Rhys wrapped an arm around her waist to stop her. "Macadams can deal with him."

He could feel the tension in her body and sensed her eagerness to break away.

"I think he has a story to tell and I think you need to hear it."

Macadams moved past her. "You're caught, Radley. I've a carriage waiting to transport you for questioning." The old man reached for the steward and the younger man bellowed as if he'd been singed.

"I won't go," Radley shouted. "Not until I've said my piece."

"Go on then, man." Rhys's impatience for the thief's nonsense was wearing thin.

Radley shot him a haughty look. "I took money from the Claremont coffers. I admit it."

"Where is it? And the money you took from the others?" Macadams asked. "We need to recover as much as we can if you have any hope of avoiding the rope."

Ignoring him, Radley continued glaring at Rhys. "Might regret what I did to other employers, but never to Claremont. He was a heartless wretch of a man."

The steward's wrath was like a palpable thing. Anger rolled off him in sickly waves, but Rhys realized the anger wasn't for him. Radley hated his father.

"Tell them the rest, Mr. Radley, so this can come to an end," Bella urged.

"The Duke of Claremont was a vile man. He used everyone that came within his circle, but there was only one who mattered to me enough to seek revenge." Radley glanced at Bella, and Rhys sensed he'd already divulged something to her. "My sister."

Bella nudged Rhys but he still didn't understand.

"Mrs. Turner," she whispered to him.

The woman his father had discarded in a town house in Gordon Square.

"Belinda was just widowed when he set his sights on

her," Radley spit out. "Thought she was lucky to catch a duke's eye. Thought the bastard loved her."

Just as he had when meeting the man's sister, Rhys felt guilt. Disgust at his father's behavior, and guilt for all the ways he'd become like him.

"I regret whatever indignities your sister suffered at my father's hands." He could muster a modicum of sympathy for the man, but not enough. He wanted Bella away from here and for Macadams to apply the law however Radley deserved.

Rhys turned his back on the man and reached for Bella.

"You're not much better than him, Claremont. Apple never falls far, does it? You needn't put on high-and-mighty airs with me."

Bella ignored Rhys's outstretched hand and kept her gaze fixed on Radley.

"Whatever the late duke did, it doesn't justify your theft, sir." Bella's tone somehow managed understanding and brutal honesty.

"He and his father and all their ilk make more money than they know what to do with," he protested. "And this one piles on even more at his Den of Dukes, or whatever they call themselves."

"They invest in people and their ideas," Bella said defensively.

"We needn't do this, Bella," Rhys told her.

"I'm more than grateful for your assistance, Your Grace," Macadams told them by way of dismissal. "I'll see to Mr. Radley now."

Rhys nodded at the man and took Bella's hand. He

was relieved when she clasped his tightly and started with him toward the door. Halfway there, Rhys stopped and turned back to Macadams.

"It wasn't me, Detective."

"Pardon, Your Grace?"

"Your thanks should go to my betrothed. It was Miss Prescott who discovered the clue that led us to Radley, and she was the one who insisted we pursue it."

Macadams worked his jaw for a moment before finally shifting his gaze to Bella. "Indebted to you, Miss Prescott. Well done," he told her with a begrudging tightness in his tone.

"You're welcome, Inspector." Bella beamed at him, despite his gruff demeanor.

Rhys didn't breathe easily until he got her outside, away from Radley's wrath and whatever danger the man might pose.

"I echo the inspector. Well done, Bella."

As soon as they reached the pavement, she released his hand and stepped away from him.

"Are you all right? Did he hurt you?"

She let out a shaky exhale before turning to face him. "That's one more part of our agreement resolved."

"One part, yes."

"But all of it is coming together. We've found Radley. Meg is well on her way to starting her Season. Mama and Papa will soon set sail for Greece." She took a step closer but he couldn't read her expression. "Don't you see? Soon we'll be able to end the charade."

"You know it's more than that." He'd said the words

but he hadn't laid out his thoughts, his desires. "The engagement may have begun as a falsehood but what I feel for you isn't false." He took a deep breath and ignored the way his heartbeat seemed to stall in his chest. "Perhaps the engagement shouldn't be either."

"No." Bella said the word with such vehemence, Rhys wondered if she'd misunderstood him.

He hadn't actually asked *the* question, but she seemed terrified he would.

"Please don't. Not now. Not like this."

Rhys raked a hand through his hair. Bella was the brightest woman he'd ever known and the most desirable. But she was also the most maddening.

"Five other men have had the opportunity to ask. Perhaps you should allow me to get the words out too."

Was this not what she wanted? Their feelings were mutual. He saw it in her eyes. Felt it in how her body responded to his. He still wasn't sure he could ever deserve her, but he wanted to try.

Bella walked away from him, pacing down the pavement, then turned back and approached until they were almost toe to toe. It was odd for her to be the one pacing, unable to remain calm, while he stood still. Waiting.

Somewhere along the way, the tables had turned.

"We should head back to the Tremaynes." Her voice held that no-nonsense quality he usually loved. "They're expecting us for luncheon."

"Very well." He wanted to push, to break through the cool facade she wore as well as he wore his jovial one. But Bella was stubborn, and he had no wish for a battle.

She walked with him to the carriage and let him help her inside. He touched her only as long as necessary and didn't linger as he'd done the past few days. When they were seated on opposite benches, he turned his head toward one window and she focused her gaze out the other.

For the short journey, they said nothing.

It was as if the past days had been nothing more than a delicious dream and they were back where they'd started, glaring at one another across the length of the Hillcrest billiard room.

He'd never had to woo or seduce a woman in any but the most carnal of ways. Bella was worth the effort to try for more.

Trouble was, he had no real idea of how to begin.

Chapter Twenty-Two

$\mathcal{B}$ella knew by all the rules of propriety, she was being an awful guest.

Rather than join the others at Tremayne House for luncheon, she asked a servant to give her excuses and remained in her room, combing the pages of her manuscript for anything she might improve.

The puzzles and problems didn't absorb her as they usually did. And of course, she knew why. She had a much greater conundrum to solve.

One that involved a man who made her breathless every time he touched her. One that made her heart race anytime she let herself contemplate the future, because every possibility frightened her. She couldn't imagine a life with Rhys, and yet she could no longer think of one without him.

It was why she'd begged off lunch. He would be there with that searching blue gaze of his, and she feared the next time they were alone together he'd ask the question she'd once longed to hear.

But that was the past, and this wasn't foolish infatuation. Her heart was torn and her head led her down winding paths of worry. If he asked, she still didn't know what her answer should be.

Rising from the settee in her guest suite, she stretched to ease the knots in her back. Glancing at the clock, she wondered if it was too late to join the luncheon.

Laughter filtered up from downstairs intermittently. The event was a larger affair than she'd imagined. She'd counted at least a dozen guests as she'd watched from her window when carriages arrived.

After nearly quarter of an hour's absence, she wondered why Rhys hadn't come up to find her and ask why she wasn't in attendance.

Pressing a hand to her middle, she drew in a deep breath. Then she turned to the mirror over the mantel and tucked a few strands of hair into pins to straighten her coiffure.

Perhaps she would go.

She started for the door and stopped when someone knocked from the other side.

"Rhys."

But when she swung the door open, it was the Duchess of Tremayne smiling at her from across the threshold.

"I wanted to make sure you were well." The duchess stepped inside and cast a glance at the pages of

Bella's manuscript spread across a table. "That looks intriguing."

"I'm working on a book. I hope to find a publisher." Bella thought the duchess might appreciate her puzzles. Perhaps one day she could present her with a copy.

"We have a published author attending the luncheon." The duchess wore a warm cajoling smile. "If you come down, I'll introduce you."

Bella grinned. "I was actually just on my way."

"Excellent." The duchess pressed her hands together and gave a little clap of victory. "We've yet to eat. Still mingling and conversing. I've saved your spot at the table across from your betrothed."

"Wonderful." Bella hoped her anxiousness didn't show.

As the duchess led her downstairs, Bella spotted Meg, who waved at her and came to meet her at the bottom of the staircase.

"I'm so glad you've decided to join us, after all." She cast a gaze toward the Tremaynes' enormous drawing room. "There are very few people here I know and I have no idea where Rhys has disappeared to."

"Has he disappeared?"

Meg sipped at a glass of what looked like punch. "He knows so many people in London. I think he drifted off to speak with a few."

Bella stepped into the drawing room and Meg was right. Rhys was nowhere to be seen. "Has the party spread to other rooms?"

Meg shrugged.

"I'm going to look for him." Bella cast the girl a look, half expecting her to offer to help in the search.

"Perhaps I'll stay put. The duchess said I should mingle."

Bella smiled. "Then you should."

Tremayne House was a surprisingly cavernous town house and designed in an unusual style, with halls jutting off from the main one and doorways nestled in corners. Most doors were closed, but a few were cracked open and Bella wondered which rooms she should explore or avoid.

Voices and laughter emerged from a few. Two men seemed to be bickering over politics in one. A few ladies whispered and snickered as if sharing gossip in another. And at the far end of the hall, Bella heard a lady's throaty chuckle and a name that set her nerves on edge.

"Claremont, how dare you?"

Bella hesitated with her palm on the half-open door. Her mind went straight to her worst fears. She had moved so far beyond that day that had haunted her for so long. She didn't want to revisit that pain.

But she had to know.

"Rhys?" She stepped inside and the room was so dim she struggled to make out anything or anyone.

Then two shapes came into view, lit by a low-burning candle sconce on the far wall. Rhys stood with his back against a bookcase, and a woman in sapphire blue stood beside him.

He smiled as soon as he noticed her arrival. "I

thought you weren't coming down." He came forward
and lifted a hand as if to reach for her.

"I changed my mind." Bella didn't take his offered
hand. She wasn't sure what she'd walked into.

His frown deepened. "I'm glad you did."

"Are you?" Bella gazed past him at the woman still
hovering near the bookcase.

She was staring back, watching her interactions
with Rhys with interest. Then she stepped forward.

"This must be your fiancée. Won't you introduce us,
Claremont?"

"Miss Jane Harrington." Rhys gestured at the young
lady but kept his gaze fixed on Bella's. "Miss Arabella
Prescott. My betrothed."

"I've heard of you, Miss Prescott."

"Have you?" Bella couldn't recall if she'd ever met
the young woman, but she was far more interested in
speaking to Rhys than becoming acquainted with her.

"You've rejected a great many suitors." She lifted
the fan strung around her wrist and tapped Rhys on
the arm. "She waited a long while for you, Claremont.
I do hope you make it worth her while."

"Would you excuse us, Jane?"

Rhys still hadn't cast the young lady a glance since
Bella entered the room, but she took the hint and made
her way out.

When Miss Harrington was gone, Rhys watched her
warily. Bella wasn't sure if she should begin, but she
also wasn't entirely certain of what she wished to say.

Rhys broke the silence. "I know my reputation and

what you must fear. But whatever you suspect that was, I promise you it wasn't that. Miss Harrington is the sister of a gent I knew at university."

Bella hated the emotions clawing inside her. Jealousy and uncertainty. She realized in that moment that she had come to trust him in the past days.

"You're friends?"

"Not really." He rushed to assure her, drawing a step closer. "We're acquainted through her brother and she expressed surprise that a man of my . . . reputation had become betrothed."

A chuckle burst from Bella's lips.

He sighed and scrubbed a hand along his jaw. "Bella, I know your trust isn't something I can demand. I must earn it and be patient as I do."

"I have trusted you in the last few days."

He swallowed hard and she suspected the same memories came to his mind that continually played in hers. Their lovemaking. Their laughter at Margate. Their growing closeness each day since he'd returned to Essex.

"But you have doubts," he said with a sadness that made her heart ache. "They creep in, even when you don't wish them to. And in a situation like this, when you find me with a stranger, how can I blame you for suspecting the worst?"

All of what he said was true. Doubts plagued her, even in the moments when she was happy and content in his arms. But the fear that she'd find him with another young lady in a hedge maze as she had so many years ago wasn't what worried her. Her fear was more about her feelings than his trustworthiness.

She was afraid of losing herself again.

He turned away from her and stalked toward a window. Bracing a hand on the frame, he stared out on the fashionable square. "Perhaps we should end this arrangement as quickly as we're able."

"Is that what you want?" Bella held her breath.

He swung around to face her. "You know it's bloody well not. You know what I want."

He'd suggested they make their engagement real. Part of her wanted that too. "Tell me what you want, Rhys."

Perhaps she was ready for the question. But rather than ask, he stalked toward her, cupped her face in his palm, and kissed her.

Bella clutched at his shirtfront and pulled him closer. It had only been hours since they'd been this close but somehow, she'd missed it. Missed his heat and unique scent and the way she felt when his body was against hers.

He lifted his head and told her breathlessly, "Showing you seemed the superior option, but I'm willing to tell you too." He slid a finger under her chin and tipped her head so that his gaze locked on hers. "I want to be yours, Arry, and I want you to be mine. Marry me."

Those two words. She'd longed to hear them from him for so long.

"Good thing you two are engaged," the Duchess of Tremayne called from the doorway.

Rhys let out a frustrated sigh.

"I only came to tell you that luncheon will be served in ten minutes. Everyone's gathering in the dining room."

"Thank you," Rhys bit out, and then strode forward to close the door when their hostess departed.

Bella stood frozen. The duchess's interruption had broken the moment and rather than savor Rhys's proposal, all Bella could think of was the past.

"You needn't give me an answer now," he told her quietly.

"I've imagined hearing you say those words. For years, it was all I wanted." Swallowing against the pain of those memories, she took a long breath. "That day of the garden party I wanted to hear those words from you."

"I know."

"You knew?" Bella turned back to find him lingering near the door, his hand still on the latch.

"I suspected. I knew you thought too highly of me."

Bella bit her lip and struggled to keep the memories where they belonged. In the past.

"We needn't revisit this again."

"When you didn't offer for me, it hurt. Deeply."

"I'm sorry." There was such tenderness in his gaze. Such regret. She knew his apology was sincere.

He started toward her and Bella lifted a hand. "I know you are. But, you see, it didn't end there. You were all I thought about for months. I struggled to sleep or focus. Nothing could catch my interest and no one else was ever going to win my heart because I'd already given it to you. Everyone else seemed lackluster in comparison."

Bella couldn't help but smile at that final sentiment. Every word was still true.

His eyes lit with hopefulness. "Is this your way of accepting my proposal?"

Yes was on the tip of her tongue. It was what her heart wanted, but her head rang with warning bells. She'd walked into the room fearing the worst of him, fearing that she would be crushed again. He'd proven her fears to be unfounded.

Perhaps she could eventually trust him completely, but the harder truth was that she didn't trust herself. She couldn't marry him if it meant she was always going to be afraid of being heartbroken again.

A gong sounded in the hallway. The signal that luncheon was served.

"We should join the others," Bella said as she made her way over to where he stood near the door.

"I need to know if you can ever trust me again, Bella. You know my feelings. My desires. I've asked you the question." His gaze held a note of sadness.

Bella swallowed hard and fought back the sting of tears. "I don't have an answer."

She didn't want to say *no* but the notion of telling him *yes* terrified her.

Rhys stepped toward the door and turned back, waiting until she joined him at the threshold. "You're worth waiting for," he told her, his voice raw, "but I can't wait forever."

Chapter Twenty-Three

Three weeks later

*A*fter years of attending balls, Bella had developed three strategies.

First, immediately discover a quiet nook for retreat. Second, always take something to read or a notebook to scribble in. Third, avoid dancing if at all possible.

She'd never imagined she'd have to employ her strategies again after her fourth Season and yet here she stood in a crowded ballroom, this time as a chaperone to her cousin rather than as a debutante.

She'd already begun drafting the letter to inform her parents that her engagement to Rhys had been called off. They'd spoken only once and exchanged a couple of perfunctory notes in the three weeks since his proposal at the Tremayne luncheon.

Bella tried not to focus on how much that hurt and how much she missed him.

Her parents were happily settled abroad, but they would have to be told the truth, especially if she and Rhys planned to call off the ruse early.

And then what? She shivered at the thought of another Season or her parents returning from Greece to play matchmaker again.

"This isn't nearly as bad as you feared it would be, is it?" Louisa approached in her pretty yellow ball gown. "As chaperone, you don't even have to dance."

Bella tried to muster a smile. "For that, I'm very grateful."

Louisa was right. As of yet, this evening hadn't been entirely dreadful. She'd stuck to her rules and, though the night was still young, the ball had proceeded without incident.

When Bella looked out on the kaleidoscope swirl of ladies in lavish ball gowns and men in ebony black, she saw only the visual puzzle she'd just been concocting in her notebook. It would be a matching conundrum that would test both memory and organizational skills.

After a second meeting with Mr. Peabody, he'd offered her a contract on her first manuscript and insisted that he wished to see another and consider a series of puzzle books.

"I'm going for the next dance," Louisa told her before heading off to find another of the bevy of gentlemen on her dance card.

The corner Bella had found to tuck herself into was well hidden but poorly lit. She tipped her notebook toward a wall sconce and bent to scribble down her idea before it slipped from her thoughts.

Her pencil skidded across the page when the pianist began playing a waltz. Memories flooded in, so sharp she could almost feel Rhys's arms around her and smell his scent in the air.

Louisa approached a few minutes later, her cheeks flushed and her eyes sparkling. "I've changed my mind. There is one problem with this ball."

"Which is?"

"Do you know whose town house is across the square from this one?"

Bella gripped the pencil so hard, the lead tip snapped against the paper of her journal. She knew, and she'd done her best to not let her gaze wander to Claremont House. Most of all, she drove away thoughts of making love with Rhys in his elaborately furnished bedroom.

"I know, Louisa."

Was he at home? Did he think of her as often as she thought of him?

"Maybe you should see the rest for yourself."

Bella tipped her head and stared at her cousin quizzically. "What is there to see?"

It had been dark when her aunt and uncle's carriage deposited them at the ball. She'd only glanced at the windows, wondering if he was at home.

"Come with me," Louisa urged.

Bella followed the girl across the hall into an empty drawing room. Louisa immediately went to the window and pulled the curtain back for Bella to see.

Across the square, one town house, his town house, had six long windows on the front facade and every single one of them was ablaze with light. Beyond gauzy curtains on the ground floor, Bella could see couples milling and on the upper floor a dozen people were dancing.

"One of his infamous parties," Louisa whispered.

Bella swallowed past the painful lump in her throat. "He didn't wait."

"What was he waiting on?" Louisa settled in the window seat to peer out toward the Claremont town house, and she looked so tired Bella couldn't bring herself to chastise the girl for wrinkling her dress.

"For me." Bella hadn't divulged what happened with Rhys to everyone. To anyone. "He said he'd wait for me." *But not forever.*

Louisa's eyes grew bigger. "What was he waiting on from you?"

"An answer." Bella took a step closer to the window and stared across at Claremont House. She realized she was looking for him, hungry for a single glimpse of him.

"I don't understand." Louisa had stopped looking out the window and was staring at Bella.

"I'm not sure I do either." Bella settled her backside against the cushioned arm of a settee. "He asked me to marry him and—"

"You refused?"

"I didn't give him an answer at all." Bella gestured in the direction of Claremont House. "And as you see he's simply gone back to being the devil-may-care Duke of Claremont."

"But why in heaven did you not say yes?"

Bella planted her hands on her hips. "He doesn't seem like the ideal husband." She nudged her chin toward the window. "Does he?"

"Some would certainly say so, but he was never like that with you. And he's the man you've always wished to marry. Isn't he?"

Louisa was being too logical, and far too inquisitive.

"There was a time I wished to marry him. Yes."

"But not now?"

Bella stood and began pacing. On a thick rug in front of the unlit fireplace, she stopped. "Perhaps I don't trust him enough. He hurt me so much."

"I remember how sad you were and that you remained so for a long time. But that was ages ago. Has he given you more reason to distrust him?"

"No. Not since he came back into my life." Bella couldn't fault him for anything but overprotectiveness and a tendency to be an enormous distraction.

"So is it Rhys you don't trust or yourself?"

Bella knew her cousin saw straight through her. Louisa had always been able to. She didn't trust herself. She didn't trust how she'd love him and she didn't trust how she'd handle the consequences if she lost him again.

"I can't ever go back to being that girl I once was. I won't allow myself to disappear into thoughts of Rhys and nothing else. And I won't lose myself in pining for him if he walks away again."

Louisa stood and approached until the skirt of her gown brushed Bella's. "How could you go back? You're not that girl anymore. You never will be. You're stronger now and not prone to infatuation."

"New Bella."

Louisa tipped her head and grinned. "I quite like her. I think you should trust her to know her own heart."

Bella let out a stifled breath, pressed a hand to her chest, and felt the round outline there. She stripped off her gloves and dipped two fingers under her lace fichu, tugging at the chain around her neck to lift the pendant out. As she pressed the daisy against her palm, memories flooded her mind.

New memories they'd made together.

She missed him with an ache that never ceased.

"You're right. I don't want to hold myself back anymore." No more cold, unfeeling debutante. No more refusals.

She'd tried to convince herself that separating from Rhys was for the best. The safe choice. But it didn't feel right. Being away from him never felt right. For the past few weeks, her life had been less vibrant. She'd smiled less. Laughed less and felt far less at ease.

Bella tucked her pendant back into the neck of her gown and squared her shoulders. She could do this.

"I should go speak to him."

Louisa nodded eagerly. "You should."

"Just a few steps and I could be at his door."

Never mind that she hadn't seen his face in weeks and wasn't sure if what he'd said when they parted was still true.

"Thank you, cousin." Bella wrapped Louisa in a hug, gave her one tight squeeze, and let her go. "Go back and find your next dance partner."

After Louisa returned to the ball room, Bella headed for the front door.

Each step she took was easier than the last. Once she'd started toward him, she couldn't stop. She refused to live her life in fear, afraid of what she felt for him. Afraid of being overwhelmed by her own emotions.

The more frightening prospect was never being close to him again.

She walked past the footmen standing sentry at the front door, both of whom gave her a look of surprise.

The evening was blessedly cool and she kept on, not stopping, not thinking. There was strategy in this plan but mostly it was instinct. Impulse. Not like her at all.

Or maybe it was exactly who she was and always had been.

Chapter Twenty-Four

*D*eafening cheers drowned out the sound of his own heartbeat. A frantic, wild chorus built from shouts of encouragement to a single demand.

"More," they cried. "More, more."

Rhys stood atop his antique cherrywood dining room table with a yard glass to his lips and was doing his damnedest to give the crowd the entertainment they demanded.

He'd only invited ten guests to his London town house, but the party had grown, as his gatherings often did. After returning from the countryside, he'd vowed to never hold another party like this one. He wanted to be a better man, one who took his duties and responsibilities seriously. But this party had been scheduled months in advance. Two friends attending, twin gentlemen he'd met at boarding school, were to celebrate their birthday.

So for this one night, he'd agreed to resume his old life and it taught him one thing quickly. He no longer gave a damn about being the best host in London.

The guests had insisted on frivolity and he'd agreed to a simple drinking game rather than a feat of daring. He'd longed for any entertainment that wouldn't mean he'd end up hanging from chandeliers or playing human dartboard for a pretty circus performer.

"Keep drinking, Claremont," someone shouted from the crowd.

He couldn't blame his friends. After all, he'd invited them and he'd been the one to set the precedent of parties filled with mayhem.

But tonight it was all so bloody loud and exhausting. Tomorrow he would start again living the life he'd come to like. A few ladies teased that he'd reformed his ways.

Perhaps he had. He only wished Bella knew. She was the spark that had changed everything in him.

Bella. Damn it. He tried not to think of her. He wouldn't. Not tonight.

Tonight he would go on doing what he once did well. Playing the nobleman jester for all those lucky enough to receive an invitation to his party.

"Empty," he shouted at those crowding around the table, swiped the sleeve of his black velvet suit across his mouth, and lifted the second empty yard glass up in triumph.

"Another!" came a reply, dreadful and immediate.

Lord Somersby, damn him to Hades, handed up another full yard glass of the most disgusting ale Rhys had ever tasted.

Glancing around the crowded room filled with friends, acquaintances, and a few rivals in business and gambling, he put on a smirk filled with false bravado.

Taking the long-necked glass, he happily sloshed as much as he could over the side on the way to his lips. It took a great deal of liquor to get him well and truly soused, and he feared that point was coming soon.

The second glass of ale had felt endless. With this one, he thought he might drown.

Bodies crowded closer. Some guests pounded on the table. Another nudged it with their thigh and some of the ale sloshed onto his face and overexpensive gold-threaded waistcoat.

He kept drinking, letting the warm ale slide down his throat. He'd had so much he could thankfully no longer taste or smell it. His senses only registered the miasma of scents in the room. Sweat, perfume, the smoke of cigars and cheroots, and the burning wax of dozens of candles.

He swallowed again and a wave of dizziness came with the gulp. With his head tipped back, dark spots danced in his vision. He closed his eyes and wished he was upstairs in his bed. Maybe tonight, finally, sleep would come. Restful sleep, uninterrupted by dreams of an auburn-haired beauty who was always just out of reach.

He choked on the last bit of ale. More froth than liquid filled his mouth and his throat refused to let it down. Queasiness came to accompany the dizziness and he stumbled forward on the polished surface of the dining table, dropping the yard glass and its final droplets of beer onto the carpet before he caught his balance and steadied himself.

"Careful, love," a buxom brunette called up.

Sylvia. Sophia? They'd been close once. Their tryst hadn't been long but he should have at least remembered her name. He hated being a man who used women for pleasure and couldn't bother to remember any of them.

"I think the party is over," he said to her quietly.

She winked and continued to watch him hungrily, as she had all night. Unfortunately for her, his desire for sleep and dreams of Bella was greater than for whatever diversion any woman might provide.

"You must walk the balcony, Claremont." Somersby spoke up again, wearing that bloody smug smile he'd perfected at university.

"Isn't it your turn, old chap?"

They'd been rivals at school. Somersby won every test of mental agility. Rhys had won any competition that involved physical strength or speed. But while Rhys accepted his shortcomings, Somersby couldn't stand to acknowledge his own. Sometimes, Rhys felt certain the man only maintained a facade of friendship in order to make ridiculous wagers intended to make his life miserable.

"No, Claremont. You said you'd walk the balcony if you didn't finish the three yards." Somersby pointed at the glass and its meager contents spilled on the floral rug.

"A few drops, I assure you, old friend."

"Our wager was quite clear, old friend."

"Walk the balcony!"

Rhys didn't recognize the male voice that called from the back of the room, and he was too bleary-eyed to focus on anyone that far away. But he did sense the gazes on him, eager expectant eyes, waiting for him to do something else daring and foolish. They came to be entertained.

"Very well. Let's do this," he heard himself lisp.

Every object in his periphery had gone a bit fuzzy, and his legs felt as solid as warm jelly, but a wager was a wager.

"Make way," he told those at the edge of the dining table before jumping down.

The hard landing cleared his head a bit but it did nothing for the beer-induced queasiness that had been building since his first sip of warm swill.

He stripped off his suit jacket as he strode through the dining room. Someone in the crowd took it from his hands. He loosened his cravat and slid it off his neck too. The room was too warm, too filled with sweaty intoxicated people. He quickened his steps to reach the balcony to get a breath of fresh air.

A few guests proceeded him into the drawing room, and the brunette pushed the upstairs balcony doors open for him. Sonya. That was her name.

"Will you bid me to be careful again?" he asked in a teasing tone.

"You're a lucky man, Your Grace. I trust your good fortune will hold this evening."

He tried for a smile but it turned into a grimace. If he were a lucky man, he'd be in his bed with Bella's soft curves nestled against him. God, he missed her warmth, her scent, the taste of her.

"One turn around the perimeter and the wager is fulfilled." Somersby was as tenacious as a terrier.

Rhys cast him a glare over his shoulder, strode out into the night, and climbed onto the ledge that ran the length of the square balcony. Finding his balance was shockingly easy, as long as he didn't look down. He wasn't too far up. A single story. A fall would perhaps break a bone or two but little else.

As he started his walk around the edge, he lifted his arms out for balance and a wave of dizziness swept over him. He focused on steadying his breathing and stopped to solidify his balance again. The party guests had gone blessedly quiet as they crowded around the terrace doors to watch. It was as if everyone was holding their breaths, yet he sensed half of them were hoping he'd tumble over the side and give them a proper show.

He started forward again, just a few more steps and this bloody nonsense would be done.

Laughter drifted up from the house across the square and he glanced over, noticing the glowing windows and people gathered in every room beyond. On the second floor, couples danced across a ballroom so large it spanned several windows. Notably none of their guests were doing a foolish intoxicated walk around a story-high balcony.

His foot slipped and several ladies gasped.

"All's well and this feat is almost accomplished." He lifted his outstretched arms a bit higher and kept his gaze as steady as he was able.

Movement caught his notice across the street. Guests still filed into the town house's front door. But looking at the front door meant he was looking down.

Not good. A very bad decision. A rusty laugh bubbled up inside his chest.

Had he ever made anything but bad decisions?

And then he saw her. She was everything right. Everything he wanted, and she was the one woman in London who he was certain didn't want him.

He frowned. He was tipsy and logic was never his strong suit but his muddled mind wrestled with the riddle of why she was striding toward his town house if she didn't want him at all.

SHE COULD DO this.

Lifting her skirts, she stepped off the pavement onto the cobbled streets and assessed the Claremont front door. No servants were stationed there. The outside sconces weren't even lit, but the door was ajar, as if in open invitation for anyone to enter.

Two steps from his door and a woman's scream

echoed down from above. Bella looked up and lost her breath.

He was standing on the balcony. Not *on* the balcony, like a normal Londoner out for a bit of fresh air. He stood balanced on the balcony's balustrade, like a circus performer on a high wire.

Bella clenched her hands into fists and held her breath as she watched him take a step forward, sliding his foot along a stone rail that couldn't be much wider than his boot. With his arms stretched out to his sides, his shirtsleeves billowed in the breeze and his body swayed to maintain balance.

Years ago, she'd watched him do the same on a tree limb that stretched out over a pond on his family's property. She also watched him fall from that limb and break his arm.

Clearly the years hadn't made him any less reckless.

If he was walking the perimeter, there were only a few more steps.

But rather than get them over with and end the journey, he stopped and turned his head as if he sensed her watching him.

"Bella?"

In the warm glow from the Wainwrights' windows, she could make out all the familiar angles of his face: sharp jaw, square chin, high cheekbones. And those lips of his, always half tilted in a smile. His hair looked darker in the shadows of evening, but the moonlight lit up a few golden highlights. It was unfashionably long, a wild tumble with strands falling across his forehead, a few waves nearly reaching his shoulders. He was wearing only his shirtsleeves, dark trousers, and a bloodred waistcoat.

As she assessed him, she sensed him doing the same. Rhys's gaze always held a unique kind of power, an intensity that made whomever he looked at seem as if they were the only person in the world who mattered.

"Is it really you?" he shouted down at her.

"Yes, of course. I'm glad you recognize me from that height." The desire to quarrel with him was just there under the surface, yearning to break free.

For weeks she'd imagined going to him, pondering everything from offering a heartfelt apology to asking if he still felt the same and receiving his mask of bravado. Then she'd be tempted to shout until she broke down the walls he was as skilled at building up around himself as she was.

"Miss Prescott." He drew out her name, lisping both words as if his tongue wouldn't quite obey. He was intoxicated. Wonderful. Drunk and inches away from a fall.

"Will you be coming down anytime soon, Your Grace? We have a matter to discuss."

He offered her nothing but a smile in reply.

A smile. After how they'd parted. After weeks of silence. Maybe this was a mistake.

"What sort of matters, my lady?"

"I'll tell you when we're both on terra firma."

"Tell me now."

Good grief, the man hadn't gotten any less bossy either.

Bella bit her lip and debated the folly of this decision.

"Marriage."

He tipped his head as if he didn't quite understand what she'd said.

She tried again, loudly. "I believe you mentioned marriage the last time we spoke to each other."

"Marriage to me?" He gestured in a big arcing movement only to finally turn a finger back toward his chest and point at himself. Bella's heart dropped when he seemed to momentarily lose his balance.

"Yes, of course you," she said, her voice suddenly shaky.

"Very well." He nodded once and then shocked her by turning his back to her. Then he crouched on the balustrade, lowered his hands to the stone railing, and heaved his body over the side.

"What are you doing?" Bella rushed toward him, but there was a cast-iron rail that kept her from getting closer and there was little she could do but stare up at the heels of his boots and the curve of his backside.

"I'm coming down to you," he mumbled.

"Not like that," Bella shouted, though he was closer now and could probably hear her if she'd whispered. "Your town house is equipped with stairs, surely."

He was tall and not far from the ground. Unfortunately, there was a servants' stairwell on one side of where he would drop and a clipped hedge on the other. Either seemed likely to cause damage.

"Quicker this way," he told her breathily as he changed his grip on the balustrade to move closer to the hedgerow.

"And more dangerous."

He tipped his head back and looked down at her. "Have you forgotten who I am completely?"

"No." The word came out too softly, too quickly.

Rhys watched her a moment and then nudged his chin up. "Clear the way."

"Don't break anything."

Bella thought she heard a chuckle in reply. Then she sucked in a quick breath.

Rhys let go and dropped, landing with a thud, though the darkness made it hard for her to see precisely where.

Stomping footsteps followed and a dozen people emerged onto the balcony above, looking over the side. A few called down to him, but he made no reply.

Bella leaned over the rail to get a closer look just as Rhys got to his feet. They were inches apart for the first time in weeks and yet he gave her a smirk that was no different from the one he'd given her a thousand times as a boy. He watched her intently, as if waiting for something. Expecting something. Hoping.

"You're not hurt?" she asked in the most unaffected tone she could muster.

"Were you wishing that I was?" His tone was teasing but when he looked up at her, his expression grew serious, weighted with an emotion she couldn't name.

His brows winged up as if he was expecting her to curse him or be angry.

"Don't be ridiculous," she told him, trying to match his light tone. "If you'd injured yourself, how could you walk me down the aisle?"

"You really do want to discuss marriage." His smirk melted into a beaming smile.

Suddenly she knew what she hadn't realized until this moment. There was never any fear when she was with Rhys. When she was with him, all she truly felt was an odd kind of relief, a rightness, as if they were both where they were meant to be.

He bit his lip and his gaze swept over her from the pins in her hair to the slippers on her toes. When he looked up again, he wore a more sober expression.

"Shall I ask you again?" He squared his shoulders, lifted his chin, and offered her his hand.

"You're intoxicated." Bella took his hand and almost gasped at how good it felt to feel his skin against hers again. "I'm sober, so perhaps I should do the asking this time."

He grinned and bent his head to nuzzle his cheek against hers. "You're intoxicating," he whispered, "so we're even."

Bella laughed, the first time she had in weeks. "Shall we talk inside the town house?"

He glanced back at his balcony and grimaced. "There are dozens of people there you probably don't know."

Turning back, he cast his gaze toward the Wainwrights' town house. "What about where you've come from?"

"A ball. I'm chaperoning Louisa." Bella peeked at the watch fob pinned to her bodice. "I should probably get back soon."

"So we must do this here? In the middle of the street."

Bella squeezed his hand. "I return to Hillcrest tomorrow. You could call on me there."

"I'm not a patient man." He reached for her other hand and brought them both up to place kisses against her knuckles. "Also, I think I should be the one to ask."

"We discussed this."

"If we had a daisy we could decide this fairly."

Bella laughed again and all the worry she'd felt for weeks loosened a bit more. "Ask. I'm ready this time."

Shock chased across his features. "Arry, will you marry me?"

For a moment, she let herself savor the words. Words she'd once longed to hear because she was infatuated and wanted him to notice her. But hearing them now was different. It felt right. Perfect. She didn't just crave his love, she wanted to give hers too. They could be good for each other. They always had been.

When she didn't answer right away, Rhys's expression began to crumple.

"Yes, I will."

"Yes?" He bent his head as if he wasn't sure he'd heard her and needed to be sure.

Bella smiled. "Absolutely without any doubt whatsoever, yes."

Rhys stared at her hungrily. She sensed he'd missed her these past weeks as much as she'd missed him. "When did you decide?"

Bella couldn't pinpoint a moment because she'd loved him for so long that she couldn't recall where it began. "I love you, Rhys. It's always been you."

He gathered her in his arms and kissed her. Tenderly. Reverently. And then the kiss deepened into something hungry and heated. He nuzzled her cheek, pressed a kiss against her neck.

When Bella finally came to her senses and realized what a spectacle they were making of themselves in the middle of Belgrave Square, Rhys leaned closer to whisper in her ear.

"It's always been us."

Epilogue

Seven months later

*S*hould we have her come down?" Meg whispered but not quietly enough.

Rhys held a finger to his lips. His wife had the hearing of a hawk, and now that the item had arrived, he wanted this to be a proper surprise.

"Maybe we could present it to her in the drawing room?" Meg held the box with all the care she'd take with the crown jewels.

"I think we should deliver it to her in her study." Rhys glanced down the hall toward the morning room Bella had converted into a space where she could write and plan her next puzzle book.

"The place where she works? It won't be as much of a surprise there. Will it?" Meg was already making her way toward the drawing room, walking backward.

"Have a care," Rhys warned when she began veering toward the crate that had come along with the very special box she held in her arms.

"I'll go and make sure everything is prepared."

"What is there to prepare?" One box and his wife's excitement at seeing its contents were the only things Rhys craved.

Meg chuckled. "Trust me. Just go and get her."

That, he was more than happy to do.

At the door of her study, he paused and leaned his head against the wood. They normally took lunch together, and he did his best not to interrupt her before then. Though he usually failed miserably.

No one had ever warned him that one of the damnable aspects of having a wife was that her nearness would mean he'd want to see her all the time. And of course, it was all so new. They hadn't yet been married a month.

If it had been up to Rhys, they wouldn't have left their bedroom for the first month. At least not very often.

Especially since they'd taken no celebratory honeymoon voyage after their nuptials. Instead, they'd vowed to visit the viscount and viscountess—how wonderfully odd that Bella's family was now his too—in Greece.

Rhys could hear Bella moving around in the morning room. Her creative methods had always involved movement. Pacing, sketching, or tapping a pencil on her lush lower lip. She really had no idea how enticing that habit was.

He rapped softly so as not to disturb her if she was in the middle of a particularly important idea.

She answered a moment later and he relished the blush that crept up her cheeks and the way her eyes lit with pleasure at the sight of him.

"Goodness, is it lunchtime already?"

"It's not."

"Then you missed me?" She slid a hand against his waistcoat and his heartbeat sped. His body warmed in anticipation.

Sometimes, when Bella took a break from her work for lunch, they didn't repair to the dining room but to their bedroom.

"I did miss you, but I also have something to show you."

"Do you indeed?" She scanned him from brow to boot, and then ran her hand across his chest, patting at his waistcoat pockets.

"If you keep doing that, I'm going to take you up to our room before I give you your present."

Bella chuckled in a husky way that was new and knowing. He absolutely loved it. "I might agree."

"Good. But first, can I entice you into joining me in the drawing room?"

She glanced back at the table where she'd spread drawings and notes, then turned to smile back at him. "Entice me."

He bent and kissed her cheek and then swept her hair back behind her ear to kiss her neck. "Will you join me in the drawing room, Duchess?"

"You have me curious now."

Rhys tucked her hand under his arm and led her back down the hall. He could sense her eagerness as they drew closer. She sped the pace of her footsteps and eventually ended up tugging him along.

Walking through the door she let out a little gasp of surprise.

"Meg, you know the secret too?"

"I do." Meg beamed and spread her hands to indicate the display she'd arranged.

Rhys could only shoot her a look of surprised admiration. In the minutes since he'd departed to find Bella, she'd gathered all the candles in the room, lit them, and set them around the box as if it was a kind of offering. She'd also found a ribbon someplace and tied it around the box in a pretty bow.

"Is that for me?"

Meg stepped back, hands clasped in front of her. Rhys gestured for Bella to open her present.

Bella tugged at the satin ribbon with an eager smile on her face, but she turned a confused look Rhys's way. "It's not even my birthday."

"A birthday of sorts."

That made her frown but she continued, lifting the painted cardboard lid off the box.

Rhys's pulse had begun racing the minute they stepped in the room. He knew how important this would be to her and he couldn't wait to see her reaction.

They'd included a wrap of colored paper, and she peeled that away gingerly.

The gasp she let out was exactly what he'd expected, but he hadn't anticipated the tears. "It's so beautiful."

Rhys placed a hand on her shoulder, rubbing gently. "You did this. It's all you."

"Congratulations, Bella." Meg stepped forward and gave Bella a kiss on the cheek. "It's an extraordinary accomplishment."

Copies of Bella's first puzzle and conundrum book were not due to be available for another week, but Rhys had arranged with her publisher for a special copy, bound in the finest red leather with gold engraving just for Bella.

She swiped at her cheeks. "Thank you, Meg. Would you excuse us for a moment? I'd like to have a word with your brother alone."

"Of course." Meg swung a bemused glance from Bella to Rhys and then exited the drawing room.

"Thank you." Bella smiled at him, one of the warm genuine smiles that made her eyes sparkle.

But Rhys had known her too long not to notice something else. There was more than loving appreciation in her expression.

"There's a *but*," Rhys said warily.

"I didn't do this entirely on my own, did I?"

Rhys squeezed the muscles of his neck. "Mr. Peabody did agree to allow me to send the manuscript to a printer who could expedite this special edition." He pointed at the volume in her hands. "But what's inside those pages is all you. I can barely solve most of your puzzles. I could never write one."

Bella grinned but shook her head. "You never give yourself enough credit, and all the compliments are overwhelming me, but—"

"I clearly need to compliment you more often."

"How well do you know Mr. Peabody?"

Rhys felt a trickle of uncertainty. "I've corresponded with him."

"Including a letter urging him to publish my book?"

Rhys ducked his head. He didn't know exactly how she knew, but she did. "I did not *instruct* him to publish your book. I simply suggested he give it due consideration. From what you said, it sounded as if he'd fobbed you off far too quickly."

"Oh, he did, and yet I told you I wanted to do this myself. Did you doubt that I could?"

"Not at all." He couldn't repress a smile. "I've never doubted your abilities in my life. I only wished to help."

She stared at him, twisting her mouth as if considering his fate. "I'm not sure whether to be grateful or cross."

He stepped closer and slid an arm around her waist. "I wholeheartedly suggest gratitude."

"Thank you." She laid the book down and slid her arms around him. Their bodies were locked tight against each other, and Rhys suddenly wished they were indulging in their usual lunchtime diversion of lovemaking in the afternoon.

Bella poked a finger against his chest. "But no more interfering, unless you ask and I approve. No more sneaking behind my back. Not with Peabody or anyone else."

"I understand."

"Do you promise?"

He'd promise her the world if he could, and he'd help her in any way that he could. But he understood. Earning his own money and becoming free of his dependence on his father had been essential in shaping his life. He knew that Bella wished to find a kind of independence too. Accomplishments that had nothing to do with her father's title or her parents' doting attention.

"I vow to you two things. I will always want to help you. But I will always seek out your approval before doing so in future."

She twined her arms around his neck and pressed her body closer. "Thank you for understanding."

Lifting on her toes, she pressed her mouth to his and for long minutes he was lost in the taste of her. The heat of her breath, the little guttural cries she let out when he kissed her deeply.

"We could simply turn this into lunch," he suggested. He shaped her backside with his hands and pulled her against him.

"Good," she whispered.

For a moment he wondered if she'd missed the euphemism. He adored her clever mind, but she did have a tendency to take everything as literal.

"I didn't mean—"

Bella lifted onto her toes again and pressed a soft hot kiss against his mouth. "I know what you meant." She scraped her fingers through his hair and kissed him again, his face, the corner of his mouth. "I want exactly what you meant."

Rhys clasped her hand and led her toward the staircase.

He'd always been told he was a man of good fortune, but he had no idea what he'd done to deserve the way Bella loved him. He only knew that he intended to savor every single moment and never take for granted that he was indeed a very lucky man.

A Duke Changes Everything

Nicholas Lyon gambled his way into a fortune and ownership of the most opulent, notorious gentlemen's club in England. But when Nick's cruel brother dies, he inherits a title he never wanted. The sooner Nick is rid of the estate that has always haunted him, the sooner he can return to the life he's built in London. But there's one obstacle—the exquisite Thomasina Thorne.

When the new heir to the Tremayne dukedom suddenly appears in Mina Thorne's life, she's flustered. Not only is he breathtakingly handsome, but he's also determined to take away her home and position as steward of the Enderley estate. If Mina learns what makes the enigmatic duke tick, perhaps she can change his mind—as long as she doesn't get too close to him.

With each day Nick spends with Mina, his resolve weakens as their colliding wills lead to explosive desire. Could she be the one woman who can help him finally bury the ghosts of his past?

Anything But
A Duke

Self-made man Aidan Iverson has seen more closed
doors in his thirty years than he's ever cared to count.
As a member of the elite Duke's Den, he has all the
money he could possibly need, but the one thing he
can't purchase is true power. If roguish Aidan can't buy
his way into society's hallowed halls, he'll resort to a
more extreme measure: marriage.

Brought up to be a proper lady, the only thing Diana
Ashby desires is to be left alone to the creation of her
own devices. But when her dreams are crushed, she
must find another way to secure the future of her invention. Knowing his desire to enter her world, Diana
strikes a deal to arrange Aidan's marriage to the perfect
lady—as long as that lady isn't her. She doesn't need
any distractions from her work, particularly of the sin-
fully handsome variety.

As Diana and Aidan set out to find him an aristo-
cratic match, neither are prepared for the passion that
ignites between them or the love they can't ignore.

In the Duke's Den, can happiness ever be a winning
prospect?

The Wildes of Lindow Castle

Wilde in Love
978-0-06-238947-3

Too Wilde to Wed
978-0-06-269246-7

Born to Be Wilde
978-0-06-269247-4

Say No to the Duke
978-0-06-287782-6

EJ6 0719

At Avon Books, we know your passion for romance—once you finish one of our novels, you find yourself wanting more.

May we tempt you with . . .

- **Excerpts** from our upcoming releases.

- Entertaining **extras**, including authors' personal photo albums and book lists.

- Behind-the-scenes **scoop** on your favorite characters and series.

- **Sweepstakes** for the chance to win free books, romantic getaways, and other fun prizes.

- Writing **tips** from our authors and editors.

- **Blog** with our authors and find out why they love to write romance.

- **Exclusive content** that's not contained within the pages of our novels.

Join us at
www.avonbooks.com